The Flowers Of May

A NOVEL

The Flight Risk Spy Series: Book Three

SHELLY SNOW PORDEA

LITTLE BLACK BOOK

PUBLISHING

Contents

Chapter One

AMANDA STOOD IN THE doorway of her small bedroom at *The Ridge,* one hand braced against the chipped molding, as if the weight of stepping inside might tip her balance. The space wasn't what she had expected when they brought her here. It wasn't sterile or clinical, but somehow, that made it worse. The walls were an unapologetic shade of purple, broken by a chaotic floral border that wrapped like a crown near the ceiling. The space looked like a bold attempt at following a home makeover trend, though the design had little chance of standing the test of time.

The room smelled faintly of lemon-scented cleaner, sharp and chemical, as if someone had tried to scrub the reality out of it. The carpet was a short, synthetic shag, with an olive tone that fought against the wallpaper like dueling swordsmen. It was dense and over-vacuumed, with tracks that never fully smoothed out.

She didn't know how much money the Hansens had to invest in this "home for troubled girls" to keep her there, but the funds were obviously not spent on decor and facility improvement. An old white wicker chair sat in the corner next to a small writing desk, and a twin-sized bed was wedged against the far wall beneath a window that refused to open fully, its metal crank stripped and rusted. A refurbished dresser held the few outfits she had been given upon arrival. The whole house felt both old and weary, and trying too hard to be youthful, like her youth group's church basement makeover dubbed as "mission work." Had that only been a year ago? It seemed more like a lifetime.

Amanda crossed the room, her hand grazing the edge of the worn dresser, pausing at the mirror above it. Her reflection stared back—a girl who was involuntarily becoming a woman. Her auburn hair was pulled into a loose knot, but stray strands framed her face in a way that made her look younger than she felt. She ran a hand over her belly, the curve of it undeniable, her skin stretching to the point of discomfort. She exhaled slowly.

She had six more weeks until her due date. No one had said it outright when she arrived, but it had become clear with every passing day: she was not going home. Not until the little life inside her was taken into their hands. Not until her body had done its part.

She made her way to the window, pressing her palm flat against the glass, the surface cool and indifferent, as she looked out at the sloping hills that cradled the winding road leading up to the house. Beyond the trees and the tidy church steeples was a world still spinning, oblivious to the fact that she was packed away there, an unspoken mistake waiting to be corrected.

Amanda's gaze drifted to the narrow bookshelf built into the corner of the desk, stacked with uplifting devotionals and several well-worn copies of *What to Expect When You're Expecting*. None of it was hers. She hadn't brought anything except the duffel bag they'd allowed her to carry, but even that was rifled through and inspected as if she might have smuggled in defiance itself. Nearly two months later, she still felt haunted by that first intrusion, as though every day since had been lived in its shadow.

It wasn't her first brush with the people who ran this place. She had attended their affiliated summer camp with her friend Julie, who was convinced that Amanda and Lyla needed Jesus. But Jesus was everywhere in White Pine. Of course, she knew him. She just didn't know many people who acted like him.

Most of the churchier adults in her life didn't remind her of the Jesus she knew. The summer that Lyla and Amanda acquiesced to Julie's insistence that they join her at Liberty Camp, Amanda had forgotten that her MP3 player was at the bottom of her travel bag. She'd known that devices were prohibited during camp week, but *not* that searching the bags of campers at any time was considered acceptable.

One day during the afternoon chapel, she watched as a rip-snorting preacher swung the little red player by the string of her headphones right into the pulpit, hitting the wooden surface with a crash. Again. And again. He spat as he warned all of them about the dangers of worldly music and what becomes of young people who go the way of the devil. "Sometimes it's necessary to flip tables in order to shake sense into people," he said, letting what was left of her MP3 player clatter to the floor.

Amanda couldn't imagine how Jesus flipping tables in the temple was similar to the preacher's actions, but she kept her thoughts to herself for the most part. And now, it was with this same group that Cooper's parents expected her to stay. To serve her sentence, condemned by others for an act of deep love. She tried, but she didn't understand the logic. She was supposed to feel gratitude and be comforted by the fact that God had allowed her to come here, as if He were the one hiding her away.

Trendy wall colors and craft activities wouldn't erase the heartbreak she had to endure—the pain of Cooper being silent for weeks on end, and her family accepting her banishment as the cost of their shame. She knew she could never go back to the house she had called home. It was never really hers anyway, and she knew it.

She was beginning to believe that the plans she and Cooper had made—getting an apartment near campus at Michigan State, morning coffee runs in a town that was far from the Hansens' prying eyes—were shredded and buried beneath a tangle of sermons: the ones preached into her now, and the ones she had never stopped carrying, each lesson soaked in guilt as proof of her unworthiness.

Amanda's throat tightened. She hadn't cried when they drove her here. She hadn't even flinched when they made her promise that she would stop contact with Cooper so he could focus on finishing school. No one asked about what *she* was going to do to keep up with her studies, and after weeks of being surrounded by brightly colored walls that screamed *be happy* while her heart refused to comply, she felt a burn rising within.

But she wouldn't give them the satisfaction. She forced herself not to cry, still repeatedly dreaming that Cooper would show up at the window, guitar in hand, serenading to get her attention, with a getaway car idling close by. But Cooper never played the guitar very well. And it was more and more evident that if anyone was going to save her, it wasn't going to be him.

"Hey, whatcha doin'?"

Amanda turned toward the doorway, startled by the voice but not surprised by who it belonged to. Ellie stood barefoot, wrapped in an oversized hoodie that nearly swallowed her frame, the sleeves chewed at the ends from a nervous habit no one told her to stop. She was only thirteen, though life had carved a tiredness into her eyes that made her seem older in some moments, younger in others.

Amanda softened. "Just... thinking," she said, but it sounded weak and disingenuous even to her ears.

Ellie padded into the room without waiting for an invitation. She had a knack for slipping into spaces as if she'd always belonged there, a survival trait Amanda recognized from experience. Ellie was the youngest in the home. The staff gave her special smiles, speaking to her like something delicate they'd been told not to damage, rather than a detainee.

She didn't carry the same shame that the rest of them were expected to wear. She wasn't whispered about in the kitchen or called into long counseling sessions about her "choices." Because Ellie hadn't chosen.

She was thirteen, still clutching the corners of childhood, when a family friend decided she'd grown up enough. The staff didn't use words like rape—that was too messy, too confrontational, but they draped her in a pity none of the other girls were afforded. Ellie was a victim, not a participant. Not like the other girls who had reportedly invited their consequences and were now learning to repent for them. Ellie was someone they could save without needing to forgive.

Amanda watched it unfold every day. The way Ellie was rolled into the group prayers with softer words, as if her redemption came pre-approved. The rest of them were projects. Cautionary tales lined up in brightly colored chairs, they were expected to confess their sins and be grateful that their flesh and blood would be placed into the arms of a better mother.

It wasn't that Amanda wanted them to treat Ellie worse; it was that she saw through the charade. Ellie's pain was palatable to them–easy to rally around. But Amanda's—that was messier. Girls like her weren't offered sympathy. They were expected to learn their lesson, and to count themselves lucky, they were given a place to hide while they *did the right thing* after such a grievous wrong.

"You shouldn't stare out the window like that," Ellie said, flopping onto Amanda's bed as if it were her own. "Miss Judy says it's a sign you're feeling defiant." Her grin was lopsided, like she knew exactly how ridiculous that sounded.

Amanda let out a breath that was almost a laugh. "Well, I wouldn't want to seem *defiant.*"

Ellie twisted onto her side, propping her chin in her hand. "You should stop fighting so hard, you know. It's easier if you just go along. That's what they want. Nod, smile, act like you're grateful. Makes everything quicker."

Amanda studied her. Ellie's case was also different because she had no desire to cradle the bundle in her womb, believing the sight of it would only traumatize her. She didn't think about genetics, or family ties, or how the constant molecular communication during pregnancy would suddenly be interrupted, not only by cutting the umbilical cord, but by complete severance. No one explained to Ellie that there was nothing written in the prenatal books for when you *don't* bring the baby home—no chapter on managing breast engorgement without your child to nurse, or the betrayal of a body that mourns in milk and blood while everyone else tells you to move on. Amanda didn't know it yet, either, but something in her ached at the thought of separating from her baby, as if her body knew before her mind could comprehend it.

But Ellie had a different approach to their common plight. There was a quiet calculation behind her casualness, like she'd learned exactly how to dull the sharp edges of her circumstance without ever truly dulling herself.

"You *want* to be here, though," Amanda said. "That's the difference between you and me." She sighed, moving to sit on the edge of the bed.

Ellie shrugged. "Yeah, you're right. I guess it is easier for me. But I've been here long enough to see girls like you come and go," she said, raising her eyebrows.

Amanda looked at her closely. "How *long* have they had you in here?"

"Since we found out. So like, seven months." She said the words as if they weren't cumbersome weights anchoring her to a new reality. As though her childhood hadn't been snatched in the cruelest way imaginable.

Amanda couldn't respond, but the rage she was carrying on behalf of her young friend bubbled beneath every gaze.

"Look, I know you wish things were different. But the more you fight, the worse it is," Ellie continued.

Amanda bit the inside of her cheek. She didn't want to be angry at Ellie, but her words pressed against still-raw wounds.

"If you let them do their thing—act like they're getting through to you when they teach you how to be sorry—they'll treat you better. You gotta make them believe that you see this whole thing like they do...as saving you from yourself," she nodded as if

"This isn't my salvation, Ellie," Amanda said quietly.

"I know." Ellie's gaze softened. "But it doesn't matter. You still gotta get through it. Doesn't mean you believe their stories. You just... survive it. Then you leave."

"But what about my baby?" Amanda stifled a tear that was begging to fall.

"You gotta let her have a different life. Could you and Cooper really take care of a baby together while you guys are both in college? I mean, even if you tried, could you give her the life you want for her?"

"I don't know..." Amanda whispered.

"Look," Ellie suddenly spoke like a seasoned instructor rather than an endearing adolescent. "This is how it goes. They bring you here; you realize that you're just a kid who made a mistake, and then they take the baby. That's the whole cycle. No one gets out of it. It doesn't matter who you are."

Amanda finally let the suppressed moisture beading at the corners of her eyes drop down her cheeks in a steady flow. They sat in silence as she wiped her face, her glance eventually drifting to the laminated "House Values" chart pinned to the back of the door. Words like *humility, gratitude, sacrifice,* and *obedience* were printed in looping script, framed by cartoon doves. There was an irony in the way they called these "values," as if they were commodities you could exchange and upgrade.

"You really think it'll be easier if I just play along?" Amanda asked.

"Easier?" Ellie snorted. "Yeah. But I'm not promising you easy," she said, widening her eyes. "They'll still make you sit in those stupid group talks and stuff. But they'll stop watching you so close. You don't want to be on their watch list, Amanda. Trust me. That's when they start poking around your file, and making decisions about you without even telling you."

Amanda winced. She had no doubt the Hansens were funding this place not just to hide her, but to control every step of what came next. They had been making every decision without her for a while now. She was collateral damage wrapped in a tax write-off.

Ellie shifted again, stretching her legs out and kicking off Amanda's pillow with a grin. "Besides, they'll probably give you extra pudding cups if you behave. That's about as good as it gets around here."

Amanda smiled despite herself. Ellie had a way of disarming her, of reminding her that rebellion didn't always have to be loud. It could be found in the way she held on, quietly, in places where they tried to make her disappear.

Ellie reached for Amanda's hand, squeezing it briefly before standing. "Come on. Miss Judy will give us demerits if we're late for the evening devotions. You don't want to be late, or there's no hope for pudding."

Amanda blew a short laugh through her nose as she followed Ellie out the door, her fingers brushing against the broken flecks of paint on the molding one more time. The room didn't feel any less like a cell. But with Ellie's wit and warmth, the walls felt a little less suffocating.

Chapter Two

Knoxville, Tennessee: April 2008, Evening Devotions

AMANDA AND ELLIE PASSED each bedroom in the hallway of the ground floor until they came to the end, where devotions were held. The room had once been a dining parlor; someone had stenciled vines up the corners and hung a cross fashioned from two pieces of weathered barn wood on the main wall. There were no folding chairs or furniture for the girls to sit on, just empty space on a thinly carpeted concrete floor. A few bean bag chairs lined the walls, but those were usually taken by staff and the early comers. Amanda never got there in time to get a bean bag. She avoided being early for anything in this place.

The room began to hum with the slow, reluctant shuffling of feet and the murmur of girls trying to take up less space than they actually needed. With a sweep of her arm and a pat on the back as each resident entered, Miss Judy waved the girls in. She then moved to the front, flipping through her worn devotional like a conductor warming up an orchestra.

She was all bright lipstick and sharp bangs, a woman who believed presentation was ministry, but who didn't realize she was selling something unattractive. It wasn't her fault. Women here were schooled in femininity and poise, but their style wasn't their own—it was an imitation of one man's desire. Pastor Harwell liked big hair, bright lips, and women frozen in the glamour of 1986. It didn't take long for that aesthetic to become law. One by one, women reshaped themselves to fit it, until they blurred into carbon copies, a congregation of clones dressed not for expression but for approval.

Tonight, Miss Judy wore a navy blazer with big shoulder pads over a floral blouse and a string of pearls that clicked faintly when she turned her head.

Amanda slid into a spot on the floor next to three girls who were forming a back row, her belly large enough to make it obviously uncomfortable to get up and down with ease. The girls furthest along in their pregnancies were usually offered a bean bag, but there weren't enough to accommodate everyone. Ellie tugged at her sleeves and lowered herself onto the floor beside Amanda. Somehow, it didn't matter how round her belly got; Ellie moved with the lively energy of any girl her age.

Miss Judy tapped the lectern with a fingernail to gather attention. "Ladies," she called, drawing the word out like taffy. "We've got a new friend with us tonight. Let's show her we are a home, and how much she's a part of our family now."

Across the room, girls whispered behind their hands, laughter like moth wings before they stilled. Their faces snapped forward as Miss Judy's gaze swept their row. It wasn't the threat of raised voices or sudden blows that silenced them, but the quieter punishments—the beckoning hand after devotions, the careful closing of the rec room door, the soft, surgical voice pressing them to confess their wayward thoughts, to dig up sins like weeds, or to name regrets that hadn't yet taken root. It was the weight of never being entirely free, the constant ache of knowing joy could be called into question at any moment, that hollowed out their smiles and taught them to guard their light.

A staffer in scrubs—Miss Marla, the quiet one—ushered a girl through the doorway. She looked to be about fifteen, with chipped black nail polish and a fall of brightly dyed red hair that curtained half her face.

"This is Savannah," Miss Judy announced, her smile a fixed beam. "She's going to be staying with us for a little while."

Savannah didn't move farther into the room. "I'm not staying here," she said, not loud exactly, but clear enough that no one could pretend they hadn't heard.

A ripple passed through the room as the girls looked on in silence. Ellie went entirely still beside Amanda, dropping her hands into her lap and settling her formerly bouncing knee. But Miss Judy's smile didn't falter; this was her arena.

"Thank you for sharing your heart, honey," she said. The words clung to every surface like a syrupy goo you couldn't wash off. "You can set your bag down and have a seat. We're just about to start."

Then she lowered her voice to a gravelly whisper and told the new girl that personal items in the devotion room were strictly prohibited. But quickly followed it with: "Unless you wanna bring your Bible, dear," and another flash of her pearly whites.

Savannah stayed silent, looking at the room, at the girls, then back at Miss Judy before Miss Marla nudged gently, "It's okay, honey. Go ahead and take a seat."

Savannah took one step and then another, walking as if the floor might give out. Every girl in the room understood her. There were no bullies here. No caddy fights or bickering except for the occasional who-took-my-hairspray incident. The girls had each other's backs. They knew that if they didn't listen to each other, no one would. But Savannah didn't know that. Not yet.

"Now," Miss Judy said, clapping her hands together with a pop. "We have a message tonight. We are going to talk about being misfits."

Amanda felt Ellie's inhale at the word. Miss Judy liked to brand her devotions the way a public speaker would brand their talks. There was always a title, an object lesson, and a moment designed as the hinge—the point where the lesson turned and the audience followed.

"Misfits," Miss Judy repeated, savoring the beat. "Such an ugly label, isn't it? Used by the world to shame anyone who doesn't tuck perfectly into its boxes. But I have good news. You have been made this way on purpose."

"On purpose," a few girls nodded, echoing the words without being told to.

Miss Judy's gaze drifted, found Ellie, and warmed with an idea. "Ellie, sweet pea? Could you come up and help me for just a moment?"

Ellie's fingers tightened around her knees, and Amanda felt the tug of her hesitation—being called up meant being made into something symbolic. But before Ellie could form a refusal, Miss Judy stepped out from behind the lectern and slipped her navy blazer off in one smooth motion.

"Come on now," she coaxed, already crossing the space, holding the blazer open like an invitation that was more like a demand.

Ellie went to the front with the practiced smile she wore for staff—the one that suggested compliance without complete surrender. Miss Judy settled the blazer over her shoulders, and it swallowed little Ellie at once. The sleeves dropped past her fingertips; the hem hit mid-thigh. The shoulder seams sagged somewhere near her biceps, as the fabric collapsed into a husk around her.

A few girls laughed—the quick, nervous kind that lives in the space between distress and misunderstanding.

"Look at our Ellie," Miss Judy said, one hand on Ellie's shoulder. "Isn't she precious?" She stepped back with a theatrical flourish, turning Ellie from side to side as if she were a mannequin in a window. "Now, does this fit her?"

"No," came the chorus, soft and uneven.

"No, it does not," Miss Judy agreed. "Because it wasn't made for her. It was made for... me." She slid the blazer back onto her thick arms with a small shimmy of satisfaction, then smoothed the lapel. "The world will hand you things that don't fit—names, expectations, so-called truths. You will try them on, and they will slouch on you or pinch you or make it hard for you to lift your arms. And then you'll be tempted to think there's something wrong with you." She leaned toward the room, voice dropping to a hush. "There isn't."

Amanda felt the room yield an inch. Miss Judy knew how to draw a collective breath and make it feel like unity. To give snippets of hope to the room of girls who constantly questioned if their very existence amounted to nothing more than wrongness.

"But here's where some of you make a mistake," Miss Judy continued. "You take that feeling—this doesn't fit—and you turn into rebellion." She swung her gaze to Savannah with a brightness so pointed it glittered. "You say, 'I'm not staying here.' You stomp your little feet. You raise your voice. You make your own rules."

The new girl's jaw flexed, but she didn't take the bait.

"And you know what happens?" Miss Judy put her hand to her chest as she tilted her head upward. "You miss the blessing. You miss the tailor."

There were murmurs, the light shuffle of the metaphor landing.

"When God brings you to a place like this," Miss Judy said, spreading her arms to act as if she was embracing the entire room, "He is not punishing you. He is—the way a seamstress is with a dress that needs taking in—He is *shaping* you. It is not an opportunity for rebellion, but for increased faithfulness. He is making you what you ought to be as you trust His authority."

Amanda sighed. *His authority or yours?* She thought, and she was almost certain she didn't say it aloud.

"What doesn't fit now can be fitted. What you call constraint just might be care." Miss Judy spoke the last part of her sentence with a staccatoed cadence that drove home the idea with quiet intensity.

Amanda watched the room absorb the words. She could feel how neatly they slid into certain girls, and how others bristled.

She thought of the blazer swallowing Ellie, the way Miss Judy had claimed it back for herself, and called the whole exchange a "lesson." But it seemed to her that the only teaching to be learned was how some people use God to invoke fear, shame, and control instead of leaning into the love they say comes only from Him.

"Ellie, you can sit, baby," Miss Judy said as she hurried back, lifting the sleeves of her sweatshirt nervously as she went.

"You okay?" Amanda whispered when Ellie sank down to her spot on the floor again.

Ellie gave a half shrug. "It's fine." But she sat rubbing her upper arms as if the fabric had left a chill on her skin.

Miss Judy stepped behind the lectern again, energized by her own momentum. "We must never quit trusting God. We're going to say this together. It's our truth tonight. Repeat after me." She raised her right hand, palm open. "I might not fit—"

"I might not fit," the room echoed, some voices clear, others landing in a mumble.

"—but I'm not gonna quit."

"—but I'm not gonna quit."

"Again," Miss Judy insisted, faster this time, leaning into the chant. "I might not fit, but I'm not gonna quit."

The girls repeated it louder, the rhythm gaining a current. Many of them smiled, a wave of laughter and giggles filling the space as they stretched out a hand to their neighbor, a new sense of camaraderie forming among them. The feeling would be short-lived, but no one remembered that in the moment. It would take getting back to the rigid schedule, being forced to spend long weeks without communicating with their family, or some weird infraction like using the wrong hand towels to shatter their illusion of hope amid a compelling talk.

Ellie's lips moved around the phrase without lifting at the corners as Amanda held her hand. And the new girl refused to engage. She hadn't been influenced enough yet. Savannah didn't need to shake her head or protest for everyone to know she refused. Because defiance has its own posture, and everyone knew the staff kept a keen eye out for it.

Miss Judy let the chant crest and then settle. "Because we are clay on the potter's wheel," she said, turning pages. "We are fabric under a master's hand. We are misfits only until we learn what we're made for."

Savannah slouched deeper, finally reaching her breaking point. "Some of us already know," she said. Not loud. Not meek. Just enough to feel *real*.

Miss Judy's eyes flicked up. "Would you like to share, Savannah?"

"No. I'd like to go home."

The whole room paused, but Miss Judy smiled again, a softness born of strategy. "Home can be a place we carry inside us, dear heart. While you're here, this is home enough."

"Not for me."

Miss Marla shifted subtly near the doorway, with a staff awareness that marked the beginning of a possible scene. Miss Judy shook her head by a fraction, keeping the situation in her own hands, but clearly annoyed that she had lost her grip on the successful moment.

"I hear your fear," Miss Judy said. "Fear is loud. It shouts, 'I'm not staying here.' It throws tantrums. But faith answers back. Faith says—say it with me, girls—"

"I might not fit," the room began, but Savannah's voice cut across them, and the two lines tangled in the air.

"It's not fear," Savannah protested. "It's a choice. I didn't choose to come here. I can choose not to stay."

The sentence landed with the clean slice of a blade. A few girls stared at their knees. Amanda felt something open in her chest that was both agreement and sudden recognition. There it was—the naked statement they all swallowed, replacing it with silence or with the tidy script the staff preferred: that they were learning, that they were grateful, that God was working on them.

Miss Judy held her smile a heartbeat too long.

"We're all here because choices were made," she said, steering the moment back to the script. "Some of them ours, some not. What matters now is the next choice. Will you let yourself be loved enough to be changed?"

Savannah looked at the floor. "I don't want your kind of love."

"You haven't tried it yet," Miss Judy answered, a sharp tang entered her tone, the smug satisfaction of bringing a stray lamb near the crook of the staff.

"Lord, make us willing," she bowed her head, beginning to pray as if it were common practice to end a conversation by turning the focus upward. The girls settled into silence, quickly bowing their heads, some folding their hands together until it was over.

They began to queue up for the sign-in sheet with Miss Marla to prove they had attended, a nightly record kept in the office for reasons Amanda couldn't understand. There were only sixteen girls there, and the home's full capacity was twenty. It wasn't as if the girls could go missing without being missed. As they finished their check-in, they all drifted toward the snack counter where a plastic tub of pudding cups waited like an altar to small mercies.

Savannah had already slipped out, unchallenged, vanishing down the hall toward her room—likely to cry herself to sleep as so many girls had on their first night. No one would rob her of that. But before the rest of the group could drift toward the door, Miss Judy clapped her hands once more, sharp enough to halt their scatter.

"Remember our truth," she said. "Say it again with me."

And the chant drifted up unevenly, a thin scatter of voices joining in the expected response.

CHAPTER THREE

Bucharest, Romania: The Morning After The Proposal

AMANDA WOKE TO THE faint pulse of a rhythm that didn't belong to the room she was in—*I might not fit, but I'm not gonna quit.*

The words floated up from the depths of her dream, stubborn and insistent. She hadn't thought about that chant in years, but Tokyo had stirred something. Seeing Cooper in a whirlwind had loosened a memory she hadn't invited. She lifted her lashes, hoping to replace the lavender walls of her subconscious with reality. As her eyes adjusted, she saw the hotel room, finally regaining a sense of where she was.

The soft charcoal curtains were cracked just enough to let a hint of gold morning in, the distant hum of growing traffic from Calea Victoriei street below. The hint of Tristan's cologne hung in the air, and Amanda breathed it in, reminding herself that she was safe, she was wanted, and she could let the present steady her before allowing the past to pull her under again.

Beside her, he was still asleep, one arm crooked above his head, the sheet tangled low around his hips. She let herself look at him for a moment. His hair mussed, the clean angle of his jaw unguarded in sleep, reminding her of the first night they spent together in Tenerife—how she had looked at him, desired him, longed to know him. She let out a belaboured breath before rolling toward the nightstand, a mix of guilt and regret stirring in her chest. She hesitated, but took her phone into her hand, thumb hovering for a moment before typing quickly.

Are you in Bucharest yet?

She hadn't told anyone, but she and Cooper had been texting. His first message came in quietly the night she had turned on her phone after fleeing Tokyo. After seeing him.

Amanda had stared at the screen longer than necessary, rereading the simple message—*"I heard you're in Romania. Are you okay?"*—before she answered him. But she didn't have the fortitude to ignore him. She was the one who gave him her number, after all.

What followed wasn't earth-shattering. Just a few cautious exchanges about the fact that he was coming to Bucharest with his dad, some kind of political obligation Amanda didn't bother to press him on, and how surreal it had been to see each other again.

It wasn't even a little bit romantic, but something in the rhythm of his words, the familiar cadence of the boy she once knew, calmed her. They didn't speak about the past or mention names and places that would revive old wounds. They didn't talk openly about their feelings, but the thread between them had revealed itself to be fully intact.

The room sharpened around her, full of reminders of her location. High ceilings framed by heavy drapes, a narrow balcony opening to wrought-iron railings, a weathered parquet floor carrying a faint scent of polish, the radiator ticking softly, releasing a heat that clung to the air. She was in Romania, lying next to Tristan—the man who had just proposed in the sweetest way imaginable. And she was texting Cooper—the man who wasn't able to find the strength to fight for her when they were plunged into adulthood much too early.

She put the phone screen to her chest, wondering if Cooper was awake, or if he was even on the same continent as she was. Her musings were all too familiar. In the first few years she spent as a commercial pilot, she'd dreamt vividly about an encounter with him while traveling.

Perhaps she'd be moving past a crowd of eager passengers already waiting at the gate, lined up to scan their boarding passes, and he'd catch her eye. She wouldn't say a word, just grin and move behind the doors of the gangway until she was out of sight, taking comfort in the fact that she was in the power seat. Perhaps she'd be standing at the door of the cockpit, thanking passengers on their way out, and he'd be stunned by her presence. She'd be the one to speak—"Enjoy your stay, Mr. Hansen,"—leaving him speechless.

It never happened, of course, but it took years for the dreams to slow and eventually stop. And she had let her mind play games for far too long. *What was she doing?* She couldn't get sucked back in.

She felt the pang of remorse settle heavy in her abdomen as she placed the phone face down before hearing it buzz.

Got in late last night. Didn't think you'd want to see me.

Her chest tightened. She stared at the words, thumbs hesitating above the keyboard. Her head was screaming to put the phone down, but her heart wouldn't let go. She quickly typed, "*I do,*" and sent it before she could reconsider.

The mattress shifted as Tristan rolled slightly, making Amanda hesitate. His breathing was slow, oblivious even, but she knew how quickly those eyes could sharpen when they opened. She forced herself to keep still, to keep her own breathing matched to his, as if the quiet steadiness could disguise the churn in her chest.

Tristan's arm slid across the sheet toward her, "Mornin'," he murmured, his voice gravelly with fatigue.

She slid the phone facedown, leaned over, and let her hair brush his cheek. "Morning," she whispered, kissing him before he could read anything in her expression. His mouth was warm, barely a hint of morning breath, tasting of sleep and last night's champagne.

He kissed her back lazily at first, then with growing insistence, his hand finding the back of her neck. She let him draw her in, her pulse jumping at the familiar press of his body against hers.

This. *This* is what she wanted. Cooper Hansen be damned.

"You always look like you're keeping a secret," Tristan murmured between kisses.

"Maybe I am," she said, her mouth curling upwards as she let the fleshy part of her bottom lip pucker slightly. She playfully skimmed the firm line of his torso, "And wouldn't you like to know what I'm hiding?"

He rolled towards her, bracing himself above her body, his knee sliding between hers as his mouth moved along her jaw, and she closed her eyes, letting the heat rise between them. Her nightgown twisted under his hands, and she felt the cool air hit her skin as he tugged it up.

He pressed against her, his breath hot in her hair. "You didn't answer me last night," he murmured.

She stilled her body, reacting to his words rather than his touch. "About what?" She tried to sound blithe.

"You know." He pulled back just enough to search her face. "The timeline."

Amanda smoothed her palm over his chest, feeling the steady beat of his heart. "It's not like I can pull up my calendar and decide how many months will feel like we've known each other long enough to get married, Tristan."

"I know. I just need to plan a few things and… well… I want to at least think there's a chance you'll say yes."

"Oh, Tristan," Amanda whispered, every word sincere. "Of course, there's a chance." She lifted herself to him, pressing his skin to hers again.

"So you're *saying* there's a chance," he said, the singsong rise and fall of his voice wrapping the tease in charm. He leaned down to kiss her, as they both let breathy laughter slip between their lips before it dissolved into desire.

Her pulse tripped in the familiar way it always did with him, the world narrowing to the taste of him, the press of his body drawing her closer. She told herself not to think about anything else—not the messages on her phone, not the name still echoing in her head—only this moment, and the dangerous comfort it offered.

His mouth was warm on hers, the kisses growing slower, heavier—until an insistent vibration of Tristan's phone shivered across the nightstand. He didn't move right away, just let his forehead rest against hers before speaking. "We have to meet Julius this morning."

Amanda drew in a quiet breath, using the pause to tuck away any thoughts she didn't want him to read in her face.

"We?" she asked, but she couldn't keep herself from sounding like a school kid dreading class.

"Of course. The European Deployment Facility tour is tomorrow, and it's become very political, as you can imagine." He grinned faintly. "Apparently, one of the visiting delegations is bringing that U.S. Governor you know… Hansen. You were talking with his son at the ball for a while, remember? What's his name?"

Amanda's pulse gave a sharp, unseen kick, betraying her in ways her expression didn't dare.

"Um, yeah… Cooper." She smoothed the words on her tongue, but inside she could feel the threat of a stutter still rattling against her teeth.

Tristan rolled away with a grin, plopping his feet on the floor. "And you guys knew each other in high school? Small world," he said, stretching his muscles upward as if forcing his personality to come fully awake with the movement. "Come on. Let's get this show on the road. I want to get some coffee before we meet anyone. They'll be expecting us soon."

"Yeah, of course," she replied, happy not to have to say more when Tristan's phone began buzzing again, and he pulled it to his ear, no longer able to ignore it.

Amanda slipped out of bed and pulled a T-shirt over her head, ambling barefoot to the closet. She sifted through the hangers with restless fingers, a small inventory of a life that wasn't supposed to be here. Most of what she'd worn in Tokyo had been rented, paraded for an evening, and then whisked back to the designers. Her suitcase held little more than a suggestion of permanence, and each outfit reminded her of how unmoored she was—someone always arriving, never staying.

She bent down to peruse her carry-on, running her hand along a folded sweatshirt at the bottom. She could feel the outline of the case Katherine had slipped into her hands. Its presence followed her everywhere, even when she managed to forget it for a few blessed hours.

She pulled out a simple black dress, plain enough to vanish in, polished enough for Julius's meetings, casual enough to excuse herself later under the guise of shopping in the city. What Amanda really needed was a day with Lyla—coffee in hand, laughter spilling into ordinary hours, and the kind of belonging you couldn't fake in a borrowed wardrobe.

She exhaled slowly through her teeth, steadying herself against the weight of her thoughts. Crossing back to the nightstand, she reached for her phone without thinking, the gesture more an instinct than a choice.

Where are you staying?

Cooper's reply to her text had come more than twenty minutes earlier. She let out another breath, the screen still glowing in her hand. Before she could decide what to say—or whether to say anything at all—the sound of Tristan approaching carried from the bathroom. Reflex overrode contemplation, and her thumb erased the thread with a single swipe. She didn't know why she did it. It wasn't as if she was doing anything wrong. And yet, the need to conceal it lingered in her chest like an echo.

Tristan appeared in the doorway, shirtless, flawless, and freshly shaved. "You want to shower now?" he asked.

"Sure," she pecked his cheek as she passed. "I'll only be a few."

Time slipped in the shower the way thoughts sometimes did—unnoticed, pooling at her feet, until she was surrounded by enough to drown in. Amanda leaned her forehead against the glass, letting the water soften everything it touched. She lingered longer than she should have, letting the quiet steady her.

She finally stepped out of the bathroom, a thin veil of steam trailing behind her as she wrapped a towel around herself and walked into the bedroom. Her cheeks were flushed from the heat, and the coolness of the room made her shiver. Tristan was dressed and sipping room service coffee he'd ordered while she washed off the morning haze.

"Just a few?" he said, offering a sly grin.

Amanda gave a half smile. "Oops, didn't mean to stay in so long." But that was only half true. She wanted to stay long enough to avoid the meeting with Julius, to text Katherine, to call Lyla—anything but meet with a man she feared.

"This stuff is gross," Tristan said, setting the cup on the edge of the desk.

While waiting, he had been reading the morning paper delivered with his coffee and croissant, a habit he had formed as a child. His father, Harold, had taught him that the two signs of a distinguished young gentleman were the morning papers he read, and the way he took his coffee—black, one cream, no sugar. Tristan didn't know if he liked his coffee or morning routine; it just always was.

He watched Amanda for a moment, as if weighing whether to hurry her, then held up his cup. "I should've asked for espresso."

She chuckled, disappearing into the closet. "Let me grab my dress, and I'll come with you. Maybe we can find something stronger before your meeting."

"*Our* meeting," he corrected gently.

"Five minutes, promise," Amanda said.

She emerged wearing the black dress she had set to the side and a slate-gray blazer that buttoned snugly to accentuate her waist. Her hair, still a bit damp, was twisted into a low bun, as she smoothed any flyaways with the bit of gel she'd run through her fingers.

"Ready?" She asked as cheerfully as she could.

Tristan stood to pull her close, wrapping his arms around her, folding her into the parts of him she craved.

"Are you?" he teased, kissing the part of her cheek just under her ear before tugging her toward the exit, leaving her wanting more.

Amanda's phone hummed as they stepped into the hall. "Give me a minute?"

He nodded and stepped away to tap out a message on his own phone, both of them effortlessly moving toward the elevator, and simultaneously stopping to address business before entering.

"Hey, Lyla. What are you doing up? It's gotta be past midnight. Is everything okay?"

"Oh, yeah, everything's fine," Lyla said, unconcerned about the time. "So hey, babe, listen, I'm flying to Paris in two days for a client who wants me to photograph her in her wedding dress. There's a whole camera crew coming to film a scene designed to look like the gown was stolen from the Louvre. Super fun. They want a movie trailer for their reception, and they hired me to do their stills. Anyway, I have a couple of free days for a shopping spree... or you know, covert investigation, whatever comes up. Want to meet there for a girls' weekend?"

Amanda blinked. "You're serious?"

"As a flash mob dance break in a spy movie," she laughed. "Come on, it'll be like old times—only with better wine and better shoes."

Amanda chuckled. "Old times? Like the times from two weeks ago?"

"Hey, that's a fortnight to you, Missy. We're fancy now." Lyla replied without missing a beat. "I already checked with Melody, and she's a firm yes. But only if you come too. So you *have* to say yes. We can do some actual shopping too, because we seriously do *not* have the wardrobe fitting of the *Spy*ce Girls."

Amanda let out a short, breathy laugh. "I'm not sure I can. Things are... complicated right now," she said, glancing at Tristan, preoccupied with his own call.

Lyla's tone softened, the sparkle in her voice dimming a touch. "Complicated is your default. Think of Paris as your antidote. Please? We *need* a girl band reunion. You can't let us go yet. And this is a good way to touch base without us *actually* being in the middle of any action, right?"

Amanda hesitated. "Let me think about it."

"Don't think. Just say yes. I'll message Melody and book the hotel. You'll thank me when you're holding a croissant in one hand and an overpriced scarf in the other."

"I promise I'll think about it. But I do really have to go, okay?" Amanda said.

"Not a no!" Lyla sang into the phone before hanging up.

"Bye, Lyla," Amanda grinned and tucked the phone away as Tristan put his phone into his pocket, too. "Everything okay?"

"Just Lyla. Trying to convince me to run off to Paris."

"Tempting," he said.

"Absolutely," she murmured, silently contemplating how to make the trip happen.

They took the elevator down to the first floor, where they gathered in the hotel's executive suite—a discreet boardroom shielded behind polished doors that overlooked a quiet terrace. Designed for confidential talks, the Handel Boardroom was trimmed in walnut and softly lit, its silence broken only by the faint murmurs of distant sounds of guests coming and going. Julius was already seated, a file open in front of him and a glass of water untouched at his side. He looked up as they entered, his expression unreadable.

"Tristan, my boy," he greeted. "Ms. Hopkins."

Amanda's heart halted. She nodded, taking the seat across from him. "Hey, Julius. Or should I call you Mr. Babb? You made quite the impression in Tokyo."

Julius steepled his fingers. "As did you, Amanda."

She smiled, keeping herself steely-eyed.

Tristan looked at his phone as it vibrated continuously, illuminating a stream of numbers. "I think this is one of our project managers. Renée said there has been a complication setting up one of the phones, and we've got to make sure we have all of our people connected with our contacts at Helion. This will only take a few minutes to fix. Excuse me, will you both?"

"Of course," Julius said, almost too happy to have a moment alone with Amanda.

As soon as Tristan had exited, Julius leaned back in his chair, examining her.

"You're not what I expected," he said finally.

"I could say the same," Amanda replied, giving nothing away.

"Still sharp," he said with the faintest hint of approval. "But sharpness alone is a liability without context."

Amanda folded her arms. "You didn't want me in this meeting for planning purposes."

"No," he said. "I asked you here because there are forces at work that you only partially understand. And partial understanding can be fatal."

She didn't respond; Amanda knew that waiting was the best way to get information. Let the counterpart babble. Gather info.

"I hear you met with Azizi Malonga," Julius said. "A man whose entire empire is built on shadows and sleight of hand."

"I spoke with him," Amanda confirmed, remembering her instruction to speak the truth in order to be believed. The irony that she'd been trained to work *with* Julius was not lost on her.

Julius leaned forward. "And you found it beneficial?"

"I found it informative," Amanda smiled.

"Informative? Did he impart any wisdom? Or did he simply redirect your trust from one manipulator to another?"

Amanda's jaw tightened. "Are you calling *yourself* a manipulator?" Her pulse pounded in her chest.

"Let me tell you a story," Julius continued. "During the Cold War, there was a man in West Berlin who smuggled classified documents out of East Germany hidden inside hollowed-out Bibles. He believed he was doing God's work—passing truth to the West, dismantling a regime. But what he didn't know was that those documents were planted. Misinformation. Lies crafted by the Stasi to destabilize NATO intelligence. He was a pawn. He died believing he was a hero. But all he did was move the pieces exactly where his enemies wanted them."

"You're saying I'm that man?"

"I'm saying Malonga plays the same game. He may be offering you something that feels righteous. But everything has a cost. The question is—have you asked yourself who's writing the check?"

Amanda stared at him. "And you think you're the moral compass in this?"

"I'm not interested in morality. I'm interested in outcomes."

He tapped the folder in front of him. "You want to save lives. So do I. But only one of us is willing to get our hands dirty to do it."

She narrowed her eyes. "And the other isn't willing to let people become collateral."

"You say that now. But soon you'll learn—everyone becomes collateral eventually."

Tristan re-entered with a sigh, "Whew, crisis averted," he said before glancing at both of them.

"Everything alright?" he asked.

"Just clarifying history," Julius said smoothly.

Amanda rose, her voice even. "I'll let you boys take care of business. Julius doesn't need me here, and I know you have a lot to do. And I could use a heavier jacket before the tour tomorrow. I assume it'll be an inside-outside thing?"

Tristan nodded, but before he could say a word, Amanda sputtered, "Good, I'll be out shopping. Call me later?"

Chapter Four

Bucharest, Romania: The Facility Tour

AT A GATE TWO hundred yards from the entrance, reporters surrounded a facility that stood in stark contrast to the rolling countryside that looked like its painted backdrop. Steel and glass angles cut through the scene, a hard geometry set against nature's warmth in the late-afternoon sun.

Politicians often flew in and out in a day, so this type of tour was set in the early evening to accommodate red eyes and ungodly early morning flights alike, and still allow for food and drinks to impress dignitaries. Flags representing nations, NGOs, and tech conglomerates whipped in the wind outside the gated complex. Government officials, reps from the Helion Group, and various investors arrived in a sleek black motorcade lining the private entrance as employees emerged with practiced efficiency. A security guard emerged from the passenger's side as the car came to a stop, who in turn opened the other vehicle doors.

Among the group were US presidential hopeful, Governor James Hansen, and his son Cooper, dressed in tailored suits, their presence underscoring the blend of politics and power brokering that defined the day's agenda.

Security was tight but discreet—high-level enough to be serious, subtle enough not to alarm, while still keeping the few journalists far outside any real view of what was happening. Inside the lobby, light filtered through glass walls and precision-cut beams, casting a lattice of shadows across polished floors. Every detail was choreographed, and no movement went unnoticed by the quietly stationed guards.

Amanda stood beside Tristan, whose smile was as carefully calibrated as the building itself. He stepped forward with his team—the decision-makers who had selected this site—but it was not their sell to make. The people who lived and worked here would do the talking; Tristan's presence only framed the choice. The facility now had to prove itself, scrutinized by Helion and by every other interested party in attendance. And this was only the beginning; in the weeks ahead, the same scrutiny would follow them from city to city, each site in turn laid bare for judgment on the world's stage.

Tristan and his executives from Envisage had been to the facility multiple times to check its capabilities, but today was the real test. Amanda tried not to dwell on the fact that it was the very city where she had landed after Tokyo. Bucharest felt almost too fitting, but it wasn't a coincidence. Russell's contacts had carved the path into this region, and Amanda had long since learned that her movements were being orchestrated, not left to chance.

Renée Cho was cool and composed as she reviewed notes on her slim tablet, and André de Villiers, head engineer, remained a few steps behind with the intensity of someone whose genius was most comfortable behind closed doors. The assembled guests included regional defense ministers, NATO liaisons, Romanian intelligence officers, and select EU diplomats, each with a vested interest in securing Eastern Europe's digital and physical borders. The American presence didn't confuse anyone, given their reputation for intel, and Julius Babb hovered near the back, watching.

The facility director adjusted the cuff of his uniform and stepped forward, his voice calm but resolute as he addressed the gathered delegation.

"Good afternoon," he began, voice low and clear, but laced with the firm vowels of Transylvanian Romanian. "My name is Colonel Filip Stoica. I oversee day-to-day operations and national coordination for this site. Welcome to Sector 9 of the Băneasa Defense Complex. If you will follow me, I'll take you through the facility, with briefings at each station so you may judge our work for yourselves."

Amanda glanced toward Tristan, who offered a small nod. This was the real beginning.

Colonel Stoica motioned to a topographical projection shimmering above a control panel positioned just inside the entry, a natural place to begin before leading them farther in.

"You may wonder why this location was chosen. Romania has long been treated as peripheral by Western defense initiatives—useful as a buffer, rarely as a center. That changes today. This site, nestled between the Carpathians and the Black Sea, provides something few other locations in Europe can: strategic obscurity with unmatched visibility."

He pointed to a zone north of Bucharest on the map, and Amanda's eyes caught on the glowing outline, the country reframed in light she had never thought to see it in.

"This facility sits atop a former Cold War signal intelligence base—deep tunnels, reinforced infrastructure, and pre-existing grid conduits that can be reactivated and adapted for secure data relay. That gave us an instant head start in constructing the subterranean containment for the Grid's sensory core."

He turned slightly, adjusting the screen to show a concentric pattern of circles radiating outward.

"From here, the Grid's range can extend in all directions across the Balkans, the western Russian corridor, the Black Sea airspace, and well into the Levantine corridor. If we had placed it further west—say, Vienna or Prague—we'd have lost critical minutes in signal reception from regions most vulnerable to hostile covert escalation."

Governor Hansen narrowed his eyes. "So Bucharest is a listening post?"

"It's more than that, sir," Stoica replied. "It's a calibration point. Every Grid node must be tuned to its geography. This site—elevated terrain to the north, electromagnetic quiet zones to the south—allows the sensory instruments of the Ocular Grid to maintain full fidelity without distortion from urban magnetic noise. A silent giant, if you will."

Tristan beamed. This was the spot he had dreamed of, and you could read the desire for everyone to buy in on his face. Guests watched as the projection shifted to reveal old fiber maps beneath the newer overlay. They could see the bones of something older—long-dead Soviet architecture reborn into the Grid's gleaming exoskeleton.

Stoica continued. "Additionally, Romania is one of the few Eastern European nations with existing NATO infrastructure, high-tech industry support, and—most crucially, in my opinion—a population amenable to increased security installations. The political lift is lighter here than it would be in Germany or France. And unlike sites in Ukraine or Georgia, this territory is not under imminent risk of kinetic conflict. It's stable, but close enough to the edge to see what's coming."

A soft murmur ran through the room. Amanda caught Governor Hansen exchanging a look with his son, Cooper. The governor spoke again, but slower this time.

"What are the local risks? Energy? Interference? Human?"

Stoica's gaze didn't flinch. "Power redundancy is managed through a triangulated hydroelectric and nuclear reserve. The sensors are shielded to military speculations and test-cleaned for sabotage vectors daily. As for human interference…" He allowed himself a wry smile. "We house personnel on a rotational basis from six agencies, three nations, and one neutral ethics commission. We've learned from the Swiss."

That earned a soft chuckle from a few members of the crowd.

"But the real reason," Stoica added, stepping away from the panel, his voice growing quieter, "is legacy."

He motioned to a small framed photograph mounted discreetly near the doorway: a faded image of radar operators during the 1968 Warsaw Pact invasion drills. Men in uniform, heads bent over consoles in the very bunker beneath their feet.

"This place was once used to suppress visibility—to blind those looking west. It is a fitting reversal that it now hosts the most powerful system ever built to *see*—to see clearly, impartially, and without delay. That is why we are here."

He let the silence settle over the room. Not sterile silence, but a kind of reverence that implies *something matters here.*

Amanda exhaled, slowly. Whatever her personal misgivings, she couldn't argue with the choice. This wasn't just a showcase. It was a fulcrum, and Bucharest had become the lever.

A woman with the delegation from France spoke up. "But if it's that powerful," she said, her voice slightly unnerved, "what safeguards are in place? Who decides what's a threat and what's... noise?"

The director nodded, not bristling at the question, but welcoming it.

"That is the heart of the ethical dilemma, madam, which is why human oversight is non-negotiable. Each Grid node will contain both automated response parameters and a manual override council. The Bucharest facility, for instance, is jointly monitored by NATO observers, Romanian defense intelligence, and The Helion Group's independent ethics committee, and will be led by Dr. Katherine Harrington."

All heads turned briefly to see Katherine step into view, composed and stoic, her gaze cool as steel. She nodded once to the crowd, a silent confirmation.

Tristan leaned slightly toward Amanda, his voice low. "This is why we're here. Not to show off a prototype. To build confidence that this thing is the future and won't start World War III."

But Amanda's eyes were fixated on Katherine. She stood holding her breath as if she'd seen a ghost.

"Hey, you okay? Tristan asked.

"Yeah, just... this is a lot. World War III? Do you hear what you just said?" She wanted to sprint out the door into the crisp air of a Romanian autumn, but Tristan's touch brought her to her senses.

He put his hand on her elbow and drew her ear close to his mouth. "Hey, it's an exaggeration—we're the good guys."

Amanda exhaled a stifled sound, somewhere between a laugh and a scoff. She tracked the screen as the Colonel spoke and the map zoomed outward to reveal more nodes—planned installations in South Korea, the UAE, and Western Australia. Not just military hubs, but technological vanguards.

"What happens," she whispered to Tristan, "if someone gets control of it *all?*"

Tristan answered immediately. "But they won't," he whispered with a shrug, and pointed to the Colonel as if telling her to be a good student and listen. The map began to display a simulation—an approaching aircraft was flagged, tracked, and neutralized on-screen before it crossed into protected airspace.

Amanda wanted to stare Katherine down or yell in her face for not giving her a warning about seeing her in public, pretending to be—or maybe *being*—the woman in charge of keeping the Ocular Grid under control. Katherine, however, never looked her way again. She seemed absorbed in the presentation, expression unreadable, leaving Amanda to wonder if she had even registered her presence at all.

Amanda knew absolutely nothing in that moment. The only thing that kept her from falling apart was Tristan's arm on hers and the fact that people were asking questions.

"Where does the data go?" Cooper Hansen asked. His voice was steady and measured, but Amanda sensed a skepticism in his tone–or perhaps she was hoping it was there. Hoping for someone else in the room to be as stunned as she was to see the vast control one system could gain.

The Colonel answered swiftly. "It goes to a distributed server matrix across multiple jurisdictions. No single entity can own or control it. That was a founding principle."

Cooper nodded slowly. "Unless they built the system." His words landed a bit like a challenge, and Amanda knew she had clocked his tone right.

But Colonel Stoica held the tension with practiced grace. "Transparency is built into the architecture. Licensing is separate from operation."

That didn't answer much in Amanda's mind, but the delegates nodded as if they understood, and the tour wound down a corridor paneled with brushed steel. These weren't the same polished insiders she'd seen in Tokyo. A handful overlapped, but the mix here was broader, heavier with officials and auditors whose job was to poke holes rather than clap at presentations. At least the movement allowed Amanda to hide her trembling hands. A new room, dimly lit and ringed with observation bays, opened before them. Inside, the hum of hardware pulsed through the floor.

This was the server room—where entire petabytes of data converged and distributed in real time. A Romanian woman in her sixties with sharp eyes and a diplomat's poise stepped forward to address the group. "My colleague," Colonel Stoica raised his palm to introduce her, "Anna Popovici."

"You are standing in the central processing hall," she began. "Each stack you see here can operate independently, but in tandem, they form the computational core of the Ocular Grid. Should a regional blackout occur, these systems will continue functioning for thirty-six hours on internal power reserves alone."

She moved toward a control console and brought up an archive of simulation files—everything from seismic activity to radiation spikes to aircraft flight paths. Across the crowd, Katherine stood with the Helion delegates, her poise unshaken. Amanda tried to catch her eye, but Katherine's attention remained fixed on the speaker, as if Amanda didn't exist.

"The Grid's design reads what we overlook," Popovici said. "Nuclear signatures. Thermal variance. Biometric clustering in refugee corridors. What we do with that data is what determines our future."

Cooper Hansen's features tightened, skepticism coiling just beneath the surface. "How does this help us sleep at night, rather than fear what it might become?"

"We don't offer guarantees, but we do understand the Grid's safeguards," Director Popovici said. "But I would argue the greater threat is ignorance, not management."

Amanda studied the crowd, her thoughts turning to Melody's folder, to Russell's warnings and nuclear references—codes hidden in plain sight. The Ocular Grid could be weaponized. Of course it could. The question was whether the right people would catch it before it happened. And the way Cooper was acting, she knew he was thinking the same thing.

Governor Hansen had listened to his son ask questions without interrupting, making Amanda wonder if he had softened or if Cooper really was in the dark about his father's dealings. "If this thing detects the makings of a nuclear threat, who sees it first?"

But when the Governor asked his question, the excitement in his tone was unmistakable—not the thrill of reassurance, but of calculation. He wasn't testing the system's integrity; she knew he was measuring how much oversight might apply if he, or someone like him, managed to seize total control. Amanda knew in her gut that nothing had changed.

"That depends on the licensing arrangement," Renée Cho stepped forward, answering calmly. She was the one who had worked with the Helion Group after their winning bid, guiding them through the details of what they were actually gaining when they bought the Ocular Grid. It wasn't full and complete control, she'd said, it was strategic control, and that was different.

"We're entering the territory of operational details about the product, not the facility, so if I may," she nodded toward Director Popovici before continuing. "In a multi-national partnership, we expect shared protocols."

"And if the data points to one of the partners?" the Governor asked.

A silence draped over the room; a few partners at Helion, visibly shocked at the American's bluntness, shuffled their feet.

Renee smiled, taking a step closer to the Governor. "When the Grid reveals an inconvenient truth, that is proof of its integrity. A system that only tells us what we want to hear isn't what we're interested in. And we've got every—"

She couldn't finish her sentence. Governor Hansen waved his broad hand upward, spouting, "I know, I know. Safeguards." He nodded, "Good to know."

The group moved in near silence, following as the Colonel led them, hearing only the clacking of shoes as they came to a panoramic viewing deck overlooking the facility's exterior network—a sprawl of satellite arrays, solar fields, and fortified towers. The Carpathian range loomed in the distance, dusted with snow at the highest elevations.

Champagne was offered, and as the group began to loosen, Amanda finally let out a long exhale. He caught her bearings, standing beside Tristan, nodding politely as officials made small talk. She could feel Cooper watching her from several paces away, but he didn't approach.

The crowd began to mingle as Amanda found her way to the room's edge, glass stretching from floor to ceiling, and as she became lost in thought, a soft voice reached her shoulder.

"It's beautiful, isn't it?"

She turned to find Katherine beside her, drink in hand.

"Yes," Amanda mumbled. "Breathtaking." She could barely get out more than a whisper. "Why didn't you warn me?" she said, turning to confront her.

Katherine let a long pause stretch between them, smiling softly. "Nice to meet you, Miss Hopkins," she said, extending her hand. "Now, shake my hand at our first meeting, won't you?"

Amanda met her palm to palm, unhurriedly moving their hands up and down. "I don't understand anything that's happening," she choked.

"You mustn't let it get the best of you, dear," Katherine muttered. "Now," she turned crisply, "Have you met Cooper Hansen?" Katherine increased her volume and extended an arm, waving Cooper over as the crowd's conversations lifted throughout the room.

He didn't object, making a few strides to meet them.

"I... have... good to see you again, Cooper." Amanda smiled.

"Ah, yes, we met at the ball in Tokyo," Cooper smiled, keeping up with the charade he assumed Amanda was attempting.

"Katherine, so good to see you again," he said, leaning in to kiss her cheek as Amanda tried to mask her surprise. "I love that the two of you have met," he said. "Amanda, Katherine is an old associate of my father's..."

"*Old?*" Katherine echoed, feigning offense as laughter rippled between her and Cooper.

Amanda didn't respond; she felt frozen. Katherine was more than Hansen's old associate—she knew that was a cover—but which direction Katherine's loyalties leaned, Amanda no longer trusted herself to guess. She had spent the whole day pretending, but with them—with Cooper—she didn't know how to *not* be herself.

"You look a little surprised," Cooper grinned.

"Oh, it's... been a lot today," Amanda's eyes widened.

"Indeed." Katherine agreed before shifting to allow space between them. "I'll let the two of you... get to know each other," she smiled, leaving Amanda and Cooper at the wall of windows.

As soon as he knew there was no one within earshot, and the noise of the room could be their protection, Cooper lowered his head near Amanda's and simply said. "Do you think we can meet for a cup of coffee somewhere before I leave the country?"

CHAPTER FIVE

Knoxville, Tennessee: April 2008

MOST PEOPLE KNEW THE university. Harwell Theological Institute wasn't just a name in American religious circles—it was *the* name. With sprawling red-brick buildings, a presidential seal, and a polished alumni network that reached into politics, publishing, and pulpit culture, the campus had earned its place on the map. Students came from across the country to study ministry, family counseling, law, ethics, and constitutional theology under the shadow of its founder's towering influence.

What most people didn't know—what *no one* outside the inner circle talked about—was what lay at the end of a small service road curving quietly off the main campus—a road the university residents overlooked. It wasn't on any of the maps they were given. Staff referred to it only as "the access route," if they acknowledged it at all.

But if you followed it long enough, past the utility sheds and weathered maintenance trucks, it sloped gently into a wooded gulley and rose again, opening up to a discreet complex of beige-brick buildings with flat roofs and lightly-tinted windows. There was no welcome sign. No school colors. Just a pair of heavy doors and a small placard mounted near the entry: The Ridge—a name as vague as it was forgettable. At the front of the small compound, where a gravel road met the pavement, stood a small house that the girls and staffers called the main office.

The girls' home didn't show up on campus tours, but it was there, just a fifteen-minute walk down a quiet gravel path through the woods. Three times a day, food from the university's main dining hall was packed into unmarked carts and ferried down the road by kitchen staff, the trays covered with lids to keep in the steam. The delivery schedule was never posted, and the carts always traveled the back route, past the dumpsters and the loading dock, where few eyes ever lingered.

To the public, Harwell's empire stood for moral clarity and academic excellence. But to the girls who lived at The Ridge, it stood for something else entirely—a place where mistakes were repackaged as testimonies, silence was branded obedience, and sob stories were currency.

Amanda had barely touched her soggy cereal when Miss Marla's cheerful voice floated into the dining hall. "Amanda Hopkins, honey? They're ready for you in the main office."

The room quieted around Amanda as the conversations lulled. Everyone knew what the office meeting meant. She stood slowly, wiping her hands on the front of her maternity jeans, and followed Miss Marla down the narrow hall lined with corkboards and motivational posters.

They felt the crunch of tiny rocks beneath their feet as they made their way along the wooded path to the meeting place, a few beige buildings over. Inside the office, the air shifted. Miss Judy sat behind her large desk, and a man in a crisp brown suit stood, tipping his head towards her as Amanda entered.

"Ladies," his gruff voice greeted them.

"Hello," Miss Marla couldn't help following proper greeting etiquette, but Amanda stayed silent, noticing a thick folder with her name stamped across the top. Miss Marla backed out of the door again, going as quietly as she came.

Miss Judy smiled, her warmth so complete it pressed down like a quilt in July. "Amanda, please, sit."

She obeyed, the vinyl chair beneath her creaking as she lowered herself into the seat.

"This is Mr. Lindell. He works with child placement services in our transition homes. He's here to help finalize arrangements for your daughter."

Amanda blinked, heat rushing to her face as she jerked her head. "Arrangements? No." Her fingers clenched against her knees. "I haven't agreed to anything."

Miss Judy folded her hands. "A lovely family in Richmond. God-fearing and stable. She'll have a nursery with lace curtains and a big yard to run in when she's older. They've even chosen a name—Faith." She cupped her hands to her heart as if moved by the thought that faith alone could place a child into the arms of a woman pining to be a mother.

Amanda felt her body tilt forward, like gravity had suddenly been redistributed. "No. I didn't agree to giving her up."

Miss Judy's smile thinned. "Amanda, sweetheart. We've discussed this."

"No," Amanda said, her voice shaking. "*You* discussed it. But I never agreed."

Mr. Lindell cleared his throat and slid a form across the desk.

"Ma'am—can I call you Amanda?" he asked with a rehearsed tenderness.

Amanda nodded as he inched his chair closer to hers.

"I know it's not easy once you're brought here. These decisions are tough to make, aren't they?" he said, taking her hand. "But it's my job to make sure your little one has a good life. Two parents with steady income and a nice home can provide the stability that you can't offer right now. You want that for your little girl, right?"

Tears pooled in Amanda's eyes as she nodded her head more out of confusion than agreement. Perhaps she didn't know what was best.

"I know you do, honey," Mr. Lindell nodded. "So, we need you to sign some papers. This one is already complete. It's the consent form from Cooper Hansen. He's signed over his parental rights already, but we need both signatures for legal purposes."

Amanda yanked her hand from Mr. Lindell's grip. "That's not possible. Cooper wouldn't do that."

"He mailed it to us directly."

"I want to talk to him," she said, panic beginning to rise. "I want to call him."

Miss Judy's tone remained sweet yet firm. "Amanda, phones are restricted. You know this. Calls home stir up old attachments, and we can't have divided loyalties when you're trying to do what's best for the baby."

"But this is different," she insisted. "We should decide together."

Mr. Lindell tapped the form. "He's made his decision, Amanda. I assure you, this is legal and binding. Your signature is all that stands in the way of you offering the best gift you can for that little life inside you."

Amanda reached for the document with trembling fingers, eyes scanning the signature. It looked like Cooper's. But it also looked… off. The letters were too neat. Too carefully aligned.

"I don't believe he signed this," Amanda said. "He wouldn't. We had plans."

Miss Judy's voice finally sharpened. "Plans change. People change. He's moved on. He's off to college soon, right? He's thinking about his future."

Amanda stared at the paper, willing it to dissolve, to shatter into a thousand tiny pieces before her eyes. Why wasn't God able to do that? Where was her miracle?

"I'm thinking about my future, too," she sputtered.

"Then make the wise choice, Amanda," Mr. Lindell said, sliding a second form toward her. "Sign. And let everyone move forward."

Amanda stood, shaking her head in disgust. "No. I can't. Not today. I won't do it without talking to him first."

Her smile having disappeared, Miss Judy painted a clear look of disappointment on her face, attempting to coax Amanda into contrition.

"Then we'll give you time. But not forever. You still need to be ready to leave for service in an hour." Miss Judy raised her voice because Amanda was halfway out the door before she finished her sentence.

"I'm sorry, Mr. Lindell, you know how these meetings go."

"Yeah, it's alright. It'd almost be too easy if they all signed at our first meeting, wouldn't it?" he joked.

"I guess it's good they're keeping us on our toes," Miss Judy agreed. "Thanks for stopping by before service. I appreciate it."

"All in the Lord's timing," he said.

Every week, the girls were instructed to wear their "Sunday best," which meant skirts that swished below the knee and cardigans that draped over flowing maternity shirts. If their hair was curled, faces powdered, and lips rouged in shades deemed wholesome, they got extra compliments from the staff.

Amanda stood in the bathroom, staring at herself in the mirror, her lipstick and made-up face feeling like a betrayal. She pressed a damp washcloth to her mouth and wiped it off, ignoring the pink smear left behind. Ellie appeared in the mirror behind her.

"Hey, smile. If you don't, you'll just get in trouble," she said, adjusting Amanda's necklace.

"I already am."

Ellie sighed, then spread her lips across her teeth in a performative grin. "Don't let them see you crack."

She took Amanda's hand as they boarded a white shuttle bus, jolting as it climbed the back road, winding its way toward the main stretch of campus. While *The Ridge* could never be revealed to be in such close proximity and affiliation to the university, the Cromwell family and their ilk loved displaying the girls themselves as a moneymaker and morality stunt. Amanda and Ellie sat shoulder to shoulder for the ride, the hum of the engine underscored by the quiet chatter of other passengers. Out the window, the landscape shifted from scrubby trees to neat brick facades—the south campus first, then the long shadow of the residence halls, and finally the gleaming glass of the business school. Each landmark revealed its slow approach into the heart of the institution, where the shuttle rolled to a stop before the massive auditorium. Its towering columns rose in solemn symmetry, framing the church's façade in a way that made the building feel like a monument to authority.

The sanctuary was cool and cavernous—its pale walls illuminated by rows of soft, even lighting that glowed from above rather than through stained glass. At the back, three cameras stood on tripods, their operators in headset mics adjusting focus and angles with practiced ease. On center stage above the pulpit, a large projection screen displayed the church's emblem: a shining crown with the words *His Kingdom Now,* which was bathed in artificial light that lent it a familiar, broadcast-ready clarity.

Two ushers approached the girls in the lobby, greeting Miss Judy with a smile. "Go on, girls," she instructed.

The men in ruby blazers funneled the girls down a side aisle like a quiet tide, and Amanda felt herself carried in a haze more than led. Spotlights warmed the stage in a careful wash—a brightness that made everything appear gentler, softer, as if holiness were in need of a lighting cue.

She'd thought Miss Judy's comment to them this morning—"the pastor wants to bless you today"-- meant a prayer and perhaps a basket of toiletries, but no. She and Ellie, along with half a dozen other girls, were quickly ushered into position between the choir risers and the gleaming pulpit, where the cameras could see them plainly.

Pastor Harwell strode out with his signature stride—the kind meant to read from the back row and straight through the lens. The pastoral swagger of a televangelist came with practiced ease, crisp sleeves, and a benevolent crescent of a smile calibrated for television.

"I was glad when they said unto me: let us go into the house of the Lord," he began, and applause rose to the rafters in the three-thousand-seat auditorium.

"This morning, we get to be the hands and feet of Jesus," he said, and the sanctuary answered with scattered amens.

On cue, a volunteer adjusted the stand of a shoulder camera at the back, and Amanda watched the red tally light bloom as a live feed streamed onto the massive screen above them. Her heart gave a quick, startled thud at her own image and the curve of her belly under the loaner maternity top.

Ellie edged closer. "Breathe," she whispered, barely moving her lips as if she had lessons in ventriloquism. "This is the part where you smile and pretend you're happy. It gets easier after the first time."

Ellie's presence steadied Amanda like a hand at the small of her back. She had told Amanda in the shuttle that "blessing" could mean anything here: a prayer, a testimony, a demonstration. Par for the course. None of it cruel, exactly. Just...part of the machine. But no one thought of this.

"Many of you don't realize," Pastor Harwell said, the cadence warming into a distinct intimacy, "that right here in Knoxville, these girls live in a beautiful home where they are safe, loved, and given a future."

A murmured awe went round the room as prerecorded footage of the town was displayed until the camera coasted toward a fringe of tall pines as if entering a secret. Before it could reach too many recognizable markers, the camera dissolved to a sunlit kitchen with a bowl of oranges, a chore chart, and a girl sitting on a kitchen chair sipping a cup of tea, her belly round and firm. Amanda didn't recognize the footage—no one had filmed *her*—but it felt close enough to prick her skin.

Harwell's voice was gentle. "These young mothers are brave."

He turned and extended a palm toward them, and the congregation applauded again, some people already on their feet.

"They chose life. They chose hope." His phrases stacked like building blocks. "They. Chose. Life. Hope. Dignity." Each word laid another brick, constructing a platform to display these lessons on.

Amanda stared at the polished wood of the pulpit to avoid the staring faces—a field of tear-bright eyes, and live TV audiences. She felt both exposed and theoretical, like a chart from a textbook—typical case, desired outcome. *Blessing*, she repeated to herself, as if the word could be broken down and swallowed.

Ellie leaned in slightly, lucky that the camera hadn't returned to a shot of them. "It'll be over soon," she said, not soothing so much as factual.

On the screen, the feed cut to a graphic with a mother holding a child, pastel serif letters splattered across them with a phone number to call. Pledge cards appeared like magic at the ends of pews, paper gliding hand to hand.

"The vision is big," Harwell said, " We believe we can plant homes like this across the nation. Not dozens. Hundreds. Imagine a network of hope from coast to coast," he bellowed, arms outstretched as another wave of applause rolled forward.

A donor video followed, stitched with swelling strings and testimonies: a house mother describing midnight prayers; a physician talking about prenatal care; a girl younger than Amanda, cheeks still round with babyhood, saying, "They told me I wasn't alone."

Each cut returned to the live stage where the girls stood in a row. Amanda steadied herself as Ellie tapped a secret code on her shoulder: *Here. With. You.* When the camera swept across them again, Amanda kept her eyes on the crossbar of the balcony rail, counting screws. *Don't cry. Don't flinch.*

"Some of these courageous young women," Harwell continued, "are still in school. Some left unsafe environments. All of them are our daughters today." He paused, and the sanctuary answered with a low amen.

"As a church, we get to say to them: You're not a problem to solve—you're a promise to keep. And it only costs us five hundred dollars a week to house them. What a small price to pay for a life. God's calling you to it today, isn't He?" Pastor Harwell stretched out his hands as if in surrender. "Answer the call."

Ushers were again deployed along the aisles efficiently as bees, collecting pledge envelopes. The band's keyboardist wrapped the moment in a soft melody while the choir hummed a familiar chorus. A camera operator crouched for a low angle like a wildlife photographer, and Amanda's belly tightened—a small, private contraction of panic—until it eased.

"Almost there," Ellie murmured.

Harwell segued to prayer, inviting churchgoers to rise as they began to ebb like a field of wheat. Amanda closed her eyes while the language flowed over her in pestilent ooze—"a hedge of protection...a future and a hope...the plans predestined for them"—and she tried not to suffocate on the shame.

"Before you go," Harwell said, pivoting smoothly to again face the girls, "We bless you. We're proud of you." He smiled, and the cameras drank it in.

A staffer at stage left stepped forward to shepherd them off in an orderly line, and as they began to move, the congregation rose in a standing ovation that felt generous and somehow far away, like heavy rain on a rooftop that you can hear the music of, but cannot let wash over your face.

Back in the wings, the girls filed in quietly. Ellie exhaled first, letting a careful laugh slip out. "You okay?" she asked her friend, already knowing the answer.

"I didn't know that's what they meant," Amanda said, her voice thin.

Ellie's mouth tipped in a smirk. "It's this place," she said gently. "They make you think love means care, but then they switch the meaning to submission. And they tell you that's all love ever was. It's temporary, though. Just remember that." She bumped Amanda's shoulder with a nudge. "You did fine."

Amanda nodded, though inside everything felt sifted—heart, nerves, and a future that was disappearing like a foggy dream. She pictured the map Harwell had conjured, homes like theirs dotting the country, multiplying under church slogans and camera lights. She couldn't let herself think about it for too long.

Ellie threaded her fingers into Amanda's as they stepped into the corridor, the noise of the sanctuary blurring behind them. "We'd better go into the sanctuary," Ellie said with a lilt that cut the haze of Amanda's scattered thoughts. "At least now we can sit in the back."

Amanda managed a small laugh. She laid a hand on her belly as if steadying both of them and let Ellie tug her toward the back doors.

Later that night, Amanda slipped quietly into the music room. Normally, the girls had to sign up for an hour or two at a time, a rigid system meant to accommodate the lessons the home paraded as enrichment—piano scales, vocal warmups, calligraphy—tokens of a "robust program" that donors could underwrite while the girls themselves remained hidden away. But on a Sunday night, the recreation wing was hushed and hollow. This was her one sanctuary, the only solace she had managed to carve out for herself in this place.

The room was barely larger than a closet, the air close and tinged with the faint scent of varnish and old wood. An upright piano crowded the far wall, its keys dulled with use. A few stringed instruments hung neatly in their mounts, silent sentinels waiting for hands that might never touch them, and a small collection of battered percussion pieces lay scattered on a low shelf.

Amanda's eyes went to the ukulele. It perched crookedly on its holder, slightly out of tune but still intact, as though time itself had passed it by. She lifted it carefully and settled onto the narrow piano bench. For a moment, she only held it, letting her palms remember the curve of the body, the smoothness of the frets beneath her fingertips. Slowly, she began to play, her fingers searching the strings the way they had once searched her grandmother's hands for guidance.

The first strum broke the silence, discordant and sharp. She winced, then leaned close, her ear bent to the sound, twisting each tuning peg with deliberate care. The notes wavered and shifted, gradually bending toward harmony. It was almost as if she could hear Grandma Nellie's voice again, steady and patient, reminding her to trust her ear, to listen for the center of the sound.

They say April showers bring May flowers,
And baby, I know that it's true.
Cause my darlin' little Daisy, that's when I know I'll see you...

A gentle crack in her voice rose, but Amanda swallowed it down and kept going, not noticing the stream of tears that flowed steadily down both sides of her face.

The world says wait—tells me to hide,
But everything within me cries,
To hold my breath, to hold the line,
Just to see it in your eyes...

Little flower... Daisy, you'll be mine.

A soft knock rapped at the door, startling her as Amanda stopped playing. The door creaked open as Ellie peeked in.

"I figured you were here," she whispered.

Amanda exhaled. "Did I wake anyone?"

"No, they're all in bed."

Amanda looked down. "I wrote it for her."

"I know." Ellie sat beside her on the bench. "It's beautiful. You're allowed to want her, you know?"

"Want her, just not *have* her."

Ellie didn't argue. She couldn't. She knew what it was to want out, to treat the whole ordeal as something to survive and leave behind. Most of them did. But Amanda...she carried herself as if the child was not her downfall but her joy. Ellie saw it clearly: Amanda wasn't dreaming of escape—she was dreaming of belonging, with her baby and the boy she loved. It made her brave in ways none of them dared to be, even if fighting the system felt impossible.

Amanda looked at the ukulele, then at her friend. "It's like they want to take her before I've even had a chance to know her."

"They do."

Amanda let the silence settle.

"But they haven't taken this," Ellie added, tapping the carved wood, the hollow sound of the instrument in her hand reverberating at her touch. "And they haven't taken you."

Amanda nodded, eyes brimming. "Not yet," Amanda said as she began to loudly strum John Denver's *Take Me Home, Country Roads,* her favorite song to sing with her grandma.

And for a moment, they let the music fill the room to the edges—two girls holding onto the only things still truly theirs, until the hallway lights snapped off, and footsteps creaked across the old floorboards.

"Girls, are you singing worldly songs in here?" Miss Judy flung the door open. She liked to think her sugar-sweet tone fooled them most of the time, but the truth was, her sharp edges always showed. And when a rule was broken, she didn't even try to hide them.

"No, ma'am. Just going to bed," Ellie said, grabbing Amanda's hand and pulling her towards the hall.

"I'll take that," Miss Judy said, snatching the ukulele from Amanda as the girls scuttled past. "You'd do well to remember your place here, Miss Hopkins."

CHAPTER SIX

Bucharest, Romania: The Morning After the Tour

"I've got a meeting downtown," Tristan said, crossing the room to adjust his tie in the full-length mirror. "But it shouldn't take too long."

The sheer layer of curtains swayed in the early morning breeze, filtering pale gold light across the polished parquet floors of the hotel suite. Amanda stood barefoot near the open terrace doors, her coffee cooling in her hands, while the distant hum of Bucharest stirred to life below. Behind her, the muffled sounds of Tristan moving through the bedroom had created a quiet rhythm—a soft cadence of drawers opening and hangers shifting, the familiar murmur of a man preparing for the day.

He buttoned the cuff of his shirt, the crisp lines of his suit already setting him apart from the softness of the morning. Amanda turned to watch him, one shoulder tucked into the doorframe, her silhouette caught between light and shadow.

She nodded, a small smile teasing her lips. "Okay. I've got some errands of my own—might do a little shopping while you're out. Take your time. Maybe we can meet for lunch?"

"That would be perfect," he said, pressing a kiss to her cheek. Then he paused, hands still at his collar, as if weighing something fragile.

"I've been thinking," he began again. "We're leaving tomorrow for the next phase. Three more facility tours—Nairobi, São Paulo, and then New York. It's six weeks total, but the pace won't be brutal. We'll have time."

He stepped toward her and took her hand in his. His thumb brushed across her knuckles with the sort of tenderness that seemed to ask for nothing and yet everything all at once.

"I want you to come with me," he said. "Not for the work stuff. Just... come. Shop today, get what you need. Cancel any flights and come, please."

Amanda drew in a breath, her fingers curling gently around his. "You're not asking me for an answer."

"No," he said. "I'm not. This isn't about that. This is just... us. The time, the places, the mornings like this. I want more of them. And I won't ask you again about marriage until you want to discuss it. I promise."

She breathed in slowly, the moment settling over her like warm silk. "I kind of want to meet Lyla in Paris."

His mouth curved at the corner, a quiet smile blooming. "Then meet her. But let me send you my itinerary so we can plan around it. São Paulo will be easy. New York, even easier."

"I don't want to tell you no," she murmured.

"Then don't," he said, brushing a kiss to her forehead, then her cheek again, before lingering for a long moment at her lips. The weight of his affection settled in the space between them like a promise.

But before she could say anything else, he was already reaching for his jacket, checking his watch, murmuring something about traffic. Amanda followed him to the door, her hand catching his one last time.

"I'll see you at lunch," she said. "Text me where, and I'll meet you."

He kissed her again—brief but full of intention.

"Sounds good. Love you," he said in a rush, then froze.

He hadn't meant to say it like that. Not hurried, not casually. But the words had tumbled out, and he didn't want them back. He had already asked her to marry him, but it wasn't until now that he realized he had never actually said the words: I love you. Not aloud. Not in the way she deserved. He hadn't told her that he had never known a love like this one before. That his heart leapt at the thought of her and capsized at the sight of her. He wanted to shout it to anyone and everyone who would listen.

Tristan loved Amanda.

He began to turn, but Amanda kept his hand in hers, holding him still.

"I love you too, Tristan," she said, reaching up to kiss him again—a short, sweet peck that sent a chill between them. "I'll see you later."

He leaned his forehead to hers. "I don't want to go," he whispered softly against her skin.

"I know," she whispered, placing her palm against his chest, giving a gentle push. "But you have to."

He nodded, then leaned in for one more kiss before he disappeared down the corridor, the echo of his departure as soft as the morning light.

Amanda made her way to the bedroom where the linens remained rumpled from the night before. The hush in the suite felt deeper, the scent of Tristan's cologne still clinging faintly to the air. She crossed to his side of the bed, intending only to smooth the sheets, but her eyes caught on the small velvet box sitting quietly on the nightstand.

The soft blue square hadn't been hidden, only left as if it belonged there. She reached for it slowly, the texture plush beneath her fingertips, her breath catching before she lifted the lid.

The large diamond stared back at her, unapologetic in its brilliance, flanked by sapphires so dark they teetered on the edge of black. Midnight stones that shimmered violet when the light struck them just so. The whole ring was almost too exquisite, like it belonged in a showcase, not a life.

She held it in her palm, letting the light catch the facets, then slipped it onto her finger with a careful slowness, as though the act itself might trigger something irreversible. It fit perfectly. She turned her hand in the light, the stone catching fire as she flexed her fingers. She couldn't help the small smile that tugged at her lips, both awed and unnerved by how right it felt—how easily it claimed space on her skin.

The subtle vibration of her phone on the dresser pulled her from thought as she picked it up to read a message flashing across the screen. It was Cooper. He had told her he was going to text.

I'm downstairs. Can we meet at the hotel restaurant in an hour?

Amanda stared at the words, her heart thudding before she typed.

Sure. See you soon.

She placed the phone face down on the dresser as if willing its existence away. She moved quickly, hoping to meet Cooper sooner rather than later—just to get it over with. She knew what she wanted to say. That he needed to stop contacting her. That the past was behind them. No hard feelings. Seeing him again had been the closure she needed. That's what she'd say.

She slipped into a burnt orange blazer and the heels she'd kicked off the night before. Her hair still held its curl as she ran a brush through it, smoothing the flyaways with her hands and a touch of gel. But standing in front of the mirror, she knew it wasn't her hair or her clothes that betrayed her. It was her eyes, just barely masking the fatigue from not being able to fully settle her nerves.

She paused, studying the version of herself who knew how to perform with poise under pressure, and she let out a breath.

When she left the safety of her suite, Amanda began mentally rehearsing neutrality like a foreign language. But as the lobby café unfurled beneath the mezzanine with its limestone grandeur, she spotted Cooper sitting in a plush chair of the waiting area.

And she forgot everything she'd planned to say.

She steadied herself, approaching carefully, letting her expression settle into a measured smile.

"Oh, hey," Cooper said, looking up. "You made it."

"I know I'm early," she said, smoothing an invisible line along her blazer, needing to do something with her hands.

He gestured toward a nearby table by that marble fountain, its soft splash masking the clatter of teacups and conversation. "Can we sit?"

"Of course," she replied, her voice barely above the murmur of the café. They walked in step, the silence between them carrying more than words could.

He pulled out a chair, allowing Amanda to sit first, his eyes never quite leaving her. She felt the weight of it—the way he searched her face like he might find the version of her he once knew tucked between lines that hadn't been there before.

"So, how are you?" he asked gently.

Amanda scoffed, glancing away. "Is that why you wanted to have coffee? To ask me how I am?"

Cooper exhaled, leaning forward with his elbows on the table. "Ugh, no. I just—" He hesitated, then surrendered the truth. "It's just good to see you."

She looked at him carefully, her face unreadable. "It's definitely something..." Her tone was dry, but not unkind. "I hear you're getting married."

"Erm... yeah. Next summer," he said, rubbing the back of his neck. "And congratulations are in order for you, too, I see." He gestured toward her left hand, offering a grin that faltered as it formed.

Amanda felt the heat rise to her cheeks. She clasped her hands together in her lap, concealing the ring she hadn't accepted but nevertheless had forgotten to remove. "Oh," she said lightly. "Thank you." She didn't owe him an explanation. Instead, she inhaled deeply, willing herself to stay composed.

A waiter arrived, offering drinks and pastries, and they placed their orders like strangers pretending they'd only just met. The silence thickened, broken only by the quiet clink of silverware and Amanda's own pulse in her ears.

"Cooper," she said finally, cutting through the pretense, "what's going on? Why did you ask for my number? And what role do you actually play in your dad's campaign?"

The words landed with more weight than she'd expected. She hadn't meant to sound accusatory, but her voice had sharpened around the edges.

He blinked. "Campaign? Oh... none, really. Dad wants me to follow him into politics, but..."

"I hear you are running for office."

He shook his head. "No, just rumors. I couldn't bring myself to do it."

"So you're not, like, a State Rep or anything?"

Cooper laughed, a dry, self-deprecating sound. "God, no. I think my dad just wanted to rattle his opponents. Show them there's another Hansen in the wings. But I've never been good at playing Daddy's pawn."

"Haven't you?" Amanda asked before she could stop herself. Her voice cracked just slightly, and she winced. "Sorry. That came out wrong."

"No. It's fair," Cooper said with a quiet nod. "When my mom told me you didn't want to see me after you lost the baby, I should've come anyway. Even just to say goodbye. I really thought I—"

"What?" Amanda interrupted, her tone sharpened by a disbelief edged with hurt. "What are you talking about?"

He flinched, his head tilting back in a quick motion, startled by the force in her voice. "You know... my mom told me when you miscarried, that you were in the hospital for observation. Before I could visit, she told me you'd been moved to some place to recover. I wanted to call, but she swore it would only set back your healing."

Words continued to spill from his mouth, but Amanda only heard a ringing in her ears—a crescendo of grief and disbelief that narrowed the world into a tunnel of sound. When the noise finally cleared, his voice found her again.

"Amanda?" he asked softly. "Are you okay? I just wanted to say I'm sorry. I didn't mean to hurt you. Not then. And certainly not now."

His voice broke at the hinges, and the weight of everything he didn't know seemed to collapse into that one moment.

"Cooper," she managed, breathless. "Do you not even know?"

She reached for her cup, her hand trembling as the stones on her ring caught the light and sent fractured color across the table.

"That place they sent me to..." Her voice caught in her throat. She tried again, but words failed. The nondisclosure agreement throbbed in her memory like a wound.

Cooper's gaze fell to the table.

"I'm sorry you went through it alone," he said finally. "I guess that's what I wanted to say. I should've called. Should've come. I thought I was honoring your wishes. But, I guess I always knew I should've fought for you."

Amanda closed her eyes, her voice cracking. "She had your eyes—our daughter. They didn't let me hold her. Only kept her in the room long enough for me to see that she was real."

The truth seeped into the space between them, and in that instant, whatever fragile tether had held the moment together unraveled. Reality broke into a million tiny fractions of time, and Cooper's breath left him in a stutter. He went rigid, as if the air had been knocked from his lungs. His face blanched, then flushed, the color rising as if disbelief and comprehension were battling for the same space.

"I..." he whispered. "Amanda, I didn't know. I swear to God, I didn't know."

For the first time, he saw a woman who had been forced to carry the unbearable alone.

"They told me... they said... that you didn't want to see me. That it would hurt you too much."

Amanda's eyes glistened, but her tears held.

"They lied to both of us," she said. "They sent me away, made me sign papers I didn't understand. And then they made her disappear."

Cooper stood suddenly, a hand pressed to his mouth, the other raking through his hair as if trying to tear the grief out of him.

"Oh God," he muttered. "Amanda, I would've—"

But he didn't finish. He couldn't. He didn't need to. And as if on cue, a gentle, calming presence approached them from behind.

"Everything okay here?" Tristan's voice cut through the tension like a clean edge.

Amanda turned slowly, her mouth parting in surprise, but words caught in her throat. She rose to her feet as time slowed and the air stretched taut between them like a high wire threatening to plunge anyone who dared walk it to their death.

Tristan remained just behind her, hands casually tucked into the pockets of his slacks, though his jaw started to tense and his eyes sharpened with quiet alertness. His gaze moved between Amanda and Cooper—not with suspicion, but like a man trained to read the room.

Cooper's posture shifted first. He stepped back instinctively, his expression becoming more composed, but Amanda could still see the pain etched behind his eyes.

"I was just leaving," Cooper said quietly, straightening his back. His voice had been stripped of pretense, softened by everything that had just cracked open between them. He looked at Amanda one last time, and when he spoke again, his voice carried a grief he could no longer hide.

"Thank you for meeting me. I…" He paused, swallowing hard. "I'm glad you're well. It's been nice catching up."

It hadn't been nice; it was cruel, and they both knew it. But there was no space for truth in the narrow silence the three of them shared. Amanda nodded slowly, her lips pressing into a line she could not bend into a smile.

Cooper turned, walking away with the uneven, weighted gait of someone newly haunted—his steps too slow to be called a retreat, and too heavy to be called escape.

Amanda remained frozen where she stood. Her heart still pounded as her breath thinned to vapor. She didn't look at Tristan immediately. She couldn't.

"Should I ask what that was about?" he said, his voice low, laced with caution rather than accusation.

She shook her head, finally lifting her gaze to meet his. "Not now."

His face softened slightly, but his eyes never left her, and he reached for her hand with a tenderness that caught her off guard. His fingers found hers, familiar and grounding. But when he felt the ring on her finger, his touch stilled.

"You're… wearing it?" he asked, his brows lifting, his voice suddenly lighter and yet disbelieving.

Amanda let a smile curl her lips slightly, nodding slowly. She reached for the warmth that had bloomed earlier that morning, willing it to rise again, even as a hollowness lingered beneath. The fragile light that surfaced felt like sunshine breaking through fog—bright for a moment, but never steady.

The echo of Cooper's words pressed against her chest, but she pushed it down, grasping for pieces of the brightness Tristan was offering her.

"Yes," she whispered.

Tristan's smile unfurled across his face like a spring thaw. He lifted her hand to his lips, brushing a kiss against her ring finger, reverent and unhurried.

"I love you," he murmured, not caring who overheard. He wrapped his arms around her waist, scooping her into him and twirling her around before setting her down again, breathless with joy. "I didn't expect a yes like this... but I'll take it."

Amanda quirked a brow, trying to rally her playfulness. "Don't make it a thing," she said with a teasing edge, though the words trembled faintly against the knot still lodged in her chest.

"Too late," he laughed, tucking a strand of hair behind her ear. "*Yes* is my new favorite word."

She leaned in, resting her head briefly against his shoulder.

"Well," she said, pulling back to meet his eyes, "I haven't said yes to the tour."

"But you said yes to *me,*" he countered, his grin boyish, and his heart on display.

He took her hand again, leading her down the corridor toward the elevators. "Let's skip the restaurant. Room service for lunch?"

Amanda exhaled slowly, letting herself be carried by the moment. "Yes," she said simply.

He stopped and kissed her again, just as the elevator chimed. "There it is," he said with a soft laugh. "My favorite word."

As the doors slid open and they stepped inside, his gaze into her eyes intensified, "I want to give you a thousand reasons to keep saying yes to me, Amanda Hopkins."

And she, without answering, leaned into the safety of his arms, knowing full well that their love couldn't erase the past. But for this breath, in this moment, it softened every jagged edge.

Chapter Seven

Paris, France: A Spyce Girls Weekend

Autumn in Paris holds an unexpected warmth with its grand apartments housing fireplaces in every room, bustling bakeries, and cozy paper shops that literally sell nothing but paper. Amanda could get lost in it. She wasn't a fan of traveling there in the summer when heat and tourists swelled the city to its bursting point, but November was perfect.

Melody had already arrived the evening before, Lyla having taken charge of accommodations like a pro. The apartment was a fifth-floor gem tucked above a quintessential Parisian boulevard, with high ceilings, soaring windows, and a wrought iron balcony draped in climbing vines that blossomed beautifully in the spring. Inside, it was the kind of place that made you feel like the main character in a film—layered with moody charm and carefully chosen decadence.

Velvet settees in saturated tones of sangria red and turquoise blue flanked a marble fireplace, where taper candles leaned like they'd been caught mid-conversation. Gilded picture frames lined the walls—some with modern art, others with vintage

Vogue covers. A sculptural chandelier dripped crystals over a round dining table set with a variety of crystal glasses and vintage china.

Lyla had been in Paris on assignment for one of her more eccentric clients, a bride with a flair for drama and a budget to match. The production was full tilt: couture gowns, a replica marble corridor, a full camera crew filming scenes with all the elegance of a European heist film. Lyla photographed the bride in a series of high-fashion editorial shots while the film crew captured slow-motion sequences meant to premiere at the reception like a blockbuster teaser.

"It's basically *Ocean's Eleven* meets *Bridgerton*, with a train of silk tulle," she said, half-laughing, half-serious. "And I got to boss around lighting techs in French." She perched herself on a window seat, sipping espresso from an antique cup.

"That's crazy. I've never heard anything like it," Melody said, shaking her head.

"It's called having too much money," Lyla said. "But these crazy shoots do pay my bills," she admitted.

"Wild," Melody scoffed, allowing a brief moment to fill the space between them. "What time does she get in?"

Lyla looked at her watch. "Should be here any minute, really," she said.

"Does she know?" Melody asked, lifting her own cup for a sip.

"Not yet. It doesn't exactly scream: *appropriate texting material,"* Lyla replied, her eyebrows raising like startled exclamation marks.

Melody nodded in agreement when a knock echoed with three crisp raps against the heavy door.

"That's her!" Lyla said, leaping up with a grin. Regardless of any pressing circumstance, she could feel nothing but excitement when it meant seeing her lifelong best friend.

Melody stepped aside as Lyla flung open the door.

Amanda stood in the hall in a belted wool coat, sunglasses, and heels that looked far too dangerous for travel. A designer weekender bag hung from one shoulder, and in her free hand, she held a wrapped bouquet of white peonies.

"Well," she said, stepping inside and surveying the apartment, "you two have outdone yourselves. Are you sure this isn't a movie set?"

"It might be," Melody teased. "We haven't ruled it out. Think of it as our Spyce Girl debut."

Lyla grabbed Amanda's hand and twirled her into the center of the room. "You're glowing. Like... suspiciously glowing. Spill."

Amanda pulled off her sunglasses and tossed them onto a velvet chaise. "I brought champagne."

"No one brings champagne unless they have news," Melody said, taking the bottle Amanda had passed her.

"I do," Amanda said, a slow smile forming as she held out her left hand.

Both Lyla and Melody gasped in unison.

"You didn't—" Melody began.

"She did," Lyla cut in, eyes wide. "Holy shit. Is *that* the ring?"

Amanda nodded. "I said yes!" She put on her best girly-girl tone, her words lilting upwards with intended flair.

The briefest moment of stunned hush overcrowded the space between the women until Lyla squealed, "Well, okay, then! Oh my gosh, are you sure?"

Amanda laughed. "I love you. And yes, I mean, as sure as I can be, right? He's such an amazing guy!"

"Yes, he is," Melody confirmed. "And you deserve to be *so* happy."

There was a moment, silent and suspended, where the weight of reality tugged at the edges of their joy, daring to intrude. But then, almost imperceptibly, shoulders softened, eyes brightened, and breath returned with a shared kind of defiance.

Lyla was the first to move, grabbing Amanda's hands and pulling her into the center of the room with a breathless laugh. Melody followed, walking to the console to flip on a record player, the soft crackle of vinyl filling the space like a memory. The three women leaned into the light instead of the shadow, choosing laughter over caution, champagne over consequence. In that flicker of time, they danced—not away from their worries, but in spite of them.

They poured the champagne as laughter spilled over like the liquid they were ingesting, effervescent and unfiltered. And for the briefest of moments, the questions could wait.

Lyla twirled her champagne flute around in her fingers, then suddenly gasped.

"Oh! I nearly forgot."

She jumped up from her perch and disappeared into the hallway, her phone already pressed to her ear.

"If I can charm a lady I know—the owner of this amazing couture gown shop—we're going wedding dress shopping today," she called over her shoulder.

Amanda blinked, laughing. "Wait, what?"

Melody arched an eyebrow as she poured a second glass. "I feel like with Lyla, champagne equals impulsive plans with very expensive outcomes."

Amanda accepted the refilled glass. "I haven't been here even thirty minutes."

"You got *engaged,*" Melody said, gesturing dramatically with her glass. "How could we just sit around drinking and not drag you into a Parisian bridal boutique?"

In the hallway, Lyla was mid-plead, slipping between French and English like a seasoned negotiator.

"Oui, oui, je comprends—but imagine the content, no charge for this influencer campaign. A newly engaged American bride to the world's most famous bachelor, très chic, très sentimental, surrounded by her *amies*—all in your vintage line. Oh, please, come on, Marie. You still owe me for my time in Saint-Tropez. I delivered so much more than you were expecting, and you know it." Lyla's singsong charm was irresistible.

Amanda leaned back against the velvet settee, letting the moment soak in. The city outside hummed softly, veiled in a silver winter light. Everything about this felt too good, too golden, almost too *right*.

"So," she said, lowering her voice as Melody settled beside her. "Was this trip really just for fun? Or are we on some kind of unofficial Spyce Girl mission I haven't been briefed on?"

Melody tilted her head. "What makes you say that?"

"Lyla mentioned the covert operation should they come up, so I assumed there might be more in store than shopping," Amanda said. "And... I don't know—call it intuition," she winked.

Melody glanced toward the hallway, where Lyla was still dramatically bartering in her half-French.

"Let's just say... it's not a bad time to be together. But I swear, this weekend is about fun. And now... it's about *you*. No dossiers. No prototypes. Just dresses and pastries."

Before Amanda could press further, Lyla swept back into the room, arms flung wide in theatrical triumph, her laughter spilling ahead of her words.

"They're in," she said, cheeks flushed. "We're officially re-booked on the bridal side. One hour. Vintage section. Champagne included."

"Of course it is," Amanda said, laughing.

"I had to offer them full rights to one of my editorial shots and promise not to bring any actual drama. So, everyone, please pretend to be emotionally stable and wildly in love."

Amanda raised her glass. "I'll try my best."

"You better," Lyla teased, grabbing Amanda's hand again. "Because after this, we're either coming home with dress options or a lifetime ban from Parisian couture."

Melody stood, lifting her glass again. "Either way, sounds like a perfect Saturday."

And just like that, the morning tipped fully into celebration—dressed in silk, sparkled in champagne, and edged with the soft suspicion that nothing with these women was ever *just* for fun.

Hours later, boutique bags swung from arms like trophies, whispering of silks, linens, and cashmere. Amanda, Lyla, and Melody emerged onto the cobblestone street with a kind of dazed elation, their laughter echoing softly beneath the pale Parisian sky.

"Did you see her face when she looked in the mirror?" Lyla gushed, linking arms with Melody as they climbed the stairs back to the apartment. "I swear, that dress changed her posture. Like it rewired her spine with couture."

Melody laughed. "You mean the one with the scalloped neckline and the illusion back? Or the one that made her look like Grace Kelly had a baby with an angel?" The champagne had been flowing freely from 10 a.m. until an acceptable wine-o'clock, and all three ladies were giddy.

Amanda trailed behind them, spinning inside, her fingers still tingling from where the seamstress had tugged the bodice into place.

"I can't believe I found it," she said, mostly to herself. *"The dress."*

"It found *you,*" Lyla corrected, digging through her purse for the apartment key. "That dress was fate."

But as the heavy door creaked open and the women stepped inside, the mood shifted. Lyla stopped short, her hand rising slowly in the air, like a conductor silencing an orchestra.

"Wait," she said, voice sharp and low. "Something's off."

Amanda blinked. "What?"

Lyla sniffed the air. She stepped forward carefully, her heels silent against the wood floor. "I left the window in the kitchen cracked this morning. But it's shut. And—" she tilted her head "—I swear that lamp was on the left side of the table."

Melody set her bag down slowly, eyes narrowing. "You're sure?"

Lyla nodded as Melody moved toward the hallway with the grace of someone who didn't want to startle the floorboards. She glanced into each room, opened a closet door, then another. When she returned, she met Lyla's gaze with a knowing, heavy silence.

Amanda crossed her arms. "Okay. What's going on?" she asked, the question hanging in the air like smoke.

Melody finally spoke. "Someone's been following me."

Amanda blinked. "What?"

"Yeah, everywhere I go," she confirmed. "At first, I thought I was being paranoid. But it's been happening since before Tokyo. I kept catching the same man near train stations, outside hotels. Never close enough to confront, but... unmistakably there."

Lyla nodded. "Same. Back in the States, it started after Tokyo for me, but... I think they know we ran together."

Amanda rubbed her temples. "Of course, they know. They can track our passports. But... why didn't either of you tell me?"

"We didn't want you to panic," Melody said. "You've had enough on your plate."

Amanda let out a slow, bitter laugh. "Right. So you thought now was the moment? After we just drank champagne and picked out a wedding dress? We'll just save the our-lives-are-in-danger part for later."

"Well, we were planning to tell you on this trip," Lyla said. "Melody's a pro at spotting them. Russell taught her, but I'm new at this. I had to make sure first."

Amanda walked to the fireplace and leaned against the mantle. "Well, I'm sorry, guys. I wish I knew how to get you out of this. But, if we're throwing cards on the table... Katherine showed up. Like, publicly. In Bucharest."

Both women turned sharply towards her.

"She was introduced as the *Head of the Ethics Committee* for Helion," Amanda said, punctuating each word like a teacher in front of a class. "Then Cooper mentioned—so casually it made my stomach turn—that she used to work with his dad. Which means he knows her. Personally."

She let out a hollow laugh. "So, Katherine is now officially overseeing regulatory clearance for the Ocular Grid. Apparently, this is her 'new' role."

The silence that followed told her everything. They all knew Cooper's father had hired Katherine's front company. But Cooper himself? That was the question Amanda could see forming on each of their faces.

Lyla let out a low whistle. "That's one way to cover your tracks. Make yourself untouchable by going global."

Melody shook her head. "Or she wants everyone to think she is."

Amanda turned to Melody. "Do you think she knows we're all here together?"

"It's possible," Melody said. "But if she does, she's not acting on it—at least not yet."

Amanda crossed her arms. "Do you believe Malonga?"

They all remembered what Malonga had laid out in the cabin: that Russell had been his partner, that Julius was compromised, that Katherine's allegiances were uncertain. He'd known everything about Amanda's movements down to her passport stamps, claimed Russell himself had sabotaged the Grid, and insisted that Amanda play the perfect girlfriend to Tristan. He offered some context, yes—but also left them wondering whether they'd just been fed another performance.

Melody hesitated. "I *did.*"

"But now?" Amanda asked.

"I don't know," Melody admitted. "I want to. He was Russell's last contact. He's been one step ahead this entire time, always showing up just in time to pull strings or offer protection. But... something doesn't sit right."

Lyla turned toward Amanda. "Do you still have the prototype?"

Amanda nodded. "Yeah. But no one knows except Katherine."

Melody sat down, drumming her fingers on her knee. "I took some files from Russell's safehouse—when we were hiding out in the mountains. I didn't have long when they came in and started ushering us out, but I had stuffed a few things into my bags before they had even come in, so I was able to grab what I could without anyone noticing. We hardly had time to think, but I couldn't leave empty-handed."

Amanda's eyes widened. "Have you looked through them all?"

"Encrypted documents, mostly," Melody said. "Some are just coordinates and dates. But a few..." She hesitated, then pushed on. "They reference Grid prototypes already seeded to multiple partners. Variants in circulation—not just the ones Russell sabotaged. Which means the version you have, Amanda, may not be the only one still in play."

Amanda's breath caught. "But Katherine said—"

"I know what she said." Melody's voice sharpened. "But Russell's notes make it sound like the system was always designed to splinter. Like the 'clean' version might not be unique at all."

Lyla frowned. "So someone else could be holding the same kind of leverage Katherine swore only you had?"

Melody nodded grimly. "And there's more. In his notes, Russell had suggestions that make me think he wondered whether Malonga wanted control as much as Julius did. He never said it outright, but I don't think he was ever sure who to trust."

Amanda's jaw tightened. The memory of Malonga's smooth assurances at the cabin suddenly felt more rehearsed than genuine. "So when we ask if we believe Malonga..." she said slowly, "the real question is whether Russell ever did."

Melody nodded slowly.

Lyla exhaled, then plopped herself onto the sofa. "Ladies, have we been played?" She flapped her arms into the air. "I will be really disappointed if we have because my bullshit detector is usually *so* good."

The woman shared a short laugh while Lyla let the moment settle in the room before a realization came to her. "Wait. I feel like we've just jumped over some really important information. Cooper? Did you talk to him *after* Tokyo?"

Amanda grimaced. "Yeah. He was in Bucharest with his dad for the tour."

"And you didn't tell *us?* Seems like we're not the only ones keeping information," she said.

Amanda didn't answer right away. Instead, she looked around the apartment—the perfect afternoon dissolving like a mirage, and in its place reality was creeping in.

Lyla leaned forward, her tone firm. "Amanda, this isn't just gossip. If Cooper knows where you are—if he's asking questions—you need to tell us how much he knows."

Amanda exhaled, her shoulders heavy. "He doesn't know enough to put anything together. Not yet. And I'd like to keep it that way." She pressed her palms against her thighs as if bracing herself.

"It's all so... messed up," she said finally. "But we need to figure out who knows what and fast."

She walked slowly to her suitcase in the corner of the room, the sound of her footsteps softened by the artisan rug beneath her, before she put the bag flat, pulling it open to reveal the contents.

Lyla leaned forward. "Wait. You brought the prototype here?"

Amanda nodded. "I didn't know what else to do. I can't leave it behind. Not in a hotel. Not in a locker. Not anywhere."

Melody stood, walking closer with quiet intent. "Amanda... this can't be safe. You're carrying it with you everywhere?"

Amanda's voice was low but steady. "Yes. In my bag. On flights. On sidewalks. Through security lines. It hasn't left my sight."

"What do you tell the TSA agents? I mean, surely they ask!" Melody gasped.

"Camera equipment," Amanda shrugged. "I mean, it passes for that, right?"

"And you're sure that's the best idea?" Lyla asked, her brow wrinkling with disapproval. "You could let one of us keep it. We can lock it up; maybe hide it better."

Amanda's eyes flicked toward her, then back to the suitcase. "I've thought about it. But Tristan—" her voice trailed off. "If it's the one brain of this system that hasn't been compromised... I almost feel obligated to know it's closest to him."

Melody stepped beside her. "But you don't even know if it works."

"No, that's true," Amanda admitted. "But right now, I think we're all safest if I'm the one holding it, right?"

The trio let every bit of uncertainty fill the room.

Lyla sighed, her voice softening. "You don't have to carry everything, you know. Not alone. Literally or figuratively."

Amanda looked up, gratitude flickering behind the exhaustion in her eyes. "I know. But until we figure out who I'm really dealing with... I need you two to be safe."

She slipped the pouch back into her suitcase, smoothing a sweater over it like it was just another travel item. She turned back to Melody and Lyla.

"We only have a couple of days here. Let's just enjoy tonight."

And for a moment, none of them said a word. Just the three of them, in a Paris apartment above a glowing street, breathing in a brief pocket of peace before the world demanded that they start moving again.

Chapter Eight

Knoxville, Tennessee: May 2008

THE RAIN HADN'T COME yet, but the sky outside Reverend Harwell's south offices sagged with its weight. Clouds curled low and thick, bruised and swollen like an injury. The cherry trees lining the quad shivered in the charged air, their pale blossoms twitching like nerves. With a storm hovering, the birds had gone still, their silence more ominous than a foreboding song. It was the kind of morning that seemed to predict an impending break.

Inside the administrative wing, a storm of its own threatened. A hush was punctured by the rhythmic quop of approaching footsteps—sharp, deliberate, and undeniably expensive. James Hansen didn't wait to be announced. He pushed through the glass-paneled doors with the impatience of someone used to being obeyed, the ease of a man long accustomed to unearned access.

The large anteroom he first entered was paneled in polished walnut, the kind meant to invoke trust and tradition. A fireplace anchored the far wall, above which hung a portrait of the Reverend himself: younger, jaw sharper, hair darker, and hands folded in his customary benevolent reverence. Hansen had walked past the secretary just outside the tall office door and let himself in before she could say a word.

Pastor Benjamin Harwell stood slowly, smoothing his tie as if time were something he had in spades.

"James," he said, offering a nod and gesturing to one of the leather armchairs arranged in front of his desk. "You're early. Please, have a seat."

"Don't coddle me," Hansen spoke sharply, his voice clipping through the room like a blade. "I don't sit when I'm angry."

Harwell dropped his hand, letting it fold into the other before his waist—an affectation he'd perfected long ago, equal parts statesman and shepherd.

"Then say what you came to say."

Without further ceremony, Hansen tossed a flash drive onto the desk. It slid across the glossy surface and collided with a brass penholder.

"You aired her face," Hansen barked, each word sharp as a gavel strike. "At a Sunday service. Live-streamed. A national audience. Did you think no one would recognize her?"

Harwell didn't blink. His expression held steady, eyes flat with the confidence of a man used to pulpits and spotlights. "She was part of the ceremony. A testimony. A reminder—"

"That life is inconvenient when it becomes public," Hansen cut in, his voice like a flint struck against steel.

A silence settled, dense and immovable, as if the walls themselves had drawn in closer.

"You've just put my son's political future at risk."

For a moment, you could hear the clock on the wall tick, the churn of the cogs distant and muffled.

"She was radiant," Harwell said finally. "Brave. Like all the others. She wasn't singled out. Our donors responded very well."

"Your donors," Hansen repeated, stepping closer, "don't control state funding or national media narratives. I do." He poked his index finger to his chest. "And I've kept this whole operation in favor with people who write seven-figure checks because you swore to me personally that no girl's identity would ever be exposed. Especially not hers."

Harwell's lips pressed together, then parted again in the same slow, pastoral way. "That promise still holds."

"Too late."

Hansen's voice had dropped to a venomous hush, taking on the kind of tone that uncoiled only in private rooms of old power.

"You think you can control this like we're still living in the eighties?" he asked. "The internet doesn't forget. That footage's already been clipped, shared, and archived. You've opened a gate that doesn't shut. Does no one have the foresight to see what is happening here?"

He flung his hands around erratically until he calmed, leaning in closer before continuing.

"Do you even understand the time we live in? Or have I overestimated you, *Pastor?*" He spat the title like a curse.

"My son is three months from entering West Point. Do you have any idea how fragile that pipeline is? How many strings I've pulled to ensure he enters with a clean record, a polished image, and a future?"

Hansen inhaled through his nose.

"And now," he continued, each syllable slower, "your little stunt might unravel everything."

Harwell remained motionless, the stillness of a man who had weathered storms before—but the room itself seemed to shift under the weight of it.

"Congressman," Harwell began, "I can assure you..."

"You've made your assurances," Hansen interrupted, "and I expect you to make good. Scrub the footage. Every trace. You make it disappear. God knows I give enough money to this place to make it happen."

"I'll do what I can," Harwell said carefully.

"Do more than that. Because if this ever comes back on my family—" He took a breath and let the threat hover in the space between them. "You'll be left funding this holy empire with bake sales and prayer chains. The Ethical Citizenry Federation won't send another cent."

As the door slammed behind him, a punctuation that ended conversations and careers reverberated through the halls.

Congressman James Hansen left the building, not so much driving as commanding the car down narrow campus roads, his hands gripping the steering wheel like it owed him penance. The rain began at precisely the moment his tires left Harwell's paved lot—first a spit, then a steady percussion that blurred the windshield despite the speed of the wipers.

He didn't listen to the radio. He didn't make any calls. He simply rehearsed.

Principal Beckmann had requested a meeting with him the day before. "It's about your son," the email had read, without elaboration, and Hansen had half a mind to cancel. But with West Point paperwork in motion and Harwell's blunder still burning through his veins, there was no avoiding it.

Cooper Hansen had been in the principal's waiting area while his father sped down the roads. The silence around him closed in with a thin, fragile texture. He leaned forward, hands clasped between his knees, watching the rain carve shapes down the windowpane. The secretary typed without looking at him, her clacking keyboard a hollow echo.

He ran his hand across his forehead, hoping it would wipe away his fatigue. Cooper hadn't slept well—again. Each morning felt like dragging himself across a battlefield no one else could see.

When the intercom buzzed, the secretary finally looked him in the eye. "You can go in now."

Cooper stood slowly, smoothing the front of his dress shirt. The collar suddenly felt too tight, his school-issued tie too knotted. The walk to the door felt a little bit longer than usual.

Principal Beckmann didn't rise when Cooper entered, but gestured calmly to the chair opposite his desk.

"Mr. Hansen. Please."

Cooper nodded and sat, palms flat against his thighs.

"I received your West Point packet," Beckmann began. "Final transcripts, leadership reviews, Coach Turner's glowing letter—very thorough."

"Thank you, sir."

"But I want to talk to you about my recommendation."

Cooper hesitated. "I assumed... I thought it was already handled."

Beckmann steepled his fingers, studying him closely.

"I've written hundreds of recommendations, Cooper. And in most cases, I don't hesitate. But with you..." He paused. "Something's been off... and I can't put my finger on it, but since spring break, you've been different."

Cooper wasn't able to keep his eyes on anything but the floor.

"You've always been composed," Beckmann continued. "Quiet and focused—that composure was one of your defining traits. But lately, there's a brittleness in you. A fault line."

Cooper swallowed hard, his gaze fixed.

"I'm not accusing you of anything. Your grades are still impeccable. Your behavior is exemplary. But I'd be doing you a disservice if I didn't say this aloud: It looks like you're carrying something you can't set down."

The room shrank, not possessing enough space for both men and the protuberance of truth between them.

"I know what West Point demands. And I believe you can rise to it. But I need to know, Cooper. Whatever's fractured, have you addressed it? Or is it still bleeding somewhere under the surface?"

Cooper's throat ached. He had nothing to confess that wouldn't unravel everything. And even if he did, who would believe him?

"It won't follow me," he said quietly.

Principal Beckmann looked at him for a long time.

"I'll write the letter," he said finally. "But don't let me regret it."

Cooper nodded once and stood.

Outside, the rain had begun in earnest. The sky had cracked open and let go.

When the congressman pulled into the school's faculty lot, the storm was fully overhead. The car door resisted the wind as he slammed it shut, but he didn't run or duck under an umbrella; he let the rain come.

Cooper had already gone to class by the time his dad arrived. Inside the building, Hansen passed trophy cases lined with faded team photos and pennants from decades past. At the far end, Principal Beckmann's office door stood cracked open.

The secretary glanced up, startled by the sight of him.

"Congressman—"

"I know the way," Hansen cut her off, pushing into the room without pausing.

Principal Beckmann stood, smoothing the front of his blazer. "Mr. Hansen," he said in his best attempt to sound neutral.

"You said you had concerns," Hansen replied. "So let's hear 'em."

"I've already spoken with Cooper," the principal began evenly, returning to his desk with measured calm. "He's submitted everything required by the Academy—grades, assessments, extracurriculars. Coach Turner sent in a stellar recommendation."

"I'm aware," Hansen snapped. "So, what exactly required my time?"

Beckmann folded his hands. "The personal letter from this office."

"You're holding it hostage?"

"I'm writing it," Beckmann said smoothly. "I told your son as much just a few minutes ago. He left reassured and encouraged."

Hansen narrowed his eyes, studying the older man like an opponent. "I'm sensing a *but,*" he said.

"I wasn't questioning his qualifications," the principal continued. "But I felt it was important to speak with him face-to-face. Something in him has changed."

Hansen waved the comment away with a scoff. "Teenage hormones. He's fine."

But Beckmann didn't hide his disagreement. "Perhaps. But I've been doing this a long time. I plan on retiring next year, and that'll put my service at a full forty years. So, I'm coming to you with compassion and a lot of experience, Congressman. I've seen students pushed to the edge—high-performing, compliant, polished on paper. Until the cracks show."

"Let me guess," Hansen said dryly. "You want me to get him a therapist now? Have him talk about his feelings?"

Beckmann's jaw tightened slightly. "I'm not telling you what to do, sir. But I am saying that the burden your son is carrying may not be academic. And if it isn't addressed, it will cost him more than a desired commission."

Hansen leaned forward, both palms pressing onto the desk like a dare.

"Let's get something clear, Principal Beckmann. I've kept this school in favor with the state board, helped secure funding, pushed your STEM initiative through committee—all without asking for a damn thing. So don't confuse your title with authority. If anyone's in a position to recommend something, it's me."

James Hansen beat his chest as if he were auditioning for a stage role as Tarzan. The silence that followed wasn't meek; it was deliberate. Beckmann let it hang just long enough to reset the balance.

"I'm not confusing anything," he said quietly. "I've already signed the letter. You'll have it by Monday."

Hansen straightened.

"But since you're here," Beckmann added, his deep love for his vocation imploring him to speak. "I'll simply encourage you to ensure your son has what he needs. I believe what he's dealing with is emotional, not intellectual. I'd hate to see him stumble under the weight of silence."

"Silence is discipline," Hansen said. "He'll be just fine."

Beckmann nodded as Mr. Hansen turned without another word and strode to the door.

"Don't harden him past repair," Beckmann said, low but deliberate, knowing the man wouldn't listen.

The only response from Hansen was the sharp thud of the door shutting behind him, a cold punctuation mark that made Beckmann's plea feel smaller than ever.

Instead of going straight home after school, Cooper walked in the park near his house mindlessly.

His shoes filled with water, but he didn't care. The rain soaked through his jacket, his collar, and the waistband of his pants. It streaked through his hair and down his back, until his shape was undone—just a boy made of skin and questions, disappearing into the tempest.

He cut through side streets and overgrown fields, taking the long way past an old chapel. The windows were streaked with droplets and steam, but he could still see inside. A dust-covered piano sat untouched. It was the one Amanda had played with her eyes closed the last time they sneaked through the woods. She played a lullaby, or hymn, or something she'd made up on the spot. He couldn't remember anything other than the way her fingers moved—graceful, like they were born knowing the keys.

She had always just *heard* music and picked up instruments as if she instinctively knew their hidden languages that took others years to learn. She hadn't been afraid then. Or maybe she had. Maybe the music was the only way she knew how to scream.

He stopped under the chapel's overhang and rested his hand against the doorframe, letting himself sob.

She'd been gone for weeks. She disappeared into the creases of polite secrecy, the kind that smoothed over anything too uncomfortable to name. At school, no one asked why her desk sat empty, why her voice no longer carried in rehearsals for the spring play. They knew better. The Hansens and her own family had made sure of that.

Even Lyla, who would have screamed the truth if she thought it would help, could do nothing but watch Amanda vanish into silence. She argued with teachers, pressed her parents and Cooper for answers, and tried to pry open the truth at every turn, but the adults closed ranks and shut her out as firmly as they had Amanda.

As for the flying lessons Amanda had started, they were casual enough that even there, no one thought to raise an alarm when she stopped showing up. It was easier for everyone to pretend she had simply moved away. Her absence had been folded neatly into silence, like the world itself had agreed to forget her all at once. But Cooper couldn't.

He remembered everything. The night they sat beneath the dogwood tree, knees pressed together, her voice shaking as she told him she didn't know what would happen next. The way she held her belly, barely rounded, with both wonder and dread. The plans they had made to go to one of the other schools they applied to, both skipping out on the more prestigious places they could attend, for the comfort of freedom.

He thought of the morning after his mom told him Amanda had lost the baby and wouldn't be returning. How he'd lain awake staring at the ceiling, his chest tight, too afraid to close his eyes in case the truth followed him into the darkness of sleep. By daylight, his father's fury filled the house, barking about discretion and forbidding even the smallest question, while his mother appeared with a bowl of soup, as though he were only recovering from a passing sickness instead of drowning in fear.

And now, the world spun toward the future. Graduation. The Academy. A pre-scripted life. But inside him, something was still anchored in the moment he was told that Amanda was gone.

He tilted his face toward the sky and let the rain fill his eyes.

Mere miles from where Cooper Hansen was walking, a woman closed a file cabinet with a soft metallic thud. The hallway outside Harwell's private office was empty, but the echo of James Hansen's earlier visit lingered like smoke.

She'd watched him storm out with a particular brand of self-importance only men like him seemed to carry. Power-suited, rain-slicked, and furious. The secretary had worked there long enough to know what came next. She adjusted the stack of forms in her arms, smoothed the hem of her blouse, and knocked softly on Harwell's door.

"Yes," she heard Harwell beckon as he sat at his desk, fingers pressed together beneath his chin.

Her voice caught as she added, "He's gone," she said, the words unnecessary but somehow required, like a confession offered to absolve her complicity. She hated the small tremor in her chest, the guilt of watching and doing nothing—but she told herself, as always, that obedience was faith, and faith meant leaving judgment to men like Harwell.

"I know."

She waited, unsure if she'd been dismissed before she'd arrived.

"I've already told the team to pull the footage from the livestream archive," she added. "I sent the full sweep to IT and legal."

Harwell nodded once. "Will it hold?"

"I don't know," she said truthfully. "But it will appear like we tried."

He leaned back in his chair, the leather sighing beneath him.

"And Amanda?" he asked.

"I spoke with Miss Judy Richards," the secretary paused. "She's pretty quiet. No incidents."

"She's not causing trouble?"

"No, sir. And she's good friends with Ellie, who, as you know, is our biggest ally. The only concern now is that Amanda isn't eating much. They say she's pale. But she hasn't signed any papers yet."

Harwell steepled his fingers. "She will. And she'll be gone soon enough."

The woman hesitated. "I know it's not my place," she said carefully, "but it might be worth pulling her from public events. No chapel appearances. No group photos. Just until—"

"She is not the problem," Harwell said flatly.

"No, sir," the secretary agreed.

"She is the evidence of this generation's sin."

The church secretary shifted the papers in her arms. She despised the way he lowered his voice, making the girl sound less like a person than a specimen—as though she were something to be studied, not saved. Like the girls in the home were merely props in a morality play, arranged for his particular brand of grace.

"There's that benefit gala next month," she reminded him. "The one in Tallahassee that's opening a new center. You wanted a testimonial from someone we haven't seen yet."

He waved his hand, as though swatting away a gnat.

"We'll use someone else. That child with the glasses. Sarah?"

She nodded. "Of course."

"And Miss Amanda Hopkins," he said after a pause, "might need to be reminded that her time here is not hers to direct. Get the documents."

Her fingers tightened around the file folder. "Understood," she said as she closed the door behind her.

In the hallway, she paused by the bulletin board. Amanda's face was still there, just a corner of it, from a group shot two Sundays before. Half-shadowed, half-smiling. Barely visible unless you knew where to look.

She unpinned the photo, slipping it between the pages of her clipboard, and walked back to her portion of the office, gathering her things to clock out for the day, her heels echoing against the tiled halls in time with the rain.

CHAPTER NINE

New York City: One Week After Paris

"Yes, I can make 10:30 work," Amanda answered the real estate agent on the phone.

The truth was, she had to work around a meeting she had scheduled with Katherine, but she was determined to fit everything in.

The city was never quiet, but this morning, her raucous noise felt personal. Tires hissed over rain-slick asphalt, scaffolding groaned in the wind, and the murmur of sidewalk conversations rose like the steam from street vents. The city moved with the self-importance of a place that never asked permission to exist, and Amanda understood that energy all too well.

Tristan was in Nairobi. He'd flown to Africa after hopping over to Paris for only a few hours to say hello and goodbye almost in the same breath. They had both decided that since she said *yes,* Amanda would find a place for them to share in New York, and Tristan would set off to the next leg of the Ocular Grid deployment tour without her.

She had told him, gently but firmly, that she needed to pause. Not to take a break from him, obviously, but from the momentum of things. From the sense that everything was happening too fast, like she was being swept downriver by a current she never asked to ride.

They hadn't set a wedding date—they would discuss that when he returned. For now, she had four whole weeks to herself. And there had never been a time in her life when she had craved solitude more.

"Well, it might not compare to the gem of a space we found Mr. Montgomery a few years ago," the real estate agent admitted, "but this place is no bachelor pad. It's perfect for raising a family in the city."

Amanda was staying in Tristan's place, tucked into a quiet corner of SoHo, its unmarked elevator opening into a private hall for the two penthouse loft apartments like a secret. Every time she entered, Amanda felt like she'd wandered into the pages of a design magazine.

Exposed brick walls bore the patina of age, softened by bright finishes and floor-to-ceiling linen drapes that flanked industrial-framed windows. A floating staircase rose like a sculpture along one wall, leading to a mezzanine bedroom with glass railings and a bed dressed in Belgian flax. Below, the living area was anchored by deep leather sofas in slate gray, scattered with velvet pillows in muted ochre and forest green.

A set of deep emerald chairs framed a reclaimed wood coffee table; its surface bearing old carpenter's marks, a tray of wine glasses, and paperback books.

Tristan's presence was barely there, which somehow made it feel more like his, and his alone. Amanda had unpacked just one suitcase—the others that she had sent from the London apartment were securely in the second bedroom, zipped tight, as she hadn't decided whether she was arriving or leaving. For now, she chose to treat the loft like a waiting room. A beautiful and borrowed one.

And yet, every corner seemed to welcome her. Much like Tristan, the loft wasn't trying to *be* anything. It didn't demand attention or orchestrate nostalgia. It simply was, and that alone compelled admiration. In a world where every move felt curated, marketed, and weighed, the loft, like him, was a rare find.

She hung up the phone and plopped herself on the sofa before realizing the time. Amanda bolted upright, quickly finding Katherine's name in her contacts.

"Hey, sorry. I'm on my way now," she muttered in a rush.

"Not to worry. I will be here when you arrive. Just use your code to buzz in."

Amanda scrambled to the lobby and out the door, adjusting the strap of her oversized bag, the familiar weight of the prototype tucked deep within the lining. Even here, in a city thick with people and constant noise, she couldn't bring herself to let it get too far out of reach. It had become second nature—like breathing, or bracing for impact.

A cab that turned too fast into the intersection sprayed cold water across the curb, and Amanda jumped back just in time, her boots catching the splash. She sighed, pulling her coat tighter, and kept walking. It was fitting, somehow, that even the weather had teeth, nipping at her with the same merciless grip she felt everywhere she turned.

Amanda's gait echoed in rhythmic dissonance against the wet concrete, her steps catching in the syncopated breath of the city. Cabs honked like geese in flight, pedestrians lingered on corners with impatience, and seemingly constant sirens sliced the air like discordant violin strings tuning to no one's symphony.

She crossed West Broadway, turned east, and slipped down a side street where the scaffolding gave way to a row of understated brownstones. Katherine's name wasn't on any buzzer, of course, but Amanda knew the code to key in as instructed, and the door gave a muted click, giving her permission to enter.

The house smelled of old books and citrus oil, like someone had just polished the banister. Amanda stepped into the front room, where Katherine was already seated at a table near the bay window, backlit by gauzy light and framed by tall calla lilies, their white petals impossibly still.

"You look tired," she said in her usual tone, not as a greeting, but a fairly harsh assessment.

Amanda exhaled through her nose. "Nice to see you, too."

Katherine gestured to the chair across from her, sliding a porcelain cup of tea in Amanda's direction.

"I trust you've settled into the loft."

"It's... beautiful," Amanda admitted, slipping her bag off and holding it loosely on her lap. "Quiet. And you just have a Manhattan brownstone now?"

"I have a place to stay while I'm here," Katherine answered plainly. "I'm only staying a couple of days. I'll join the group in São Paulo next Friday."

Amanda didn't reply; she just leaned back, letting the faint hum of the heating duct fill the silence between them. Her arms crossed, more instinct than posturing, wrapping around the unease in her chest.

"So, you were announced in Bucharest," she said finally. Her voice didn't crack, but it carried an edge. "You're the Helion rep now? The head of their *ethics committee?* Standing there like you'd been on the development side of things all along." She turned her head, her gaze locking onto Katherine's with more vulnerability than anger.

"I don't get it, Katherine." Amanda's voice cracked, caught between anger and exhaustion. "Some days I feel like I can trust you—like I *have* to, but then you pull a stunt like this."

She slouched back, the fight draining out of her. "And if I'm just putting it all out there... in Tokyo, you ghosted me. I risked everything, and you disappeared. Then Bucharest happened. Now, out of nowhere, you text me—tell me you're here, and I need to meet you? What is this?"

Katherine didn't move. Amanda pressed on, her words gaining heat.

"Do I not deserve an explanation? I know I've been naive—maybe stupid—but the positions you've put me in, the money you've wired to my account? None of that is imaginary. It's real. And I don't know whether to cut and run and pray you can't find me, or to trust that somehow you're on the right side of history and I'll understand later. So, what do I do now?"

The question lingered in the space between them like a lit fuse. Not quite aflame, but flickering.

"I told you my front company was involved with Hansen, didn't I?" Katherine asked, as if Amanda's question was rhetorical. "I needed to leave Tokyo before setting up my current post. I am, for all intents and purposes, the Head of the Ethics Committee for the international rollout of the Ocular Grid's deployment efforts. I have been hired as a consultant by the Helion Group. That is entirely true."

Amanda's expression darkened, but she said nothing. She let the words stagnate between them as she tried to process.

"And I can see you're questioning," Katherine said.

"You think?" Amanda scoffed. "You're saying that these people from the Helion Group just trust a British intelligence officer with all of this?"

Katherine's head tilted, a small concession of acknowledgment. "Amanda, think it through."

Her words were soft, but they carried the weight of someone who had watched far too many young operatives mistake impulse for instinct.

"Helion doesn't trust me," she said at last. "They trust what I represent. A negotiator, an ethicist, the semblance of a moral compass. It gives them something to point to when the world grows suspicious. To them, I am a shield, not a confidante. But that is precisely why it works. Their need for my skills keeps me close, and for the moment, it is the safest place I could stand. And whether you like it or not, Amanda, it keeps you safer too."

Amanda's gaze faltered, but Katherine pressed on, her voice unhurried.

"As for Tokyo, silence was the safest language I had. Sometimes absence says more than presence. I left to set the stage I stand on now. Without it, I could not be here with you."

Amanda's lips parted as though to argue, but nothing came.

Katherine's eyes softened, but her tone didn't. "You survived, Amanda. With half the truth and less than half the guidance, you still made the choices that kept you alive. That is what matters."

She leaned back, her posture deceptively casual, as though they were discussing the weather. "The question is not whether you can trust me wholesale. The question is what you will do when you cannot. That is the measure of whether you will last in this game."

Amanda swallowed, her voice low. "And what do I do now?"

Katherine allowed the faintest curve of her mouth, something between pity and pride. "Decide what you are willing to protect, what you will never become, and how much risk your soul can bear. Those are your only instruments. Learn to read them, and you won't lose yourself."

"So, why am I really here?" Amanda exhaled. "I assume this was not just a meeting to check on my well-being."

Katherine smiled faintly. "You are here to exhale. To recalibrate. And—" She reached beneath the table and produced a slim, hard-sided case the color of pewter. "To make a trade."

Amanda sat straighter, shoulders coiled. "What is that?"

"Your decoy. Identical in weight and design, down to the internal chip mock-up. No one outside our circle will be able to tell the difference. I've already taken the liberty of registering its signature on the secure channel. From this point forward, this is what you keep close."

Amanda's breath caught. She opened her mouth as if to answer, then shut it again, her hand brushing unconsciously against the edge of her bag.

Katherine tilted her head. "Unless... I do hope you're not in possession of it at this very moment?"

Amanda hesitated, then drew the oversized bag onto the table. She unzipped the hidden lining and withdrew the prototype—unprotected, wrapped only in a silk scarf. She set it down as though revealing a sacrament.

Katherine did not reach for it. She only stared. "Amanda," she breathed, her scolding soft with disbelief.

"I didn't know where else to put it," Amanda said, her voice tight. "I've barely let it out of reach. It felt safer with me."

"It's a machine, not a talisman," Katherine said, her tone firm but not unkind. "And the weight of it is already crushing you. You cannot continue this way."

Amanda bristled. "Then what am I supposed to do with it? You told me to guard it with my life."

"I did, and I do not take that back," Katherine replied, her eyes softening. "But guarding it doesn't mean carrying it like a burden strapped to your back. It means being wise enough to keep it out of reach of those who would twist it for their own ends. Julius believes he should be the one in control. The Americans will insist it should belong to them. And men like Malonga..." She paused, choosing her words. "They see it as leverage in a game where none of us can afford to lose. That is why I trusted you. Because unlike them, you do not want power for its own sake."

Amanda swallowed, searching Katherine's face. For a flicker of a moment, she felt the same warmth she had clung to when she spilled the truth of her past to Katherine in Rome. She leaned into the sense that this woman—however shrouded in secrets—truly wanted her to survive.

"That may be true," Amanda said, "But this is the only model you say you can trust—and I still don't know if it's the only one that hasn't been compromised."

Katherine huffed, sharper than usual, and leaned forward. "And when someone shoves you in a crowd? When a hand snatches your bag? You don't even carry a weapon."

"I carry instinct," Amanda shot back.

Katherine's lips thinned. "A most fragile currency in this economy."

Amanda shoved the prototype toward her. "Fine. Take it. I don't want to be its vault anymore."

But Katherine didn't move. At last, she said, "No. I want you to leave the original at Tristan's loft. It belongs there, not dangling from your shoulder."

Amanda frowned. "But—"

"The safest place," Katherine cut in, "is always the one no one thinks to search. Whoever shadows you will be watching when you hand this decoy off. Let them. Meanwhile, the original stays stowed, untouched. They already suspect you carry it with you, use that."

Amanda's breath hitched. "And you don't think someone will break into the apartment?"

"My dear, they already have. If they've swept it and decided you're the carrier, then you're in more danger than I feared. No, this way buys you cover." She slid the pewter case across the table. "Stow the original, for God's sake, put it back in its shell, and carry this instead until the handoff."

Amanda sat back, pulse hammering as the decoy settled between them, gleaming like a second choice that might save her life.

"I want you to give this one to Melody when she returns," Katherine said, tapping the decoy case.

Amanda stiffened. "She's in Croatia. And I don't want to put her in any more danger."

"She'll be in New York soon enough. We'll arrange it."

Amanda shook her head. "I don't like this. Why her?"

"Because someone already has eyes on all of us," Katherine said evenly. "We need multiple threads to follow. If they intercept the prototype, better they chase the wrong one."

Amanda's brow furrowed. "You think it's Malonga? Is he playing us, too?"

"For all I know, it's nothing but players playing players, Amanda. And that is the only rule you must remember."

Amanda exhaled slowly, as if trying to press the tension back into her own bones. "Does he know I met the girls in Paris?"

"Of course he does." Katherine's tone was almost indulgent. "But he likely believes you're only a woman with girlfriends. Good cover—shopping for wedding dresses." She gave a small approving nod, and in that instant, Amanda was reminded just how closely Katherine had been watching, too.

"Anyway," Katherine continued lightly, "I doubt he suspects I would ever trust you with the real one."

Amanda's eyes narrowed. "But you did."

"I had to."

Amanda held her stare, searching for cracks. "You think I'm breaking."

"I think you're human. And that's the part people exploit first," Katherine said, lifting her cup with unhurried elegance. She sipped her tea as if nothing in the world demanded haste. "This isn't about paranoia, my dear. It's about containment."

Amanda stood abruptly and crossed to the window. Outside, a man in a red raincoat tugged at a stubborn dog who refused to cross the street. Steam from a nearby vent curled around them like fog on a stage, blurring the edges of the scene. For a fleeting moment, she wondered if the man was watching her, an informant waiting for the signal to move. The thought sent a chill up her arms. She pulled the curtain across her face, a small gesture, but one that betrayed how much her nerves had frayed.

"I want this to end," she whispered, her voice carrying a raw edge.

"It won't," Katherine said. "Not soon enough. But it will change shape. That's the best we get."

Amanda exhaled sharply, turning towards Katherine again. "Then help me do what you asked. Help me think it through. What do you make of Tristan in all this? He isn't a man who lusts after power, but power tests everyone who touches it. And if he fails that test, what happens to me?"

Katherine's expression was unreadable, the stillness of her face its own kind of answer. "It's not wrong to love him. Many agents marry their targets."

Amanda's eyes widened. "That's not comforting—and not what I asked."

Katherine smiled faintly, as though Amanda's resistance amused her. "He believes in the technology, and he isn't wrong to. But belief clouds judgment. Belief makes people careless. And he has chosen to trust the woman he sees before him—the version of you that keeps much hidden. You mustn't forget that. So yes, I think he is who he claims to be. But the question you should ask yourself is not whether he is true—it is whether he is careful enough to remain so."

Amanda's voice thinned. "And you? Are you always careful with what you believe?"

"I don't have the luxury of carelessness," Katherine said, blunt and unadorned. "I have no one left to lose."

The words fell heavy between them. Amanda reached for the pewter case, fingers brushing the cold edge before she drew it close. She did not open it. Instead, she slid the decoy into her bag, her movements sharp with reluctance.

"I swear, if anything happens to Melody—"

"It won't," Katherine interrupted. "I'll see to her myself. She'll take this to Croatia and let it sink into the sea. Let the men chase what is not real while you remain untouched."

Amanda slung the strap across her shoulder, a gesture of compliance that felt like surrender. "This better work." She studied Katherine's face, searching for something solid, some glimmer of truth in the shadows.

"Does Cooper know?" she asked suddenly, the words escaping before she could weigh them. "The lengths his father is willing to go for control? He must see you as part of it—a way to steer me, to keep me in play."

Katherine didn't blink. "Cooper is not the enemy."

Amanda frowned. "And that's supposed to comfort me?"

"No," Katherine said softly. "It's supposed to sharpen you. What you think you know is never the whole of it. Hold that truth close."

Amanda let out a short, incredulous snort. "If that isn't the understatement of the century."

Her phone buzzed with an appointment reminder from the real estate agent. She nodded once, more to herself than to Katherine, and turned toward the door.

"I have to go. But you were right about one thing," she said over her shoulder. "I am human. And the people you work for? They left their humanity at the door a long time ago."

Katherine's voice followed, gentled now, threaded with a sound resembling regret. "But—"

Amanda spun, cutting her off. "No. No more riddles. No more elusive excuses. Instinct is all I have left, and it's what will get me through this. I will find a way out."

And before Katherine could reply, Amanda was on the street again, stepping into the buzz of traffic, voices, and clattering footsteps. Her surroundings were chaos, yes, but chaos that carried its own strange music, a sound almost comforting in its disorder.

Chapter Ten

Knoxville, Tennessee: May 2008

Amanda sat cross-legged on a chair in her room, the vibrant purple walls casting a faint lavender shadow over the paper sitting on her small writing desk. She rolled a soft knitted blanket beneath her knees. Evening devotions were going to be held in less than an hour, and outside the small window, dusk was sliding into night. She knew she had enough time to write the letter she had been planning to hide in her underwear the next time she went to run any errands on campus. Miss Marla had let her grab copy paper and office supplies a week before, and she knew they were getting low on tissue boxes and soap, so she was going to offer to get toiletries in the morning.

The main campus maintenance staff outfitted all building supplies at The Ridge, and the last time Amanda had made the thirty-minute walk to the utility sheds, she'd found a campus map, revealing every location: dining hall, residence apartments, office buildings, sports fields, and—most importantly—a post office. That's the one communication she knew she could afford to try. Cooper's home address was etched in her memory like a handprint pressed into wet cement.

She bent over the notebook pages, words coming slowly at first as her pen halted before pressing down. She steadied her hand, the pen heavy with everything she hadn't said, and began.

Dear Cooper,

Amanda paused, staring at the name of the boy she loved, her chest aching in places she was learning to ignore. She knew she'd be in trouble if she got caught, but this message had been scratching at her ribs for weeks, begging to get out. If she didn't do it now, she wouldn't reach him in time.

I don't know if you'll ever read this. I don't even know if this will get to you. But I need to try. I'm not sure if you know what's happening.

She adjusted slightly, brushing the edge of her sleeve across her cheek, her hand trembling.

I'm at a place called The Ridge. It's a home for girls who get pregnant too young. They told my family it was safe and that it would help me. They say it's a place to start over. But no one tells the truth here. Not really.

Her throat tightened. She stared at the sentence, knowing if someone found the letter, this would be the most damning part of it, but she promised herself she wouldn't cross out the words.

This is a place where girls disappear. Not forever. Just long enough to give birth and be forgotten. They want to take the baby, Cooper. They said it'll be easier this way. They tell me that you already signed papers. I don't know if that's true, but...

Amanda blinked a tear away as her hand clenched the pen, determined to finish what she had started.

Cooper, I don't want to let her go. I don't want to pretend she didn't exist. I feel her inside me every single day. She moves when I sing. She kicks when I'm still. She knows me. And I know her.

The next words came in a rush.

They said you gave up your rights on those papers. Did you?

She stared at the question for a moment. Everything inside her throbbed at the possibility it could be true. If it was, it'd be easier to just ignore—to put him out of her mind forever, but she had to know.

Please tell me you didn't. Please tell me someone forged your name or pressured you, or lied. Because the boy I know—the one who held my hand on that rainy day when we found that old abandoned chapel and promised we could do this together—he wouldn't just vanish. Not like this.

Amanda swallowed, pressing the palm of her hand against her chest. She let the tears flow for a moment before she wiped her eyes and began again.

I don't blame you for what happened. I know your parents were furious. I know your life was planned out differently than this. But you told me you wanted our family—that we'd figure it out together. If you've changed your mind, if you never see me again, I need you to at least know she exists. She's real, and she's ours. And I love her like I always promised, but loving her may not be enough. They're already telling me what's best, already pressing me to believe I can't raise her, not like this, not alone. I don't want to let her go, but I can feel the choice slipping from my hands.

Her pen faltered near the end of the page, the ink beginning to run light.

Cooper, if there's a part of you that still cares—any part of you that remembers what we were before all of this—I need you to try. I don't even know what I mean by that, but there it is. Please, just try. For her. For me. For us.

She signed—*Love Amanda*—with as much intensity as she'd ever felt for him, folding the page with slow, deliberate hands. She slipped the letter into a bright pink envelope from the kitchen drawer, the ones the girls use to mail thank-you notes to donors, slowly wetting the seal with a kiss and a prayer.

The next morning, she followed the plan, offering to get the waning supplies. Miss Marla was happy to be free of the task since it was early spring, and the path between The Ridge and the main campus was muddier than normal. Amanda didn't mind the dirt, making her way down the path quickly, running as soon as it was safe to do so without being seen. She came to the supply warehouse where trucks and employees scurried in and out, stopping at the main desk.

"Can I get four hand soaps and a six-pack of tissues for Miss Judy Richards?" Amanda asked in a hurry.

"Alright, sure," a young college student on a work scholarship said. "Just sign them out here." She gave her a sign-in sheet, something the whole campus seemed incapable of running without, and Amanda scratched her name, Miss Judy's, and the number of items she was taking before turning to leave.

"Hey, you have to wait for the supplies," the student pointed to the pickup corner. "They'll be up here in a few minutes."

"Oh, yeah," Amanda said. "Sorry, I guess I'm a little scatter-brained today," she smiled, feigning airheadedness.

But the work scholarship student didn't acknowledge her further, answering the phone with a cheerful, trained greeting: "Harwell University Maintenance."

Amanda picked up a large tote by the loading corner and put the supplies in quickly when a young guy placed them on the counter. She exited in haste, turning towards the gravel road that led to the girls' home, and coming to the line of trees. She hesitated at the edge, finding a large pine near the path and concealing the bag in its littered pinecones. They would expect her back soon, because they always did. But if she was fast enough, she might return before anyone bothered to notice.

And if she wasn't, the risk was a lighter load to bear than the weight of Cooper's silence.

She glanced down the path both ways, then sprinted down the tree line, hoping she'd be able to see the landmarks she'd committed to memory. By the time she ran out of breath, she eyed the small gray building labeled *Campus Mail Center*. She took only a moment before approaching the office with a cherry red sign on the window and a little bell that jingled as she opened the door.

"Good morning, sweetheart," a woman greeted her behind the counter, smiling beneath thick glasses. "How can I help you today?"

Amanda reached under the stretchy fabric of her maternity jeans and pulled out the envelope, smoothing it like it hadn't been burning against her skin all morning.

"I'd like to mail a letter," she said softly.

The woman took the envelope with a warm nod. "No problem. Just need a stamp?"

Amanda nodded.

"That'll be forty-two cents," the campus postal worker said.

Amanda handed over the two quarters she'd found while on cleanup duty in the rec room, and the woman peeled a stamp from its strip and placed it on the corner of the envelope. She set it gently in the outbox with a practiced flick of her wrist.

"There you go, hon. Mail's picked up every afternoon at three."

"Thank you," Amanda whispered.

She stepped back into the sunlight, a weight lifting from her chest. It was a tether cast into the world, aimed in the direction of someone who once loved her, and that was as much as she could hope for in the moment.

But inside the mail center, the woman turned to her desk, eyes narrowing slightly as she watched Amanda walk out the door and down the steps of the entrance before heading in a direction that led away from the main campus. She re-read the name on the envelope before it could disappear into the outgoing bin: *Mr. Cooper Hansen.* She chewed the inside of her cheek, then reached for the phone.

"Judy Richards speaking," the familiar voice of a coworker chimed at the other end.

"Hi, Miss Judy—it's Carla from the mail center. I just wanted to check... did one of your girls run errands on campus this morning?"

There was a short pause before Miss Judy clipped, "She dropped off something?"

"A letter, addressed to a Mr. Cooper Hansen. Just figured I should ask."

"Thank you, Carla. That was the right thing to do. It's one of ours, trying to stir up trouble. I'll come take care of it."

By the end of the hour, the envelope had been pulled from the bin, opened behind closed doors, and filed under a lockbox where so many others had gone before it.

Amanda had walked back toward The Ridge, the wind lifting the ends of her jacket, and for the first time since she had arrived, didn't scold herself for believing the outcome was not going to be as bad as she imagined. And she didn't get so much as a side eye when she walked in ten minutes late.

But days passed, blurring into one another, measured only by the shuffle of mealtimes and the slow, deliberate tick of the rec room clock. Shadows shifted across the floor like silent witnesses, stretching longer each evening, as if the world itself were holding its breath.

Ellie had marked her calendar with careful Xs, each one bringing her closer to a date the girls both longed for and feared. She and Amanda shared the same due date—perhaps the thread that had first stitched them together as allies, then friends, and finally as sisters in a kind of battle neither of them had enlisted for.

Amanda had stopped marking her days, though. She didn't want to count anymore. She didn't want to hope or to look forward. All she wanted was to go back. Something in her ached for Cooper, for the thought that maybe she didn't have to hate him for leaving her there.

Her belly was rounding as much as felt humanly possible, her body shifting in ways she hadn't expected, even though she'd read every pamphlet, taken every class, and tried to stay two steps ahead of what was coming. But no book or nurse or whispered piece of advice could explain the way the baby kicked hardest when the world was still—when it was just the two of them in the quiet. As if the little girl knew she had her mother's ear, and wanted to remind her she was real. Amanda would press her hand to the swell of her stomach and breathe deep, anchoring herself to that tiny rhythm within. It was the only conversation that mattered anymore.

Every day passed coiled in sadness, Amanda's only joy found in the girl who calmed her nerves. Then, just before dawn one morning, a deep spasm of pain ripped through her lower back and seized her breath. Her hand flew to the bed frame, but she didn't scream or gasp. Amanda just braced herself with the guttural certainty that this was it.

She had never had a baby before. She had vowed to never do it again. And yet, her body knew. Without instruction and without permission. Nature took over.

Her contractions came like a rising tide, each one pulling everything taut, holding her hostage, then crashing back into her with primal force. She gritted her teeth and steadied herself against the edge of the narrow bed, her knuckles blanched white. She stayed silent, refusing to cry out, hoping to keep something—anything—sacred.

But, soon, the pain grew too loud to hide. By morning check-ins, Ellie found her biting down on a pillow, tears and sweat mingling at her brow, her breaths short and fractured.

"Oh God," Ellie whispered, rushing to her side, her own hand trembling. "I'll get the nurse," she told her with the composure of a woman far beyond Ellie's years.

There was no ceremony or panic. No dramatic call to action. Although it wasn't common, the staff was well-prepared for a first-time mom to give birth a week early.

Ellie was given permission to ride beside Amanda in the backseat of the van. It worked out, Miss Judy said, because Ellie had an early morning prenatal visit scheduled anyway. It was as if fate had been penciled in between appointments.

The clinic on campus was a plain, self-contained building that didn't have regular hours. Someone had radioed ahead that the doctor needed to go to the office on a Saturday. Girls from the home weren't allowed to deliver in hospitals. They got clean sheets, locked doors, and walls that didn't echo. Harwell had a system for everything—a clinic, a rehab, an adoption agency, a school. Their every need taken care of, and their every would-be problem solved.

Amanda was led to a room with a thin mattress and a shared bathroom with fluorescent lights humming overhead. No one asked her what she wanted or how she felt. They just told her to breathe.

Two women in scrubs moved in and out of the room like a metronome, and Amanda asked them if they were nurses or midwives, but they didn't answer. Because skills were less important than ideology, titles here didn't always come from training. Some were just bestowed, like blessings—or curses. She clung to her belly and begged, whispered, and pleaded for someone to call Cooper. Or her parents. Or *anyone*. But the only reply was the same clipped response she'd received before.

"Phones are not permitted."

She sat in a haze of pain, delusional with the piercing ache of each tightened muscle, imagining that perhaps none of it was real. But then the pressure came again. She moaned low, feral and unfiltered.

"I need a moment," she rasped, barely audible over the buzz of the room. "Please… just give me a moment with her. When she comes," she begged between breaths.

The woman seated between her knees didn't respond as she adjusted her gloves, casting a disapproving glance that needed no explanation.

Amanda screamed as the next surge tore through her, a raw sound that rose from a place deeper than memory, older than language. She instinctively reached down to feel the life that was coming from her.

"Don't interfere," a voice said briskly, and hands caught hers, moving them away.

Time lost shape for a moment too short to fully recall after it had passed. The minutes would plunge too far into the deep for Amanda to hold the full memory of it, to save what she stored in her bones. Consuming pain was eventually followed by a strange, terrifying release, and then a silence that pressed against her ears like the hush before a storm crackles through a solemn night.

But what broke through wasn't thunderous. It was a small, sharp, breathtakingly simple cry in all of its aliveness. She lifted her head, straining toward the sound of that tiny voice, desperate to see, to speak, to claim whatever she could before the moment slipped through her fingers.

Amanda strained toward the sound, reaching desperately with her hands, her eyes—anything that would stretch in the direction of her own flesh and bones, clambering relentlessly with her soul, but her body was held fast while nurses pinned her arms against the bed.

"Please—*please*—just let me..." Her voice broke.

She caught a short glimpse of Daisy's face—her eyes glassy and blue. Amanda watched in agony, catching only the soft curve of a newborn's shoulder, the side of a gel-covered cheek, and the gentle jiggle of a tiny limb before one of the women wrapped Daisy in a blanket, bundled her into practiced arms, and walked away. Her baby's cry faded down the hallway like a memory that hadn't even had a chance to begin.

A scream tore from Amanda's throat, "Give me my baby!" she demanded before collapsing back into the mattress from exhaustion and blood loss, her body unrecognizable, emptied of her soul along with her child.

Her chest heaved, vision blurring as the staff moved around her, cleaning and stitching, but she couldn't feel them. She couldn't hear them.

Her only perception of reality was the cavernous and hollow echo of her baby's cry.

And so her thoughts sang a song—not to soothe, but to remember the truth.

A lullaby for the girl she couldn't hold.

They say April showers bring May flowers,
And baby, I know that it's true.
Cause my darlin' little Daisy,
That's when I know I'll see you...

Chapter Eleven

New York City: Two Weeks In

THE TAP-TAP-TAP OF THE knock was soft but insistent, a sound that should've startled Amanda more than it did. Visitors were meant to be announced through the intercom long before they reached the penthouse door. But for some reason, it didn't scare her as much as it made her curious. She wouldn't put it past Tristan to come and surprise her for a twenty-four-hour stay before he jetted off to his next meeting on another continent. Her heart kicked with hope against her ribs, warmth rushing to her cheeks.

She grinned, moving slowly, one hand still curled around a mug of tea that had gone cold when it occurred to her that if it wasn't Tristan, then the concierge had either gone soft, or whoever was there had somehow snuck past security. But, before she could think twice, she pulled at the door.

Cooper Hansen stood on the other side, a thin layer of New York drizzle beading on his wool coat.

"Amanda." His voice cracked around her name.

She felt the ground sway slightly beneath her feet, but her posture didn't falter. "Cooper, how did you get up here? You shouldn't be here."

"I know," he said, his gaze dropping, shoulders bowing as if under a weight.

And yet Amanda stepped aside, the motion almost involuntary, her hand tightening on the doorframe as though to anchor herself. She swung the door wider, her silence forming an invitation he didn't need to question.

He entered cautiously, as if every step deeper into Tristan's space would cost him something. His eyes darted to the view beyond the windows, the curve of the staircase, the plush leather sofas juxtaposed against the rigid lines of the loft. He turned to view her, noticing the mug in her hand, her soft fingers curled around the handle, no ring to be seen. But neither his eyes nor his thoughts lingered on anything too long.

"I... I was in the city," he stuttered, though she hadn't asked. "And I couldn't..." His voice caught. He let out a breath, sharp and short. "I had to see you."

Amanda gently closed the door behind him as if something might shatter if she made too much noise.

"I'm sorry that you came all this way, Cooper, but I don't know what we can say to each other now that could possibly fix anything. I should have just kept my mouth shut." She moved to the countertop island, placing her mug down and busying herself with the task of making a fresh cup.

"But… I don't know," she shrugged. "There are so many unanswered questions when it comes to you. And I don't seem to be myself when you're around. Can I get you a drink?"

"Got anything stronger than tea?" Cooper let out a soft, exasperated laugh.

Amanda pointed to a liquor cart against the brick wall. "Help yourself," she motioned.

She watched him walk away, wondering what it would have been like to know Cooper as an adult. What his drink of choice might be, what he acted like when he got a little bit tipsy, or if he'd made a fool of himself during college drinking games. She shook her head, attempting to shoo the thoughts away as she watched the water in her mug curl into steam.

Cooper poured himself a shot, swallowed it, then poured another, the amber liquid catching in the low light. By the time Amanda crossed to the couch, the sharp scent of whiskey hung in the air.

"Does your father know you're here?" Her voice broke the silence, steady but gentler than she expected it to be.

"No," he said, taking off his coat and sinking into the emerald chair across from her. "I don't report to my dad every day."

Amanda's shoulders flicked upward as she took a sip, attempting to prevent herself from saying anything that could sound like an insult. She reminded herself that she had known Cooper as an eighteen-year-old boy, not a man. What she thought of him now was based on things that may not have held true.

Cooper didn't let the silence linger. "I haven't stopped thinking about you. About what you said in Bucharest. These past two weeks have been hell."

Amanda's throat tightened. "Yeah," she managed, the word carrying more ache than agreement. The scene at the restaurant had replayed in her mind again and again—his hollow voice admitting he didn't know, the stunned grief that crossed his face when she blurted out that their daughter had his eyes.

The memory pressed between them, as tangible as breath. Silence swelled, not empty but heavy, ballooning into the room until it felt like another presence they both had to reckon with.

"What do you want from me?" Amanda finally muttered.

Cooper dragged a hand through his hair, his eyes rimmed red from the battle to keep tears from overtaking him completely. She'd seen him under stress before, and apparently, those idiosyncrasies didn't change with time.

"I don't know. I thought I did," he said. "But after seeing you, and hearing—God, Amanda." His voice broke open, rawer than she'd ever heard it. "All this time—"

She looked away, pressing her lips together until they blanched. Her arms crossed, not in defense but to stop her own hands from reaching for him. It was something she couldn't make sense of. How she wanted to comfort him after all of this. But, she had mastered stillness in emotional earthquakes—an art learned the hard way, a discipline she could call on like muscle memory.

But with Cooper, that stillness frayed. Restraint in his presence felt less like control and more like bracing against a storm with no shelter. The effort left her nearly breathless, as though the air itself had thinned.

"You came all this way," she managed, her voice steadier than she felt. "What are you hoping to find?"

For a moment, he held himself still, fighting the inevitable. Then the tears came, slow at first, until they fell unchecked, darkening the floor at his feet. Amanda couldn't look away. When he finally raised his hands, it was less to wipe them clean than to gather himself, lifting his face so she would see the truth unhidden in his eyes.

"I guess I'm here to find a version of the truth I can live with. Do you... Do you know anything else? About her, I mean."

Amanda shook her head slowly. "Only what the papers said. She was placed with a family out of state. No names. No photos. It was a closed adoption." She lifted her glass, buying herself a moment before she went on. "I was told that anonymity was part of the arrangement. It was pretty much standard practice there."

Cooper gave a short, bitter laugh. "Standard practice for what? A way to erase people? To make them disappear?"

Amanda studied him, wishing she could step into his shock and carry part of it for him. But the truth had calcified inside her over nearly two decades, and far from being a discovery, it was peeling back a scab that had bled many times before.

"I signed an NDA," she whispered, the words as brittle as glass.

Cooper's head dropped into his hands, his body folding as if the weight of it finally buckled him. "God, Amanda."

"I didn't think I had a choice. After what we saw with your dad and grandpa... I—" Her voice faltered. She wasn't sure how much more to say.

Did he even remember that night? The shadows stretching across the water, the low voices, the sound that didn't belong. Most newspapers never used the word, probably because they knew what alleging something against the Hansens would mean, but Amanda had long since admitted it to herself. Murder. A cover-up so complete that his father walked away untouched. Maybe Cooper buried the memory, convinced himself there was nothing to see. That his father was still a good man, trying to take care of everyone. How else could he keep living as if the world made sense? How else could either of them?

"She's almost eighteen," Cooper said at last, his voice rough. "Just a few months away. I did the math." He let out a brittle laugh, shaking his head. "I've been doing the math every day."

Amanda's breath caught. "Eighteen years. It doesn't even seem possible, does it?"

"I think we have the right to find her," he said firmly. "Once she's eighteen, we don't need permission. Not from anyone."

"No." Amanda's stomach dropped, the word tumbling out before she could stop it. "Cooper, you don't understand. Your dad..."

He lifted his head, eyes raw but steady, anchoring her in place.

"I don't want to crash into her life like some long-lost savior," he said. "I just want to know she's okay. That she had love. That she wasn't just a transaction."

"You can't do this." Amanda stopped, meeting his eyes. The words clung in her throat before she forced them out. "I've never told anyone about her."

"But you've *known*," Cooper pressed, the ache in his voice undeniable. "All this time you've carried that truth—that our baby is alive, that she's out there in the world—and what about me? I didn't even get the chance to have a say."

Amanda's composure cracked. "But your family sure has!" The words shot out sharp and direct. "If you think your dad is going to let you escape politics forever, you're dreaming. And the last thing you need is to go chasing after an illegitimate daughter while they're grooming you for office."

"Do you even hear yourself?" Cooper said breathlessly. *"Illegitimate?* We were going to build a life together," he insisted.

She scoffed. "Yeah, and who changed those plans?"

"That's not fair. You said it yourself. We were both lied to."

"Okay, sure, that may be true, but I was the one with the least amount of power and the most to lose, so spare me if I don't feel too sorry for the way your life turned out."

Cooper stood, brushing his hands down the legs of his trousers.

"Maybe I shouldn't have come," he said.

And Amanda rose to her feet as if to agree. "Yeah," she whispered, moving toward the door while he reached for his coat, still damp with evening rain.

Her hand touched the knob just as he stepped closer. "Cooper, I..." The words faltered. "I didn't want any of this."

"I know," he murmured, reaching for her arm in apology.

But the moment his skin brushed hers, Amanda leaned in, her body betraying her resolve as if it had been waiting years for this collision. His fingers tightened, and then his lips found hers—hungry, desperate, drinking in all they had lost.

In the next breath, they broke apart with the same intensity that had flung them together, his hands still knotted in her shirt.

"I'm sorry," he whispered, though he didn't let go. The kiss hung between them like smoke—sweet, choking, and impossible to breathe without wanting more.

Amanda's voice trembled. "I... I used to dream she'd find me."

Cooper's arms fell slack, his eyes searching hers.

"I never let myself dream of finding her myself," she went on. "Sometimes I just picture her knocking at the door, asking questions I'll never know how to answer." Tears slipped down her cheeks, stripping her of every defense.

Cooper's chest ached with the urge to touch her, to pull her in and trace the familiar texture of her hair between his fingers. But all he managed was her name. "Amanda... I should... go." Releasing her shirt, his hand moved toward the door.

"Don't," she breathed.

He froze, leaning his forehead against the wood, a low cry slipping out of him. "Amanda. When you left, it broke me."

She pressed her palm to his back, her head settling against his shoulder. "I never let myself believe you were the bad guy. Not fully. So, I'm not sorry we've said this much—cleared the air, at least."

He gave a strained laugh. "Is that what this is? Clearing the air?"

"Whatever it is," she said, voice low, "and whatever we had—we have to let go."

But Cooper turned, slow and deliberate, switching places with Amanda and pressing her against the door, his thigh wedging close, his hands moving with the ache of someone gathering what had been lost. "God, Amanda. I didn't come here for this. I swear."

"I know." She moved away from the door and into his frame, only to slip out of his hold, cupping her face in her hands, trembling.

"But I can't just let you go," he muttered, and before she could speak again, he wrenched open the door and slipped into the hall.

Amanda let the door click shut behind him. The echo carried through the penthouse like the hollow strike of a dissonant final note, unresolved, and when silence rushed back in, she felt its weight press down against her chest. She leaned into the door, palms flat against the wood as if steadying herself against the aftershock of an earthquake.

Her phone still waited on the counter where she had left it, screen black, a lifeless rectangle in the dim light. For a moment, she only stared at it, unwilling to move, her body heavy as stone. When she finally crossed the room, her legs felt unreliable beneath her. She hadn't even noticed her tears until one fell, splashing against the back of her hand as she reached for the device.

Her swipe was clumsy, but her muscle memory carried her to Lyla's number as she pressed the call through without thinking.

"Hey," she breathed.

"Amanda? What's wrong?" The concern in Lyla's voice nearly undid her.

Amanda pressed her fist to her lips, biting down until words would come. "He didn't know," she whispered.

"Who didn't know?" The pause was brief but telling. Words weren't needed; Lyla already understood. "Cooper?"

"Yes. All this time… they told him the baby died. That I had a miscarriage, and then I was just… away, recovering." Her voice cracked, raw and jagged against the truth she had carried in silence for so long.

On the other end, Lyla sighed, low and unsurprised. "Of course they did."

Amanda blinked through her tears. "You're not shocked?"

"I'm not ever shocked by them," Lyla said, her voice hardening with steel. "I'm not shocked by what power does to people desperate to protect an image. But Amanda… his not knowing doesn't erase what he didn't do. He never came after you."

Amanda sank onto the couch, curling her legs beneath her. "I know. I keep circling it in my head—whether he could have, if there was some chance..."

"No," Lyla said gently, cutting her off. "He chose silence. He chose distance. Maybe he thought he was protecting you. Or maybe only himself. Either way, you deserved more than a boy who let other people tell him how to live."

Amanda closed her eyes, the words falling over her like both balm and wound. "I told him tonight. Not everything. Just enough. And—God, Lyla—it hurt. Like tearing a scar back open after all these years."

The line held steady with nothing but Lyla's breathing, deliberate and present.

Then her voice softened. "Listen. I got the invitation today. Tristan's family is throwing that big New Year's party, and Kyle and I are coming. I'll see you in a few weeks, but if you need me before then—say the word. You know me. I'll be there in a New York minute."

Amanda let out a small laugh. "No. Don't. I'll be okay. I just... I needed to hear your voice."

"You sure?" Lyla pressed. "Because you know I'd drop everything."

"I know." Amanda leaned back against the cushions, tracing the curve of her knee with her fingertips. "I promise, I'll be fine. I'll see you at the party."

"Good. You're going to need me too—because we both know these people have no idea how to throw down properly," Lyla teased, trying to ease the weight.

Amanda smiled faintly. "For real. Katherine's already told me she wants me to hand the decoy off to Melody before the gathering, since everyone will be there. She made it sound simple, but nothing ever is with her."

"Simple isn't Katherine's style," Lyla said dryly. "But Melody will be all right. She's steady."

Amanda hesitated. "Do you still think we're being followed?"

The line went quiet, just long enough to matter, before Lyla answered. "Yes."

Amanda inhaled slowly through her nose, bracing herself.

"It's not constant," Lyla added quickly. "But enough. Enough that I can feel it at the fringes. And I don't imagine these things."

"I know," Amanda whispered. She pressed her forehead to her knees, eyes closed tight.

"Just promise me you'll stay alert," Lyla said. "If I'm wrong, then good. But if I'm right... don't let them catch you off guard."

"I promise. You too."

Silence lingered again until Lyla's voice came through, raspy and calm. "Get some sleep, okay? And remember—you are not alone, no matter how much it feels that way. You've got me. Always."

Amanda's lips curved into a small, tired smile. "Always," she echoed.

She set the phone down, leaned back, and closed her eyes, listening to the rain tick against the glass. Beyond it, the city pulsed on, oblivious to her woes. And somewhere out there, a girl with eyes like Cooper's lived her life, unaware that the two people whose love made her had as many questions about her as she had about them.

Amanda breathed in, knowing that this night would have to be forgotten, and her one focus must be to pretend the world hadn't already split open.

Chapter Twelve

White Pine, Tennessee: June 2008

"Well, baby," Grandma Nellie said, shuffling in from the pantry with a lopsided cake balanced on a ceramic stand, "you've done it. Eighteen."

Her eyes shone with the kind of pride that didn't need speeches. The weight of joy from a life she had prayed over, tended, and believed in from the very first breath was simply felt.

The air inside the farmhouse kitchen was thick with sugar and old memories. A boxed fan hummed in the window, barely denting the Tennessee heat. Amanda sat at the table in a faded tank top, her damp hair coiled in a loose braid down one shoulder, bare feet propped on the lower rung of the chair. Her legs still ached from her nightly shift at the local diner.

Pink icing bloomed along the top of the cake like a crown of magnolias—hand-piped, no less—and a single candle leaning precariously in the center.

"Officially a grown woman, which means I get to brag even more shamelessly from here on out." Nellie wiped her hands on her apron and leaned over to kiss Amanda's head.

Amanda smiled. "Thanks for the cake, Granny."

"Oh, you know I wouldn't miss it. It's tradition." Nellie lit the candle and nodded toward it. "Go on. Make a wish."

Amanda hesitated, then leaned forward and blew, the flame disappearing in a curl of smoke.

Nellie sat across from her with two chipped floral plates and began to cut a slice. "You got your papers for flight school in order?"

Amanda nodded. "Starts next month. Tuesdays and Thursdays."

"Well, I'll be the one crying when I see you in that uniform. You're gonna be the best pilot Tennessee's ever raised."

Amanda swallowed, blinking hard. "You're the only one who thinks so."

"That's not true. I know someone else who would be proud." Nellie paused, then stood. "Hang on."

She disappeared into the hallway and returned carrying a weathered hatbox wrapped in a thick fabric ribbon. Amanda knew what it was before Nellie even set it down. It was a tradition hidden from everyone else in the family. When one sister gives birth to a child and the other raises her, there's no open dialogue about feelings on the subject. The silence wasn't reverence—it was shame, and pride, woven tight enough to choke out the truth.

Grandma Nellie had two girls, and even though Kate made mistakes, she loved her daughter and the little girl she had brought into the world just the same. So, once a year, Nellie refused to let the silence win. She uttered the words everyone else was afraid to speak—but only when it was the two of them, and always on Amanda's birthday.

"You sure?" Amanda asked, voice barely above a whisper.

Nellie nodded. "If you are."

"It's tradition," Amanda repeated with a grin, lifting the lid carefully.

Inside, yellowing Polaroids and colored prints with curled edges, plastic barrettes, handwritten notes in swirly pink ink. She pulled out a photo—two girls in matching Easter dresses, one with tangled red curls, and the other smiling too wide to make out the shape of her eyes.

"There's Kate and Genny," Nellie said, peering over Amanda's shoulder. "Lord, they were a mess. Kate used to get out of her chores and hide in the barn to read, and when I'd get upset that nothing was done, Genevieve would tattletale just to get her in trouble, even though she'd been fooling around too."

Amanda smiled faintly, her thumb tracing the contours of her mother's face in the photograph, wishing she could fill in the blanks the picture couldn't give.

Kate had given her life, but Genevieve had raised her, carrying the mantle of motherhood. Nellie had always been the one who favored her, though—the grandmother who slipped her little kindnesses, who saw her without judgment. Genevieve hadn't resented Amanda outright, not until the pregnancy presented an opportunity. After her time at The Ridge, Amanda couldn't bear the thought of going back into that house, pretending everything was normal. So she came here, to Nellie, who let her belong without demanding silence.

"I wish I knew her better."

"She loves you, baby." Nellie's voice softened, the lines around her mouth folding into a shadow of sorrow. "I know people say a lot of things about folks who leave, but it's true—she loves ya. Kate just... wasn't built for this world. Not in the way that sticks. Tennessee's good for some folks, but she ain't that kind."

Amanda kept her gaze low. "Do I ever remind you of her?"

"All the time," Nellie said with a chuckle. "Especially when you get stubborn. But you've got your own fire, too. You stayed. You didn't run. And you're fighting for something now that's as big as the sky." She gave a little snicker, pleased at her own turn of phrase.

Amanda laughed, a short huff that didn't quite shake her thoughts.

"If you've ever heard someone act like you're a mistake, you ignore 'em, alright?" Nellie went on, her tone firm now, one hand tightening around her coffee mug. "You know you're not. You're the best damn decision your mama ever made."

Amanda's eyelids fluttered. She didn't want to cry on her birthday. Instead, she sent up a prayer—every day she did—that little Daisy might have a grandmother who would one day tell her she wasn't anyone's mistake to fix either.

Nellie reached across the table, her hand warm and sure over Amanda's. "Flight school is just the beginning, sweetheart. I'm so proud of you. I hope you know that."

"I do," Amanda whispered. "I really do. Now, let's eat this cake so I can go change for work and pay for that education of mine."

"I wish I could help you more, baby," Nellie said, glancing at the lopsided cake as though it should've been more.

"Oh, Granny, you help me plenty. You're the only one who still believes in me after—" Amanda's words tangled and fell away. *After what? Her mistake?* She refused to see it that way.

"Oh, now." Nellie flicked her hand through the air, dismissing the thought. "You believe in yourself and that's enough. That's all you need, you remember that."

Amanda smiled and nodded, placing her hands on her grandmother's, while across the half-acre yard, behind a small tool shed, Cooper Hansen peered past the wall and into Grandma Nellie's kitchen window.

His fingers curled tightly around the warped edge of the tool shed, splinters digging into his palm, but he didn't notice. His gaze was fixed on the kitchen window like it was a movie screen, and Amanda was the only actor who mattered.

She looked older than the last time he saw her—softer in her movements, a little thinner in the cheeks, but still unmistakably her. The braid down her back, and the way she tilted her head when she smiled, was a drug to him. He didn't get close enough to see the flicker of sadness she tried to bury.

He hadn't planned to show up. Not really. He was just... driving. And then somehow he ended up back in White Pine, back at Nellie's old place. He knew his dad would kill him if he knew. Everyone was telling him it was time to move on, as if Amanda had been a fling and not a romance. But after five months had passed, and he still hadn't heard a word from her, he felt empty. Hollow.

He watched as she blew out the candle, Nellie reaching for her hand, the two of them talking. He couldn't hear what they were saying, but he didn't need to. He imagined it. A proud grandmother, a girl trying to grow into her future with all the weight of the past pressing on her ribs.

When he saw a flash of movement, he ducked behind the ridge of the shed, barely catching sight of her when Amanda stood and walked toward the hallway, her fingers grazing Nellie's shoulder. They laughed together, and Cooper swallowed his pain down, remembering the way her voice would tilt upward when she laughed.

He wanted to knock on the door. To just stand there and ask if he could come in. If they could talk. But fear tangled with shame—fear she'd reject him, shame that he'd stayed silent for so long—and he couldn't make himself go any closer. Besides, it must have been true what everyone was saying—that she was happier without him; that they both needed to move on, and start their lives afresh. But she still felt like the only reason in the world to wake up in the mornings.

Amanda reappeared a few minutes later in a crisp black blouse, her apron balled in one hand, and her hair pulled into a neater braid. She looked like she was late for something, and Cooper smiled. She was always rushing. She hugged Grandma Nellie, said something at the door, and slipped out to the beat-up Corolla parked beside the porch. Cooper ducked lower, peering out enough to trace her movements. As the car backed out slowly, she slung her arm over the passenger seat, and her face was half-illuminated by the slanting afternoon sun.

He waited until the dust from the gravel drive settled, then jogged to his own truck parked under a patch of shade a block over. She was heading toward town. He knew every turn, every stop sign, every dip in the road. It was the route to the diner.

He didn't know what he was doing—just that he couldn't lose sight of her again. Maybe he'd sit at the counter. Order coffee. Smile like it was all normal. Like he wasn't the guy who'd been forced to leave her alone in the wreckage of their relationship, of their lives.

Cooper turned the key in the ignition and pulled onto the road, staying a safe distance behind until he spotted the diner. He parked across the street at a gas station, just far enough to avoid suspicion but close enough to see her.

The diner's red neon sign buzzed faintly against the fading daylight, casting a soft glow onto the gravel lot where Cooper sat in his truck. He'd angled it behind a row of ice machines, close to the propane tank cages, where no one would notice.

Amanda made her way inside the window-lined building, smiling at her coworkers as she entered. She was magnetic. Everyone was drawn to her; it wasn't just him. He watched her through the plate-glass windows as she tied her apron, grabbing the notepad from the pocket, her movements automatic and graceful. She had the kind of rhythm you didn't earn without showing up tired and leaving later than you should.

Hours passed, but Cooper didn't leave to eat, go in for snacks, or turn on the radio. He just sat in silence as the dusk deepened into evening, then night, headlights streaking past him every few minutes. He imagined walking in and catching her eye—daydreamed about her running into his arms. Instead, he stayed in the shadows, watching her serve up slices of pie and refill water glasses.

When she slipped out of the side door for a break and sat on a crate near the dumpster fence, she sipped a bottle of water, rubbed her temples, and looked up at the stars. That was when Cooper leaned forward, one hand flat on the steering wheel, barely breathing. Her profile was perfect against the blackened sky. Her fingers lifted to her lips at times, like she was praying.

He wondered if she ever thought of him. If she ever looked at the moon and remembered their whispered promises.

When the last of the lights dimmed to close off the back half of the restaurant, and the overnight crew took over, Amanda stepped out into the night, her hair loose, and her apron folded under one arm.

Cooper stayed perched in his spot, waiting until she'd gotten to her car safely, and watched her pull out of the driveway. He waited until her taillights disappeared before he turned the key in his own ignition.

He promised himself he wouldn't follow her home. So he drove the opposite direction. When he pulled into the circular drive of his house, the gate clicked shut behind him as his headlights briefly illuminated the manicured hedges and tall columns that framed the entryway. He killed the engine and sat motionless, hands still gripping the steering wheel. The dashboard clock glowed like an accusation.

He went through the side door, the house dim but not fully dark. A single pendant light burned in the foyer, casting a golden pool onto the marble floor. His footsteps echoed slightly as he entered, his sneakers a quiet rebellion against the polished silence of the estate. He'd hoped—rather naively, knowing his father—that the house would be asleep. That maybe he'd slip in unnoticed. But as he moved past the sitting room, a voice sliced through the air.

"Where the hell have you been?"

James Hansen stood at the edge of the hallway, hair rumpled, and collar undone. He hadn't even bothered to change out of his shirt and slacks, though the jacket had been tossed somewhere hours before. His eyes were bloodshot and sharp, locked on his son.

Cooper froze. "I—just went for a drive."

"At one o'clock in the morning?"

"I lost track of time," Cooper lied. It sounded ridiculous the second it left his mouth.

Hansen advanced, his voice low and vibrating with fury. "You've been out all night, your phone's off, and I'm sitting here wondering if I need to call in the state patrol to find my son in a ditch. You think that's acceptable behavior for someone with your future?"

"I'm sorry," Cooper said, but his tone held no weight. The truth of where he'd been pressed against his ribs like a bruise. Watching Amanda through the window of the diner, heart lodged in his throat, waiting for something—he didn't know what. Maybe just a glimpse of the life he'd been told to forget. Why couldn't he let go of it? Of her?

His dad stepped closer. "Tell me the truth."

Cooper hesitated. "I went to White Pine."

A thick and dangerous pause followed as James Hansen's nostrils flared.

"You what?"

"I just... needed to see her." The words sounded pathetic even to Cooper. "That's all I did, though. I didn't talk to her. I didn't—"

"You turned off your phone and drove in the middle of the night to *see her*?" his father spat the words at him.

"She's not a criminal," Cooper snapped. "She didn't do anything wrong."

Hansen's voice dropped to a lethal whisper. "You listen to me. You think you're smarter than me? You think sneaking around and playing the tragic lover changes anything? You made your choice—to throw it all away for one reckless night with a girl who would ruin you. We *all* made sacrifices to protect you after your screw up. And I *will not* let you throw that away because you can't control your urges. Grow up, Cooper. No girl is worth throwin' your life away for."

Cooper's hands curled into fists at his sides. "You mean *you* made that choice. I didn't. I never would have—"

"Enough!"

His father stepped back, beginning to pace. The air was tight with a frantic type of fury and restraint all at the same time. Then, with sudden resolve, Hansen turned to his son.

"You're leaving tomorrow."

Cooper blinked. "What?"

"There's a program. Summer readiness. A boot camp that starts before West Point's formal orientation. I'll pull some strings to get you in early. You're going."

"You can't just—"

"Oh, but I can." James's voice rose again, no longer bothered by the idea of who he might wake up in the house. "You're still under my roof, and you're going to walk into that academy with discipline and focus, not pathetic sentiment."

Cooper looked at him, jaw tense. "You think you can erase her from me? From *who I am*?"

"I can erase *distraction*," James growled. "And don't be foolish enough to think this doesn't affect me. You think voters want to have a leader whose son knocked up a slut in White Pine and has no self-control?"

The slap of the words hit harder than any hand could.

"I'm done arguing," James said, voice cold as ice. "Pack your bags. Your driver will be here at six."

He turned, disappearing down the hallway without waiting for an answer, and Cooper was left standing alone in the grand foyer, surrounded by marble and silence and the ghosts of everything he wasn't allowed to want.

Chapter Thirteen

New York City: Three Weeks In

6:30 P.M. BRYANT PARK. *Corner bench near the carousel. Bring the case. Stay visible. M. lands at JFK shortly. The world is your stage. —K*

Amanda's mouth curled at the corners when she read Katherine's text—enigmatically cryptic, dramatic, and poetic all in the same line.

She had felt a shift in the air before the notification on her phone even came through. It was a near-electric stillness, as if the whole atmosphere paused mid-breath. She read the message twice, then, pressing the phone to sleep and sliding it back into her coat, she picked up her pace.

It was only five o'clock, and Amanda had spent half the day looking for a dress. Tristan would be coming home soon, and despite the mayhem of what had become her life, she needed no further reminders that she was a woman in love. Tristan was more attractive to her than ever, and after a regretful moment with Cooper Hansen that had jolted her emotions, the one thing she settled on was this: Tristan Montgomery was the man of her dreams. In fact, he was almost *too* perfect, and if she knew what was good for her, she'd lock it down and fast.

She couldn't wait to see him. She wanted him to look at her like he did that first night in Tenerife when she walked onto Julis Babb's terrace and felt Tristan's eyes settle on her skin like the morning dew. She looked down at her shopping bag with the black slip dress and smiled in satisfaction.

Amanda made her way to the apartment building and pushed through the revolving doors, greeting the concierge before stepping into the private elevator, lost in thought until it chimed at the top floor. She slipped out, shoes clicking against the polished concrete, her mind racing through the timing, the decoy handoff, and the risk this posed. But when she turned into the narrow hallway between the twin loft apartments, she froze.

Cooper Hansen leaned against the opposite wall, his eyes dark with whatever storm had driven him there.

Amanda's chest tightened. "You can't keep doing this," she said, her voice low but sharp. "Showing up here."

He pushed off the wall, closing the space, his gaze fixed on hers as though daring her to look away first. "Then tell me how else I'm supposed to see you."

"I told you *not* to," she reminded him. "You have to leave me alone."

"I just want some details. I can't stop playing and replaying everything, Amanda. You've had time to move on. I haven't."

"I'm not staying," she said flatly. "I have a meeting. I'm just dropping off my bags."

"Just tell me where they sent you," he murmured.

Amanda angled past him, every nerve alive with the danger of this convergence: Cooper in Tristan's hallway, the prototype and decoy only steps away, Melody approaching Bryant Park in less than an hour, and an informant lurking around a corner somewhere below.

"Why do you want to know now? What does it matter?" she barked. "And you couldn't have texted me your burning questions? Cooper, seriously," she said, frustration sparking through every line of her body as she made for the door, determined to brush him off completely.

"But–" Cooper began, keeping his distance. "What if it's still there? That place. What if…" he almost didn't let himself say it. "What if my dad funded the place that took her away from us?"

Amanda's shoulders sank, the bags slipping from her grasp to the floor as she turned to face him. In that moment, she pitied him, though she knew he would despise her for it. Whatever stories he had spun to survive, about Governor James Hansen, about the man he called father, had splintered beyond repair, fragments too jagged to piece together again.

"They called it The Ridge," she murmured. "You might Google it, but I doubt much would appear. It was tucked behind the University, hidden in plain sight, the sort of place people pretended not to know about. And now that Harwell's gone..." She exhaled softly. "I wonder if they've let it wither away."

"Well, I aim to find out," Cooper said, the sound of gratitude evident on his lips.

"But why?" Amanda insisted.

"Because you're probably right. I don't know if I have it in me to stand against the man I call Dad. But if I play his game, maybe I can beat him at it." Cooper nodded, his jaw tight with resolve.

Amanda stared at him, bewildered at first—until she understood the gravity of what he was saying. Cooper wasn't planning on stepping into his father's shadow; he was preparing to break away from it.

It struck her as almost laughable. "So what, you'll run for state office? Promise to rid Tennessee of the homes that take babies from girls who can't fight back?" She hadn't meant the words to land so sharply, but they did.

"If I have to," Cooper said with a short nod. He shifted back, already turning on his heel. "I'll let you get back to your evening."

"Cooper." His name left her lips like a request before she even realized it had slipped out. She hesitated, then added, "Meet me for drinks later? You can ask me anything. Just... not here. It'll be easier in a public place."

The flash of the two of them on the other side of that door lit his eyes with an almost boyish grin, but he didn't hold onto it. "Okay. Thanks. Text me?"

Amanda nodded, fumbling for her keys. She unlocked the door, gathered her bags, and slipped inside without looking back. She listened for the hum of the elevator as it carried him away.

Amanda took the long way through Bryant Park, cutting diagonally past the library steps, avoiding anything that might look routine. She forced every movement to appear deliberate, as if the mission alone occupied her mind.

She had clocked two men on the walk over—at least she thought she had. Maybe they were just ordinary pedestrians, maybe not. But they looked too much like the same shadows she'd seen before, lingering a moment too long when her reflection caught in the glassy towers of Midtown.

The carousel spun ahead, bulbs glowing, painted horses bobbing endlessly to a tinny, cheerful tune that mocked her unease. She crossed to a bench, folding her legs neatly. A large shopping bag rested loosely at Amanda's feet, its handles slack against the bench slats, as though it contained nothing more important than a box of holiday scarves. She kept her posture easy, the faintest smile playing on her lips, until Melody emerged from the blur of foot traffic.

Amanda rose at once, her movement fluid, greeting Melody with the ease of true friendship. "Hi," she said.

"Hey," Melody replied, wrapping her in an embrace that looked effortless—warm, familiar, the kind of greeting no one would question. To anyone watching, it was simple and unremarkable: two friends meeting by chance. And that was exactly the point.

"Welcome back."

"Thanks," Melody said, her smile never wavering, but her eyes swept the park in quick, practiced arcs—cataloguing shadows, watchers, the men posted at angles meant to look casual.

Amanda gestured lightly toward the carousel, where the music tumbled out over the chilly evening air. "Wanna ride?" she teased, her voice bright.

Melody gave a small laugh, lowering her tone as they resettled on the bench. "Better not. Anything too out of character, they'll know it's staged."

Amanda matched the cadence of her whisper, then deliberately brightened, her voice pitched high and cheerful, as if they were two women trading vacation stories. "Are you enjoying Croatia?"

Melody slipped easily into the role. "Oh, you'd love it. But wait until summer—the water is perfect, and it doesn't get too hot. You should come." Her words carried the natural rhythm of idle chatter.

"Sounds amazing." Amanda leaned in like she was sharing a bit of gossip. "Though I might be a little preoccupied with wedding plans..."

Melody's brows lifted in feigned delight, though her voice cooled a degree. "This summer? Wait. Don't tell me you've picked a date?"

"No, not yet." Amanda kept her expression bright, but a slight tremor crossed her words. "But when he gets back, I want to at least talk about it. I don't know if I want to wait anymore."

"Why the sudden change of heart?" Melody asked, suspicion edging into her tone. She tilted her head, but kept her smile steady for any audience. "Don't tell me this is because you saw Cooper Hansen."

Amanda's eyes widened, guilt written plainly across her face. Her lips barely moved when she whispered, "He's in New York."

"Amanda." Melody's warning was gentle but firm. "Be careful."

"I know. It's just…" Amanda exhaled, her breath visible in the cold air. Her mouth fumbled for words that never came clean. She pivoted. "I love Tristan. Whatever threw us together, maybe it wasn't an accident. Maybe it's fate."

Melody only inclined her head, keeping her smile, wise enough not to press. "Then prepare yourself. Evelyn Montgomery will expect the most classic, extravagant wedding New York has ever seen. You'll be busy. Just promise me you'll still come see me."

"I promise," she said, her smile carrying a quiet warmth that belonged less to the ruse and more to the woman behind it.

"Good," Melody said. "I'll be here for the New Year's party too. I was glad for the invitation—though I'm fairly certain Julius had more to do with it than the Montgomerys. Call me if you want to meet before then, okay?"

Amanda noted the name but didn't press. Julius lingered at the edges of everything—sometimes an ally, sometimes a threat. For now, she could only treat him as both. Instead of lingering on the thought, she nodded to her friend. "Have a wonderful Christmas."

"You too. The boys are flying in this week. We're doing every single New York holiday tradition we can cram in before school starts again."

"That sounds perfect," Amanda smirked, standing to hug her goodbye, the embrace lingering just long enough to show a genuine friendship.

Melody bent gracefully, retrieving the shopping bag from beside the bench. The gesture was seamless, ordinary to any passerby, yet its precision gave the exchange the polish of rehearsal.

Amanda turned east, her breath visible in the cold, while Melody walked in the opposite direction, her phone already in hand. Amanda typed quickly:

My meeting's over. Bryant Park Hotel? I'm grabbing a drink at the bar.

Three dots appeared almost instantly before Cooper's reply came.

On my way.

The warmth of the hotel lobby wrapped around Amanda like a hush after the raw winter air. She crossed the marble floor without stopping as the lounge opened before her like another world.

Lanterns glowed in intricate latticework, scattering amber light across velvet banquettes and arched alcoves. The air carried the scent of citrus and spice, with the faint sting of gin and clove. Conversations rose in layered undertones, softened by music that seemed to belong nowhere in particular—nomadic, borderless, as though it had traveled the world on waves of sound only to find its place right here.

Amanda slipped onto a seat at the bar, tucking into the curve of polished wood where she could watch both the entrance and the mirrored wall behind. It was becoming a habit of hers—choosing positions that offered her more than one line of sight. She asked for wine almost by reflex, the words spilling as easily as breath. The glass warmed against her fingers, less a drink than an accessory to her posture.

She saw Cooper first in the mirror—the unmistakable breadth of his shoulders cutting through the lantern-lit crowd, and her breath caught before his gaze found hers. He looked every bit the polished young aide his father had made him, tethered full-time to James Hansen's office, mastering the handshakes and speeches that would prepare him for a campaign of his own. Yet he hadn't ever run for office himself, never ready to give himself over to politics entirely—and looking at him now, she wondered if it was true resistance or only delay.

She smiled in the mirror as he approached, turning slightly on her stool, the stem of her wineglass cool in her hand.

"Hey," she said, voice low, nearly lost beneath the hum of music. "I'm glad you came."

He let out a slow breath, his voice rough with restraint. "I'm glad you asked," he said.

Cooper took the stool beside her, the bar light striking the planes of his face. For a heartbeat, neither spoke; the silence between them encumbered with words they both knew were too dangerous to blurt in haste.

"Should we move to a table?" Cooper asked at last.

Amanda nodded, setting her glass down. "Sure."

"The corner?" He motioned to the bartender. "And a couple of menus?"

"Absolutely," the bartender said with easy warmth.

They crossed the lounge in silence, each step carrying the heft of everything said and unsaid. Beneath Moroccan lanterns and velvet shadows, the world narrowed to the two of them—no fathers, no handlers, no partners. Only secrets pressing at the edges of their breath.

At the corner table, Cooper ordered without hesitation: charcuterie, hummus, flatbread, wine, and a tall bottle of sparkling water. Amanda lifted an eyebrow, a small smile tugging at her lips.

"What?" he asked. "You're not hungry?"

"Actually," she laughed, the sound breaking the icy veneer between them, "I'm famished."

The tension shifted, still palpable but less fragile.

"Good," he said with a grin.

Amanda tipped her glass toward him as if toasting his choices.

"So," Cooper leaned back slightly, studying her, "you said I can ask you anything?"

"Within reason," she said through her teeth, lifting her glass to her mouth for a sip.

"Fair." Cooper contemplated for a moment, not rushing to fill the silence.

"You didn't come prepared? That's not the Cooper Hansen I remember. Lists, forms, checked boxes—those were your love language," Amanda teased, finding it almost surreal the way she slipped back into familiarity with him.

He grinned. "You're not wrong. I've had a whole hour to prepare since your invitation. Should've used my Notes app or something." He shifted in his chair. "But my mind jumbles when it comes to you, Amanda." His voice roughened, almost coarse.

"Cooper." Amanda lowered her voice. "I'm engaged. And so are you. What happened the other day—it was unfinished business, that's all. And that's why we're here, isn't it? To tie any loose ends?"

"I guess." He rubbed one hand against the other, too forceful not to be noticed as a stress relief tool, then set them flat in his lap. "Except—I broke up with Paige."

Amanda's eyes widened. She drew breath, ready to scold him, but he cut her off.

"It wasn't because of you. Not directly, anyway. It was me. I knew I was with her out of convenience, out of expectation. And she deserves better than that."

"That's... kind of you," Amanda said into her glass, taking another slow sip.

"Anyway," Cooper shifted, almost shaking off the confession, "we didn't come here to talk about Paige or Tristan."

"No," Amanda agreed. "So where do you want to start?"

"Maybe I just want your side of it." His voice steadied. "One day, you were just gone. I went looking for you once, you know."

"What?" Amanda's breath hitched.

"You'd been gone for months. It was your birthday."

Amanda gasped. He offered nothing more, the silence widening until she stepped into it.

"I…" For a heartbeat, she nearly told him how often she'd imagined chasing him down, demanding answers from the past. But she swallowed it back. "I sent you a letter," she whispered.

His head jerked. "What? I never got one."

"I figured." A tear burned at the corner of her eye. "When you didn't come, I assumed you didn't want to. Or that they'd been as forceful with you as they were with me."

She shifted in her seat, pushing the words out. "Don't get me wrong. I hated you for a while. Part of me still did—until Tokyo."

"I'm so sorry," Cooper said, his voice raw.

"Yeah," she exhaled, blinking fast. "Me too."

Amanda dabbed the corner of her eye with her napkin, steadying herself. Cooper leaned closer, about to speak, then stopped, his jaw flexing as though wrestling with something unplanned.

"What was her name?" The question slipped out in a rough whisper, startling even him. "Our daughter. I keep saying *she,* but I don't even know—"

Amanda's breath hitched. For a moment, she couldn't speak; the name caught like shards of glass in her throat. Finally, she let it out, so soft it could have been mistaken for a delicate wish she was afraid to utter aloud. "Daisy."

Cooper's hand found hers across the table, his palm warm, firm, and trembling all at once. His eyes closed briefly, as if he were anchoring himself to the sound of it.

And then the air seemed to shift, thickening like fog, as two figures cut across the lounge. Katherine appeared first, her silk scarf draped with practiced elegance, while Julius strode beside her, radiating his signature mix of charm and command that bent rooms toward him. The lantern light caught in his silver hair, gilding it as his gaze swept the tables. It landed on Amanda and Cooper without hesitation.

"Hello," Cooper said, springing to his feet, surprise flickering in his eyes at Katherine.

"Well, what fortune," Katherine exclaimed, her delight threaded with warmth. She drew Cooper into a quick embrace before turning to Amanda. "Nice to see you again, Miss Hopkins."

"Yes, you too," Amanda swallowed.

Julius turned to Cooper with a grin. "So, Mr. Hansen. What brings you here? Did your father send you on ahead for the next facility tour?"

Cooper cradled his elbows in his hands, a flicker of embarrassment narrowing his gaze. "Yes. I didn't expect to be here either, but my dad seems incapable of functioning without me."

Julius beamed, gripping Cooper's shoulder with a touch that felt both hearty and controlling. "Of course not. Flesh is thicker than water, my boy—and a father couldn't ask for a better ally."

Amanda forced a smile, careful to mask her unease. "What brings you both here?"

"We've taken rooms for the week," Katherine said gracefully, the words smooth as glass. To Amanda, the lie struck like a hit between the eyes. She knew exactly where Katherine was staying.

"Tristan arrives next Friday, as you know. Julius insisted we come early. The New York site is nearly finished, and we're thrilled to present it before Christmas. A little holiday respite before the big party never hurts," she added, her voice smoothed with social gloss.

"Business with a touch of celebration—that's the way," Julius chuckled.

"That does seem to be Tristan's M.O.," Amanda replied lightly, though her pulse quickened.

Katherine's eyes lingered on Amanda with a familiarity Cooper did not miss before she turned to address him again. "So delightful to see you again. You must come up for a drink before the week is out."

"Thank you," Cooper said with a polite nod. "But I'll be upstate for a few things before the tour, and then in Tennessee with my family for the holidays. We'll be back for the party, though. My momma never misses an excuse to wear a sparkly dress and drink champagne."

"Oh, lovely. It will be nice to see her again," Katherine said just as Julius spotted an empty table across the room, far enough to give them their privacy.

"Shall we let these two get back to their—" Julius gestured between Amanda and Cooper, his tone laced with mock innocence, "whatever this is?"

Amanda exhaled. "Just two old friends catching up," she said with a smile.

"Ah, that's right." Julius's eyes gleamed. "Katherine tells me you went to high school together. What a small world."

"You can't exactly call it that," Cooper laughed.

"No, it's true enough," Amanda interjected quickly. "Simpler than explaining that my public school had a fine arts program without any proper facilities, and Cooper's fancy academy let us use their campus every week—probably as a tax write-off."

"Ooo," Julius bristled with offense. "That cynicism toward the government might not sit well in this company. Am I right, son?" He winked, clapping Cooper's back.

"Let's just say Amanda hasn't changed much since high school," Cooper replied smoothly, keeping it light.

"Ha!" Julius barked. "Well, you two have a good evening. We'll see you around."

Cooper nodded to them both before sinking back into his chair. Amanda reached for her glass, her smile gone as he studied her. The thoughtful, easy grin from earlier was nowhere in sight. He let the quiet hum of the music stretch before leaning in.

"How exactly do you know them? They seemed awfully familiar for just being Tristan's business associates. I don't know Katherine well—never have. And Julius…" his voice dropped, "I mean, who really knows Julius Babb?"

Amanda's fingers faltered on the stem of her glass. "Julius and I spent some time together earlier this year. When Tristan and I first started seeing each other."

Cooper cocked his head slightly, waiting for her to say more. Amanda caught the hint.

"Well, Katherine… we met in Bucharest, remember? You told me she was an acquaintance of your father," she said. Not a lie, though not the whole truth. Cooper's silence suggested he knew the difference. And a new list of questions was already beginning to form in his mind.

The lantern light fractured across the table, shadows sliding in restless patterns, and they both knew this wasn't the past intruding—it was the present pressing in.

Chapter Fourteen

Knoxville, Tennessee: June 2010

"Ladies and gentlemen, it is my honor to present to you the graduating class of 2010!"

The small crowd erupted before the man's words had fully settled. Cheers bounced off the hangar walls like a rising swell and clapped against steel beams, sailing through the open bay doors where the afternoon sky stretched in endless blue. Banners fluttered in the breeze, and beneath them, three rows of graduates stood in crisp navy jackets, gleaming flight wings pinned near at their hearts.

Amanda blinked into the noise, her breath catching as if her lungs didn't quite know how to hold this moment. Sunlight broke in patches across the hangar floor, and she spotted Grandma Nellie, cupping her hands around her mouth to shout her name over the din.

"Amanda!" Nellie cried, waving both arms like she was guiding in a plane herself. "That's my girl!"

Streamers rained from above in a surprise that made everyone laugh. Cameras clicked in a fever, and someone let off a party horn. One of the flight graduates shouted, "Let's fly, Class of 2010!" to wild and hearty agreement.

Amanda weaved through the crowd until she reached Nellie, who opened her arms without hesitation.

"You did it, baby," Nellie whispered against her ear. "You made the sky yours."

Amanda leaned back to see her grandma's face, eyes shining. "You gave it to me first."

"Pfft," Nellie grinned. "I just pointed up. You're the one who took off."

Behind them, a prop plane buzzed overhead in a flyby salute, its engine purring like applause. Amanda tilted her head, watching it bank and climb. For a moment, she saw herself in the curve of its ascent—not the girl who had arrived, unsure and full of ache, but the woman who now carried sky in her lungs and wings on her chest.

"Look at you," Grandma Nellie took Amanda by both shoulders. "My little aviatrix."

Amanda laughed, caught off guard by the word. "Granny, where'd you learn a term like that?"

"Read it in a crossword last week. Been saving it up just for today." Nellie's eyes gleamed with pride, a heavy, quilted cardigan draped over her shoulders despite the June heat.

They took pictures in front of Amanda's favorite plane, the instructor chuckling as Nellie insisted on climbing the ladder to the wing to get a shot "just like Rosie the Riveter." Amanda held tight to her hand, steadying her the whole way down.

Later that night, they sat on the farmhouse porch swing with slices of lemon meringue pie and glasses of sweet tea, as fireflies blinked across the yard.

"Yup. You really did it, baby," Nellie repeated after their long day of celebration, her words drifting out with the dusk.

Amanda leaned her head against her grandmother's shoulder. "Couldn't have done it without you."

Nellie didn't respond. She just reached over and squeezed Amanda's hand, her thumb rubbing slow circles against her knuckles. Less than twenty-four hours later, Amanda would find her in another chair, body slumped, and eyes closed.

She didn't suffer. Just drifted off like a leaf on water, her body cool in the light and her hand still curled as if ready to hold Amanda's again. Grief, Amanda learned, could move in as silently as cloud cover—one moment bright, the next obscured.

The week after the funeral, after seeing the aunt and uncle who had raised her in Kate's absence, and the siblings she still kept in contact with when she could, she climbed back into the cockpit of an old Piper Cherokee. She convinced herself that all she needed was air, altitude, and distance.

But when she pulled up the throttle and the nose lifted, emptiness struck harder than gravity. Her hands trembled against the yoke, and the headset muffled the world. She was alone—truly alone—in a way she had never been before.

Tennessee stretched out below her in patches of green and gold. From up there, things were small. Her childhood, her mistakes, even the memory of Daisy—all buried somewhere in that mosaic.

She exhaled hard through her nose, the headset hissing with static before clearing. "Skybound One, maintain present altitude. You're looking good."

She managed a smile, knowing this—the magic of flight—would be her saving grace. It had always been a bit of a drug to her, but now, it was oxygen. And she needed more and more of it.

Amanda stepped into the air-conditioned hush of the pilot's lounge—the fixed-base operator, or FBO—where a bearded man in a headset looked up from his clipboard. The shift from the heat of the cockpit to the fuel-tinged air of the tarmac, then into the sterile lobby, felt abrupt, almost jarring. A vending machine hummed against the far wall, and the faint tang of burnt coffee clung to the air.

"Back already?"

She forced a casual shrug, though her pulse still thudded from the flight she'd just cut short. "Just need to log another one," she said, sliding her license across the desk with practiced ease. "I filed for Stewart."

The man's pen hovered mid-page, his expression caught between curiosity and surprise.

"I need cross-country hours," Amanda added quickly, flipping open her logbook without meeting his eyes. Her thumb pressed hard into the paper, as if she could smooth out the lie in her voice. "Figured I'd go stretch out a little." It wasn't untrue—just skewed enough to give her the keys she wanted.

He studied her for a beat, his gaze sweeping over her flight jacket and the taut line of her shoulders. Whatever he saw, it convinced him. With a short nod, he reached for the clipboard.

"Cessna 172's gassed and ready. Just filed?"

"Yup." She made herself meet his eyes this time, steady and focused. "VFR to SWF." The shorthand rolled off her tongue—pilot code for flying by sight to Stewart International.

The man raised a brow, a half-smile tugging at his beard. "Fancy airport for a solo joyride."

She smiled, thin and practiced. "Just felt like flying north, I guess. Maybe they're gettin' a break from this heat."

He handed over the keys and stepped back into his office with a grin, the door clicking shut behind him. Amanda stood for a beat in the quiet, just long enough to feel her pulse thrum behind her eyes. But she turned, took a breath, and walked across the tarmac to climb into the cockpit.

The aircraft smelled the same as always—vinyl, sweat, and sun-warmed metal. She ran through preflight mechanically, checking the gauges and confirming radio frequencies with steady hands, but her breaths were shallow. Grief had lodged itself somewhere below the clavicle—tight and constant, like a seatbelt she couldn't unbuckle.

As she climbed to altitude, leveled off, and pointed the nose northeast, the sky thinned, but her chest opened. Up here, the air was scarce, yet Amanda could breathe more freely than on the ground. The flight would be long—nearly four hours with a stop for fuel—but her cargo was light: a small bag, an unwritten letter, and one photograph of her and Cooper, tucked into her jacket like a compass pointing its way home.

In the days since Nellie died, Amanda kept reaching for things that were no longer hers. More than once, her fingers hovered over his number, begging to call. Her mind circled the memory of his voice, the shape of his face, the way his touch had once steadied her.

As the propeller thrummed beneath her feet, clouds stretched ahead in layered sheets, and for a moment it felt like she was flying through stacked memories—each version of herself flickering past the windows. The girl who had been brave. The girl who had faltered. And the woman who now gripped the yoke too tightly, chasing something that was clearly out of reach.

Words rose and broke inside her—what she might say, what she would keep forever unsaid.

What am I even doing? She thought, her musings incessant.

And when Stewart Tower came into range, she pressed the mic for landing, her voice low and clear.

The descent carried her easily, wheels kissing earth, the plane obedient beneath her hands. As she was taxiing to parking, she could hear her instructor's voice again: *You fly like someone who already knows the sky wants you.*

Amanda smiled, sitting for a moment before she moved—before the reality of her choices solidified beneath her.

She made her way to a point where taxis lingered as a cab rolled to the curb with the weary slowness of a man who had nowhere else to be. She leaned down, gave him the address, and slid into the back seat, her bag anchored tightly against her lap.

The ride carried them past clipped hedges and stone walls, the kind of curated neatness that made the town feel more like a museum than a place where people actually lived. Neither of them spoke. Amanda always appreciated that in a driver, but today, she craved the distraction of small talk. But only the hum of the tires, the buzz of the crackling radio station, and a faint rattle of the car filled the silence.

Turn around. Tell him to turn around. Her logic implored.

When they pulled into the visitor lot, Amanda pressed folded bills into the driver's hand and stepped out into the late afternoon glare. She squinted her eyes, light bouncing off the Hudson where it curved beyond the hills. But her gaze fixed elsewhere—on the gray geometry of the academy buildings beyond the gates, stone and shadow rising like sentinels over a world so far from her own.

Clusters of cadets streamed along the walkways inside the fence, uniforms sharp, movements synchronized, as if each one knew exactly where he belonged. Amanda lingered at the edge, beside a weathered bench where a laminated map buckled and flapped against the wind.

And then—without warning, as if conjured directly from memory itself—there he was.

Cooper appeared through the main gate flanked by two others, the line of his shoulders unmistakable even after all this time. He seemed taller somehow, posture sharpened by years of discipline. But even at that distance, the tilt of his head, the curve of his grin, Amanda knew the sound that would follow. She could almost hear it, his familiar laugh, carrying across the years even if the air refused to deliver it to her now.

God, let me get close enough to hear it again.

She dropped her head, fingers stiff around the photograph, and his name rose in her throat but never made it past her lips. She forced herself to look again, deciding she was at least strong enough to watch—but he and the others were already turning, moving away with whatever task awaited them.

In his gray uniform, he looked almost carved and chiseled, hair neat, stride confident, as if he had become precisely what they demanded he become. There was no trace of the Tennessee boy in him now—no late-night porches, no hurried touches in shadowed spaces or reckless hours spent slipping around corners just to be together.

Amanda took half a step forward, her hand trembling at her side. She could cross the lot, say his name, touch his arm. Offer the letter she'd only scribbled one line on, or the photograph she clenched as proof they'd once belonged to each other.

One step. Just one step.

Her whole body begged questions she couldn't speak.

Did you ever mourn? Do you wonder about me? Do you feel whole again?

The group disappeared down the main road, his silhouette shrinking with every step. And then—he looked back.

Amanda froze.

Please come closer.

Please don't.

A bird startled from the fence beside her, wings rustling like paper, and she glanced upward. But when she looked his way again, Cooper was gone.

She placed the photograph on the bench as if setting down a piece of herself, then moved toward the waiting taxis. Each step measured, each breath tight. She didn't run. She didn't turn.

Please let this be enough to get him out of my mind.

She let the sorrow root itself deeper into an ache she would carry in the marrow of her bones as she climbed again into the night, the propeller steady where she was not. The sky was bruised violet and indigo, the last veins of gold strung thin on the horizon, and she gripped the controls as if her grief had weight enough to tilt the wings.

Her headset carried nothing but static, while below, the Hudson bent like silver, mountains rolling into shadows. She told herself that flight was salvation, and air could stitch her back together. But everything in that moment felt hollow.

Far below her, evening spread across the parade grounds as Cooper lingered by the gate, his friends now gone. He was being drawn back toward the visitor lot. A shadow of someone he knew, or the memory of one, pulling him there with a force he couldn't deny. He came to the bench where a photograph lay, edges curled, faces familiar. His breath caught in his throat as he lifted it, thumb brushing worn paper, and for an instant, the air smelled of Tennessee grass.

No—it can't be her. Not now.

He looked to the road, but it was empty; the space there held only the hush of evening against pavement and manicured lawns. Overhead, a single plane droned across the darkening sky, its course steady and unremarkable. Cooper didn't think to look twice, but Amanda was up there as he walked back through the gates, the photograph pressed against his heart like a question neither of them could answer.

Chapter Fifteen

New York City: Tristan's Return

Amanda stood barefoot on the wide-plank floors of Tristan's loft, the city whirring beyond the windows like a pulse. Dusk had only begun to settle, streaks of molten orange and violet trailing behind the buildings, its glow washing over her bare shoulders. The slip dress—black silk, delicate as smoke—fell against her body like poured ink. It felt a bit over the top, maybe even a little foolish, but she wanted him to see her in it the moment he walked through the door.

The penthouse had become familiar these last weeks, though it never lost its ability to stun her. She had been waiting all afternoon, nerves riding like a tide she couldn't still. He was back—from São Paulo, from Nairobi, and from the endless circuit of flights and meetings that seemed to eat his life whole. She had told herself she would be calm, that she would meet him with grace, perhaps even with restraint. But as the key slid into the lock, her pulse betrayed her.

The door opened, and Amanda's world shifted.

Tristan stepped inside, dropping his leather weekender onto the bench by instinct, the sound of it thudding against wood. He wore a navy suit, the collar of his shirt loosened, the long hours of flight and business clinging to him in the slight slump of his shoulders. But when his gaze found her, the exhaustion cracked, giving way to something sharper—heat, surprise, hunger.

"Amanda." His voice caught on the edge of her name, low and unguarded.

She let a smile tug at her lips, slow and deliberate, and tilted her head. "Welcome home."

He crossed the space faster than she could draw a breath. One moment, he was by the door, the next his hand was at her waist, pulling her into him as though the miles between Europe and New York had never existed. She laughed, breathless, the sound breaking against his mouth as he kissed her—hard, possessive, as if someone might steal her away if he didn't hold on.

The silk slid beneath his touch, her body yielding against the firmness of his chest as she wrapped her arms around his neck, feeling the stubble from travel still on his jaw, and the faint coolness of the evening air clinging to his suit. He smelled like airports and musk, exhaustion and power, the complexity of a man who nowadays didn't belong to any one place.

She pulled back just enough to meet his eyes. The city shimmered behind them, alive with its own relentless rhythm, but for the first time in days, she felt the world narrow to the space between them.

"You're late," she teased, though her voice wavered with the thrill of having him in her arms again.

He touched his forehead to hers, his breath unsteady. "I would've been here sooner if I knew this was what's waiting for me."

Amanda's smile flickered, and she kept her body pressed to his. "You didn't think I'd be here?"

"Not like this... even though I did let myself imagine it. Not gonna lie," he said, a sly smile spreading across his face.

"Well, usually I'm the one disappearing into the world, but being on this side of things—the one waiting—I just hope you'll remember where you left me."

His hand tightened at her waist, thumb brushing the silk as if to anchor her. "Don't say that. I carry you with me everywhere. It's the only thing that makes those rooms bearable."

She searched his eyes, wanting to believe, almost afraid to let herself. "Do you?"

"More than you know." He leaned in again, softer this time, lips grazing the corner of her mouth, words spilling warm against her skin. "Every mile back here, I thought about this.

About you, in my home, waiting to meet me. It drove me half mad."

Amanda laughed, the sound hushed and trembling. "Well, here I am. Mad enough to dress like this just to see if I could get a reaction when you walked in the door."

His gaze swept over her slowly, openly, with no pretense of restraint. "Mission accomplished," he murmured, before kissing her again, this time unhurried, the kind of kiss that drew breath and blood into a single current.

When they broke apart, the city lights had burned brighter behind the glass, the sky deepening into night. Amanda let her fingers trail down the lapel of his jacket, tugging him closer. "At least you're staying for a while this time and don't have to vanish tomorrow."

They made their way to the couch as Tristan took off his jacket, unbuttoning his shirt and freeing himself of any constraints. His sigh was long and deep as he rested himself on the cushions, and Amanda leaned her head briefly against his chest, listening to the faint echo of his heartbeat. Everything slowed as Tristan's eyelids threatened to droop.

"You'd better shower before you collapse. I didn't put this dress on for you to fall asleep on me."

His laughter rumbled low, reverberating in his chest. "Trust me, sleep is the last thing on my mind." He stood and took her hand into his, keeping his voice to a whisper as he pulled her to him. "Coming with?"

Steam blurred the glass shower door, softening the edges of the world until there was only skin and heat. Amanda pressed her palms flat to the tiled wall as Tristan's lips traced the slope of her shoulder, the water coursing over them both in hot rivulets. His hands mapped her waist, firm and searching, as if he were relearning the geography of her body after weeks of distance.

She leaned into him, laughter catching in her throat when he caught her mouth again, the kiss deep and unrelenting, the taste of travel finally washed away. For a breath, she let herself drown in it—the heat, the press of him, the steady drum of water against her back.

"How was New York without me?" His voice came low against her ear, breath mixing with steam. It wasn't just a question—it was a claim, a reminder that he felt her absence as much as she felt his.

Amanda tilted her head, her lips brushing the line of his jaw. "Lonely," she admitted, then added, quieter, "though not empty."

For an instant, a thought rose unbidden, the ghost of another presence—Cooper's eyes, his lips, the feel of a different touch on her skin. The memory sliced through her before she could shove it back into silence.

Tristan pulled away just enough to catch her gaze, water running down the sharp cut of his cheekbones. "Yeah, you filled it with parties and celebrations?"

"Ha, not exactly. We have a couple of apartments to look at if you have time before the facility tour." The words slipped out soft and inviting, at odds with her shifting internal state.

Tristan stilled, the steam curling between them, tightening the space.

"Hmmm," he moaned. "I'll make time. Setting up a home here with you sounds like heaven. A top priority," he said before his mouth began exploring more and more of her skin.

She turned to see his face, water blurring every line. "Yeah," she agreed, breathless. It was easier to let her body answer than to quiet the noise in her head, easier to act as if she were still wholly his.

Tristan pulled her closer, letting the cascade of warmth wash over them before Amanda broke the silence.

"We should definitely wait until the new year to make any moves, though. After everyone is out of our hair and it's just us," she said.

Tristan paused, taking a step back. "Erm, I'm doing some of my best work here," he teased, trying to mask his annoyance.

"Oh, sorry," Amanda said. "I've just been thinking a lot about all we have going on."

She almost said more, almost asked about how each facility tour went, but she buried it under the press of his mouth and the weight of his body. Easier to lose herself in the heat than to name any question gnawing at her.

"Let's not think about anything but each other right now," Tristan said, hands pulling her close until every inch of her body was locked into his.

"Yeah," she repeated stiffly.

Tristan stopped, feeling her body tense in his arms. He dropped his arms to his side. "Did I miss something?"

Amanda searched his face, trying to read the man beneath the exhaustion and heat. "Uh, no. I'm sorry." She put her hands into his. "I'm good."

"Babe, you gotta talk to me," Tristan insisted.

"I just... I guess I'm preoccupied. I saw Katherine and Julius the other day, and I've just been wondering about this whole thing with the Grid and your work. It's a lot, Tristan."

She hadn't meant to say it. The words slid out before she could pull them back, the heat and closeness stripping her guard.

Frustration flashed in his eyes, bright even through the veil of water. "And you choose this moment to bring it up?" he sighed. "Bringing up Julius and work right now? Talk about a mood killer."

The steam felt heavier suddenly, the water hotter. Amanda pressed her palm to his chest, trying to steady the rhythm between them. "I didn't intend to, Tristan. Obviously. I just feel like there's a lot I'm expected to accept at face value when there's clearly so much I don't know."

He let out a laugh that was low and humorless. "It's not like there's something I'm not telling you." He turned away, bracing his hands on the slick wall, the muscles of his back taut under the cascade. "Is there something you're not telling me?"

"No," she said, her denial uttered too quickly not to carry a tinge of guilt.

The distance between them couldn't be measured in inches, their intimacy dissolving into something brittle. Amanda stared at the rivulets sliding down his spine.

"Babe, I'm sorry," she said.

"It's fine." Tristan grabbed a shampoo bottle, prepared to let the moment pass. "I'm gonna finish up and get some sleep. I'll be less tense in the morning. I'm just tired and irritable, I guess. Let's just call this our first fight," he breathed out a short exasperated chuckle.

Amanda slipped from the shower without a word, pulling the robe from its hook and wrapping herself in its plush weight, as though fabric might muffle the regret clinging to her. In the kitchen, she filled the kettle and set it to boil, the eventual hiss a poor substitute for conversation. If she couldn't smooth the air between them, she could at least give him the small comfort of ritual.

By the time Tristan emerged—silent and unreadable—she had placed a cup of chamomile-mint on the nightstand, steam curling like an apology she couldn't form. Only then did she change into her pajamas, the ordinary gesture feeling strangely foreign in the quiet of the room.

They had only known each other for seven months, but it was long enough to learn their most telling resemblance. Neither of them erupted when pressed; they receded. They folded instead of opening, closing like shutters against a storm. What others might release in fire, they carried inward, pacing their own minds until the world stilled enough to speak again.

Tristan sat on the edge of the bed, robe loose at his waist, shoulders slumped as though the miles of travel had finally landed on him all at once. He took the mug from the nightstand, cradled it for a moment, then set it aside untouched. His head tipped back against the wall, eyes closing in surrender.

Amanda brushed a hand over his hair, the gesture brief. "Rest," she whispered. "I'll let you be."

He gave a faint nod, already half-gone, and she slipped from the room, pulling the door until only a sliver of light escaped into the hall.

The loft felt cavernous in its hush as Amanda curled into the corner of the couch, scrolling absently through her phone, chasing distraction in headlines and endless photos of people she didn't know, until a new message from Cooper lit the screen. Her pulse jolted, the quiet air of the loft suddenly charged. It was the first time she had heard from him since Bryant Park.

She swiped, the screen resolving into words stripped bare of anything but intent.

We need to talk.

"Shit," she whispered to herself, pressing the phone to her chest. The last thing she wanted to do was see Cooper again.

Tristan slept, but Amanda lay restless on the couch, her phone still warm in her hand. She stared at the message, turning the words over, trying to decide how much truth she could bear to give him. Their meeting in a public setting had been risky enough since they had been seen, and nothing in her world went unseen for long. Which meant every move she chose now could ricochet in ways she couldn't predict.

Chapter Sixteen

Croatia: On the Adriatic Sea

While Manhattan glittered in a deceptive calm, the Adriatic was restless. Waves slapped against the hull of a small fishing boat, spraying water cold enough to sting; the sky was a bruised slate with clouds knotting low on the horizon. Melody braced herself at the rail, the decoy case clutched against her chest, its weight out of proportion to the lie inside.

"And *you* wanted to tackle this alone." Lyla's voice was steady, though her knuckles whitened as she gripped the edge of the cabin door.

Melody gave a short laugh. "I suppose I'll be thankful for the company when this goes wrong."

The boat pitched, and Lyla staggered before regaining her footing, eyes narrowing at the dark water. "Wrong or not, I wasn't about to let you come out here by yourself."

Melody swallowed back her desired reply—that she'd already spent a lifetime alone in things that mattered—but instead, she turned to the task. She opened the case, verifying that it was there. Of course, it was there, but her mind kept playing tricks on her. She wasn't the one usually carrying out covert missions, just observing them. This was different, but she couldn't help thinking that Russell would be proud. He wouldn't have been surprised she had it in her, though.

The casing was brushed titanium, matte and smooth, and warm from her touch, giving the illusion that it was purely inert hardware. In the gray light of the Adriatic afternoon, it almost disappeared into the haze, absorbing the leaden tones of sea and sky.

The design was seamless—no switches, no ports, no indicators. Just one narrow, recessed panel etched faintly with the insignia of a concentric grid, like an iris, embedded at the top right corner.

A rogue gust of wind pressed her hair into her mouth, and the boat swayed beneath them like it was reconsidering its place on the sea. They had already pushed off from Krk, the island's shoreline thinning behind them, but across the cove on the mainland, half-shrouded by windblown mist, two silhouettes lingered long on the bluff. The captain muttered something she couldn't understand. Her Croatian hadn't gotten anywhere near conversational, and she just nodded as he throttled the motor down, drifting them farther into the channel as the water deepened to a black mirror, and the town lights stretched thin.

"This is it," Melody said, her breath catching in her throat. She hefted the case, fingers tingling from cold and adrenaline, and flung it over the side. For a moment, it hovered on the surface, a pale outline against the swell, then the sea pulled it down, swallowing without ceremony.

Lyla let out a sharp breath, but Melody's eyes stayed on the shoreline. The men had moved to a small boat, trying to be inconspicuous in the night, but unable to advance without their flickering lights on.

"Not exactly a night for sightseeing," Lyla murmured.

"No," Melody answered, her voice clipped. "But it looks like this worked. Let them come; we're outta here," she said, gesturing to the captain.

"Idemo natrag," Melody waved, and he snapped to attention, understanding her and the basic phrases she'd been working on. It wasn't exactly the right way to say *take us to shore*, but *let's go back* did the trick.

The engine rumbled back to life, churning the dark water as the boat swung toward the mainland shore. Spray leapt over the bow, the rocky swells pushing against their speed, but the captain kept his hand firm on the wheel, guiding them swiftly through the chop. Melody held to the railing, her breath sharp with salt spray as the Adriatic surged restlessly around them. Behind them, the island of Krk receded into a blur of stone and shadow. A ferry lumbered past in the distance, its deck strung with light like a drifting constellation. Closer by, a fisherman's boat dared the swell, bobbing stubbornly against the chop.

Lyla's hair whipped across her face, her voice nearly stolen by the wind. "Do you think we're just paranoid? I mean, maybe no one followed us, and we're not a part of a crazy global conspiracy at all. Amanda's the one in real danger, and this almost seems too crazy, doesn't it?"

Melody swallowed the unease pressing at her ribs. She forced a tight smile, putting her arm around Lyla. "I don't know. Nothing about any of this has seemed real. You hear stories about the world operating this way, and even when Russell was alive, there were hints everywhere. But they're good at what they do. Making us believe that there's nothing to see, all hiding in plain sight."

Lyla sucked in the cold, misty air as both took a hard turn into a wave that bounced them enough to startle everyone.

"Yeah, it scares me how easily they can make us doubt our own eyes." Lyla sucked in the cold, misty air. "Honestly, I think it's gettin' to me," she admitted, blowing out a shaky breath before smirking and putting her arm around Melody's shoulder with a pop of her hip. "Listen, our spy team is sexy and all, but I'm really second-guessing its appeal right now,"

Melody grinned. "Then at least this part is finished. We chose to trust Katherine and Amanda with this, and now it's out of our hands."

For a moment, they allowed themselves to believe the possibility that they had been imagining the eyes on their backs, that the sea itself was their only pursuer. The boat pressed forward into the night, the shoreline of the mainland ahead a faint promise of safety.

But the darkness held more than waves. Far astern, another vessel slid into their wake, its running lights extinguished, its engine throttled low to mask the sound. Two figures stood on deck, their windbreakers plastered to their bodies, and their eyes fixed on the black water where Melody's hand had released the case.

"Got it marked," one murmured, slipping a beacon into the swell. The device blinked faintly red, a solitary star vanishing into the troughs.

The other man pulled his hood close, his voice low and measured. "I'll let headquarters know we're on-site where they offloaded the module in question. This may be another dead end, but we're not leaving the Adriatic until we know if this is the original prototype."

The first agent's gaze followed the small vessel carrying the women until it slipped deeper into the haze. He drew a steadying breath; his words meant more for himself than his partner. "We've been chasing their shadows long enough. This is a huge step."

He adjusted the earpiece hidden beneath his hood, listening for the beacon's crackle of confirmation that never came.

"They're pawns," he muttered, glancing at the fading silhouette of Melody and Lyla's boat. "Women pulled into something they don't even understand. If someone has planted the module on them, they're being used as bait."

His partner shook his head slowly, eyes narrowed against the spray. "Or they're smarter than they look. Julius Babb never lets anything out of his grip unless there's a reason. And Katherine—she's been playing angles since Berlin. If she trusts one of them, then we pay attention."

The younger agent gave a humorless laugh. "Trust? Katherine doesn't trust anyone. She uses them. And the brunette—Melody—she's a widow, not an operative. One of ours, Russell Drake, was his name. I read the file. She's vulnerable, chasing ghosts."

"Exactly," the other replied, his tone cool. "Sometimes the vulnerable ones are the most dangerous. They're willing to believe, willing to run, willing to burn. That makes them harder to predict—and harder to control."

The boat rolled on its axis, a wave slapping hard against its side, but neither man flinched. Their eyes remained fixed on the retreating lights ahead, tracking every shift in the distance.

"Orders stand," the agent said at last, his voice as even as the hum of the hidden engine. The small crew beamed their dive lights into the blackness, but it was no use. They would not be able to secure the small case hidden in the depths.

"We have to come back in the daylight. It's too dark, and the waters are getting too dangerous. The beacon never gave confirmation, so we've marked the site as best we can. We'll sweep again in daylight," the search crew chief said.

The agents nodded, well aware that a mission takes on many phases before it's complete. The sea closed over the beacon's glow, leaving only darkness.

Back in New York, Tristan had already succumbed to the pull of jet lag while Amanda remained wide awake, scrolling mindlessly on her phone until another text rolled onto her screen.

Will you be at the facility tour?

Cooper's reply slid in beneath the unanswered text she'd left hanging thirty minutes before.

Cooper, I can't do this.

Amanda, please. I think you know we can't leave things as they are.

I can.

Amanda wrote back as fast as her fingers could move. She waited for a reply longer than she expected, almost regretful that her attempts at blowing him off might have worked.

I think you're in danger.

The text finally appeared after Amanda had gone back to browsing her social media feed. Her heart pounded as she reread the message, the glow of her phone pooling against the dark fabric of Tristan's sofa. He slept in the next room, his breathing even, unbothered, while her chest felt like it might split from the weight of the words on the screen.

She wanted to type something scathing, something final, but instead she set the phone on her lap, the silence swelling around her. Cooper wasn't guessing blindly. He had always read people well—better than most people had ever given him credit for.

But she wondered if it was Tristan he thought she needed to worry about. If Tristan was as manipulative as the men he surrounded himself with.

Did Cooper think she was in danger because of that... or had he begun to grasp the darker truth? He knew about the baby, about the lies that had sent her to The Ridge—but did he realize how easily his father could still use it to blackmail her? Did he see the use his father could make of it?

James Hansen wanted the Grid. Tristan fell in love with a woman whose past was supposedly buried, but Hansen knew every detail of it. Put those two truths together, and her secret became the perfect leverage to access the thing Hansen had only proximity to and not possession of.

She pressed her palms into her face, forcing back the burn that was just beneath her eyelids. Cooper was circling a truth he couldn't yet name, and that scared her more than his father lurking in the shadows for some reason. When Cooper was involved, her logic was fuzzy, and she didn't want to risk more than she already had.

She felt another vibration.

I'll just say this. I'm not sure Tristan is who you think he is. At least, not all of him. I just want to talk. Try to figure things out. I haven't always done right by you, and I couldn't live with myself if I didn't at least try this time.

Her pulse caught, the words slicing through the veil of denial she had fought to keep in place.

Tristan sleepily shifted in the bedroom, the rustle of sheets and covers faint through the open loft bedroom. Amanda stared at the screen, every part of her braced between two worlds—one where she confessed, and one where she carried the burden of lies, pretending not to notice the walls closing in.

She typed, erased, then typed again.

Meet me tomorrow. Birch Coffee. 8 a.m.

Her hand trembled as she hit send, not sure whether she was agreeing to illumination or to ruin.

A bell above the door gave a muted chime as Amanda stepped inside, shrugging the chill from her shoulders. The café carried its own kind of hush—low conversations beneath the steady hum of an espresso machine, the air thick with roasted beans. Exposed brick walls and shelves lined with books lent the place the air of a library that had forgotten its silence.

Cooper sat in a far corner beneath a row of bulbs glowing like drops of amber. His jacket slumped over the back of his chair, tie loosened, a steaming cup untouched before him. He looked as though sleep had abandoned him for days, shadows carved beneath his eyes.

"Amanda." He rose slightly, her name stretched and brittle on his lips.

"Hey, Cooper." Her voice stayed measured, though her pulse thudded at her throat. She slid into the chair across from him, forcing stillness into every limb.

For a long time, neither one of them spoke. A steam wand hissed at the counter, punctuating their silence with airy squeals.

"I thought you might back out," Cooper said at last.

"So did I." She let a grin slip, her shoulder tilting almost imperceptibly.

He leaned forward, forearms braced on the table. "Well, I'm glad you came. There's something I need to tell you—and I need you to hear me before you shut me out."

She folded her arms, feigning calm. "Okay."

"My father is about to announce his candidacy for president."

Amanda nodded, relieved it wasn't anything she'd be surprised about. "I think we were all expecting that."

"Well, the talk isn't just whispers anymore." He dragged a hand down his face, the gesture raw with weariness. "I thought it was just ego, another rung on his ladder, you know? But it's more than that. His whole candidacy is about the Grid."

"The Ocular Grid?" she said, disbelief catching on the words. Yet the thought settled fast, like puzzle pieces sliding into place. A sharp pressure coiled around her ribs. "But wasn't he always gunning for the presidency?"

"No. If there's one thing my father knows, it's that you can control more behind the scenes than you ever can as the front man. Keep just enough power in your hand, and the world looks elsewhere when it wants a fall guy." He paused, eyes flinty. "But the Grid changes that equation."

Amanda's nod was slow. "So the Grid rewrites his philosophy? Makes it worth it to be the front man?"

"Yes. It's that powerful. You've seen what they're claiming."

"And you think your dad wants control of it?"

"I don't think—I know." His jaw tightened. "He's been maneuvering behind closed doors—licensing, partnerships, political deals you wouldn't believe. It's not just ambition. It's dangerous. The Grid would tip everything. With it, the title of 'Most Powerful Man in the World' wouldn't be hyperbole anymore. A U.S. President who controlled this operation would literally be unstoppable."

Amanda's fingers curled in her lap. Tristan's voice echoed in her memory—earnest, certain—that the Grid was about progress, about safety, about vision. She wanted to believe him, needed to believe him. But she knew this was the premise of her entanglement.

She'd bent before—when Katherine demanded, when Tristan charmed, when Julius manipulated—but Cooper's father was different. He was the only one who could force her hand outright, because the power he held over her wasn't a strategy. It was personal, and it left her defenseless, as if no years had passed since she was seventeen and stripped of every choice.

"And Tristan?" she asked carefully. "You think he's part of that?"

Cooper's gaze sharpened. "Don't you?"

Her breath faltered. "No. Tristan... he's not like that."

"You love him." It came not as a question but as a truth laid bare, a line thrown between them to hold the conversation steady.

Amanda swallowed hard. "Yes. I do. And he's a good man, Cooper. He believes in what he's building."

"Or he believes in what it gives him." Cooper's tone sliced the air. "The Grid isn't neutral, Amanda, no matter what they tell you—or what they might even be naive enough to believe themselves. It's a weapon. Who decides how it's used? Who decides what's ethical? Don't you see? My father wants it for power. Tristan wants it for influence. And everyone else is too blinded by what it *could* be to question what it *is.*"

The words weren't new, but they crashed through her defenses, echoing the doubts that had haunted her since Rome, since Tokyo, since Katherine pressed the prototype into her hands. Questions she had buried beneath Tristan's warmth, beneath the illusion that love could nullify the shadows gathering around them.

Her eyes burned, but she blinked hard, refusing the relief of tears—refusing to let them soothe the sting. "You don't know him."

"I know enough." Cooper's voice cracked before steadying. "I know that when men start speaking of the future as if it belongs to them, it's everyone else who pays the price. And you're standing in the middle of it. You can't tell me you haven't asked yourself the same questions. How can this possibly be ethical? Who will control it? Are we all this gullible?"

Amanda's lips parted, but no words came. The café walls seemed to tilt, the books looming like silent witnesses.

"I can't—" She pressed her palm to her forehead. "I can't do this right now."

"Yes, you can." His voice was quiet but fierce. "You owe yourself the truth. You owe the world the truth."

Amanda's defenses buckled, her breath shuddering. "I fell in love with him. That's the truth I know. And I want to believe in him. Is that so wrong?"

"No." His voice softened, aching. "But it's not enough. Love doesn't make this safe, and it doesn't make it right."

Tears finally began to blur her vision. She wanted to tell him everything—that Katherine had bound her into this web, that she had the prototype in her possession, that the line between loyalty and betrayal had dissolved long ago. The confession clawed at her throat, but she held it back. To speak it would unravel everything.

"I can't," she whispered.

Cooper searched her face, grief etched into the lines of her profile. "Then promise me this. Promise you'll think about what I've said. Promise you'll remember who you are when the time comes to choose."

Amanda's head bowed in the smallest nod, though it split her chest like a fault line.

"Because that time has come for me, Amanda—and it will come for you too," he said.

Silence fell again as the café hummed beneath the tension crammed between them. Amanda sat hollowed, torn between the man she loved and the man who knew her too well, between the truth demanding her voice and the lie she wasn't ready to release.

Cooper's eyes said he knew better than she did, that he saw through the story she was still telling herself. But he didn't press. He would wait for her to catch up, and somehow that was worse than judgment. Finally, he rose, slipped on his jacket, and kept his eyes on hers.

"Take care of yourself, Amanda. More than that—be careful."

He left her in the cafe, their coffees cooling untouched. She folded her arms on the table, lowered her head into them, and let the tears come, salt mingling with the bitter scent of coffee grounds.

She wished she could vanish into the rows of books, slip into another story where the weight of the world belonged to someone else.

Chapter Seventeen

New York City: Tristan's Apartment

"Hey, babe. Where've you been?" Tristan's voice drifted from the loft, warm and casual, as Amanda nudged the door open with her shoulder. Two paper cups steamed in her hands, sleeves damp from the chill outside. A brown bag of pastries crinkled beneath her arm, the scent of butter and cinnamon trailing her in.

She let the door fall shut behind her and crossed the threshold. "Coffee run," she said with manufactured brightness, as if that explained everything.

Tristan leaned against the kitchen island, hair still mussed from sleep. He looked at her with a half-smile, though his brow ticked faintly. "That was kind of a long run for coffee."

Amanda set the cups on the counter, grateful for the excuse to busy her hands. "The line was longer than usual. Everyone must have decided today was the day they couldn't live without their lattes." She tore open the pastry bag and slid it toward him. "I brought reinforcements."

He reached for one, eyes flicking back to her with a mixture of amusement and curiosity. "Over an hour, though?"

She let out a soft laugh, trying to shake it off. "You've been timing me?"

"Not exactly." He took a bite, brushed a crumb from his lip. "But I notice when you're gone longer than I expect."

Amanda lowered herself onto a stool, wrapped both hands around her cup as if the heat might anchor her. She forced her shoulders to relax, her tone easy. "Sorry, I lost track of time. I didn't grab a cab; I needed the walk. I should've told you, but it's not like you were awake when I left."

"Yeah, I guess that's why it surprised me," Tristan said, studying her for a moment longer than she wanted him to. She kept her gaze on the steam rising between her fingers, willing her expression to remain composed.

"Well," he said finally, his smile softening. "You do look...fresh. Like the air did you good."

She returned his smile, careful not to let it falter. If only he knew that her lungs still felt tight from the conversation she had left behind, that she had nearly unraveled across a café table. She sipped her coffee, letting the chocolaty taste give her a moment of pleasure.

"Also," she said, placing her cup down, "I figured you could use a little indulgence since you've been traveling so much. And what's a good morning without croissants?" she winked.

"I couldn't tell ya," Tristan's lips stretched across his teeth playfully.

"Well, it's been studied. Pastries make any morning better. It's a proven fact."

"Scientific, huh?" He reached for another bite, going along with the bit. "I'll take your word for it."

Amanda let the moment ease between them, small talk flowing like balm. She clung to it, to the illusion of normalcy—to the two of them in his Manhattan loft, coffee cups and crumbs scattered on the counter, sunlight spilling over exposed brick. It looked like the life she was working so hard to make true. Secure, ordinary, and safe.

But beneath her calm, she replayed Cooper's words in her mind with merciless clarity.

Love doesn't make this safe.

She lifted her coffee again, the sleeve damp against her palm, and smiled across the counter. "Worth the wait, don't you think?"

Tristan raised his cup in mock salute. "Worth every minute."

His easy confidence wrapped around her like a comfort she didn't deserve. And still, she let herself breathe it in as he crossed the room in barely more than a stride, closing the distance between them. He slipped the pastry bag from her hand and set it aside, his palm sliding to the back of her neck.

"You know how much I hate it when we're apart," he murmured, pressing his mouth to hers.

The warmth of him flooded over her as she leaned into the touch, craving the solidity of him even as her mind churned with everything she couldn't say. His lips brushed hers, searching, first slowly, then again with the sexiest bit of urgency.

For a moment, Amanda let herself drown in it—the weight of his hands, the insistence of his mouth, the familiar fire between them.

But when he pulled back, breath uneven, and his eyes searching hers closely, he paused longer than expected. "You sure it was just a coffee run?" he asked, eyes squinting slightly.

The question cut through the warmth, snapping her back into the walls she had built around herself. She broke their gaze and slid off the kitchen stool, angling past him toward the opposite counter.

"Yeah, of course," she said softly, forcing a smile that didn't reach past her lips. "I wanted to surprise you. That's all."

The silence stretched, charged with slightly more than just desire. Finally, Tristan exhaled, his thumbnail worrying at his teeth before he pulled his hand away, the gesture betraying any hesitation his words did not.

"Okay, I need to get ready," he said, already turning to leave the kitchen.

He disappeared into the bedroom with his coffee, placing it on the dresser before tugging at hangers, shirts, and slacks lined like soldiers at inspection. Amanda slipped into the bedroom after him, perched at the bed's edge. She watched in silence as he slid his arms through his shirt sleeves, shoulders filling the white cotton, fingers moving with mechanical precision down the row of buttons.

"You've got the tour today?" she asked, even though she already knew the answer.

He glanced up, one brow arched. "Yeah. This is our home base site. Investors, partners, half of D.C., if the RSVP list is right." He turned fully toward her, cufflink glinting in his hand. "But the way you said that—it sounds like you're not planning on coming."

Amanda smoothed the rumpled covers beside her, pressing the creases flat as if order could steady her. "I don't think I can today."

Tristan stilled, the cufflink frozen between his fingers. "You don't think you can, or you don't want to?"

She lifted her gaze to him. "I still have some Christmas shopping to do. And I just... really don't feel up to it."

"You don't feel up to it," he echoed slowly, fastening the cufflink with even sharper precision than before. "Amanda, these tours matter. You were in Bucharest, and I asked you to come with me for all of them. You didn't come to Nairobi or

São Paulo; you explained you needed some downtime, and I was happy to oblige. Now that we're home, I assumed you'd be right there at my side. Why not today?"

Her throat tightened. The truth hovered too close—Cooper's voice still echoing, the risk of being forced to stare down the Grid's ethical fault lines was something she wasn't ready to face.

"I just need some space," she said, the words slipping out before she could catch them. Regret stung instantly.

Tristan's jaw tightened. He shifted the jacket over his arm. "Space. From me? From public events? Which is it?"

"No, not from you." Her voice thinned, softly betraying her. She hated that she sounded exactly how she felt: unsure of herself. "I just need a break from everything else. I didn't travel with you to the other sites for a reason. And it's not that I don't care. It's just—it's not my work. I don't understand it the way you do. Can't you see how overwhelming it is for me?"

For a long beat, he studied her, expression unreadable, as if weighing words he couldn't trust himself to speak.

"This feels eerily familiar," he said at last. "Last night—I hadn't seen you in weeks—you pulled away. Right in the middle of us—my homecoming. One second, you were right there with me, and the next, you were talking about the Grid. Asking questions I couldn't answer without shattering the moment."

Amanda felt heat climb her cheeks. "I wasn't trying to ruin anything. I just—"

"You just what?" His voice sharpened, then faltered into a sigh. He swept his hands through the air in a frustrated arc. "Look, last night, something was off—whatever. I don't want to rehash anything that isn't worth examining. But this…" His eyes searched hers. "This feels like more than that. Like you're not telling me something."

Her chest constricted. Of course, he was right—it *was* more. She was drowning in secrets and torn between truths she couldn't speak. But she forced the words out, as steadily as she could: "I'm not trying to push you away. I support you."

"Then what is it?" His frustration weakened to a raw grumble. "Because it feels like something's breaking down, Amanda."

A hush fell between them and drew taut, every second heavier than the last. She glanced at the jacket tailored perfectly to his shoulders, the sheen of his shoes catching the light. Everything about him was polished, stage-ready. But there was no rehearsal for this. No script for how to hold a love together while standing on shifting ground.

Finally, she whispered, "Maybe it's the engagement. The stress. I'm so overwhelmed by everything right now."

Softening, Tristan sat beside her. He took her hand, his thumb grazing the edge of her palm.

"I don't know, babe." Her voice cracked. "It's just...a lot. This is your place, and it's amazing. But you said yourself that you want us to find somewhere we can call ours. Then there's the holidays, your family's huge New Year's party—I'm the new piece in all of it, remember? I didn't get a playbook."

What she wanted to say was that it wasn't the apartment—it was the feeling of living in his world instead of theirs, but like so many other things, she left that unsaid too.

Tristan's jaw tightened, but his eyes softened. "You don't need my playbook. Write your own, and I'll adjust. I want this relationship to be better than any I've had before. No more guessing games. Open communication. So tell me—what helps when you're this stressed?"

Amanda gave a helpless shrug. "I don't know. I guess...I just fly."

That response earned a smile as Tristan brought the back of her hand to his lips and pressed a soft kiss on her skin. "Well, that can be arranged. Antigua? My parents and sister are there for Christmas. You can register the flight yourself, right?"

She shook her head, her hair brushing her cheek. "That sounds nice, but I thought maybe we could spend our first Christmas here. For some reason, I don't want to leave New York. It'll be just us."

"I'd like that." Relief eased the tension in Tristan's shoulders. He pulled her close, pressing his lips to hers with renewed certainty. His lips brushed her temple, the deep tones of his voice low and warm. "We'll fly soon enough, okay?"

Amanda managed a nod, her smile small but convincing. He kissed her once more, then turned back to the mirror to adjust his tie. She sat on the bed, coffee cooling on the nightstand, her chest tight with the weight of all she had left unsaid.

Outside, Manhattan's late-morning hum rose from the streets, steady and indifferent. Amanda let the sound wash over her, trying to tether herself to something ordinary.

But across the ocean, there was nothing ordinary about the day.

Sharp winds carried sea salt through the harbor air, the faint stink of diesel fighting for space as fishing boats rocked against chipped docks, nets heavy with the evening catch. Fishing boats rocked against the docks, their paint chipped, their nets heavy with the night's catch. Tourists drifted toward cafés along the waterfront, but Melody and Lyla kept their pace brisk.

"You know," Lyla said, clutching her cross-body bag as though it held more than lip gloss and a passport, "when I pictured the Spyce Girl cinematic version of our mission, this wasn't exactly what I had in mind. That Paris apartment? Much more my speed."

"Yeah, well, we had to get out of there. That hotel lobby was compromised the moment we checked in," Melody murmured. "You didn't see the man at reception take our photo?"

Lyla's breath caught. "What? No."

Melody only lifted her brows in a wide-eyed look that said *pay attention, rookie spy,* though she didn't voice it. She slowed near a stack of crates, phone in hand as cover, her eyes sweeping the pier.

A black sedan idled too far down the street to be casual, its tinted windows dark, and its engine still running.

Lyla followed her gaze, then quickly looked away. "So...that's kind of ominous."

"And a little too expected, I think," Melody said evenly, lips quirking without humor.

They moved deeper into the small town of Crikvenica, a rugged lane narrowing between stone facades. A few woolens hung stiff on a line above, refusing to dry in the damp air. The faint brine of fish lingered from kitchens that still served the locals who stayed year-round, though most windows were shuttered tight for winter. Laughter spilled from a balcony overhead—too carefree, too ordinary—against the prickle along Lyla's neck.

"You've done this before," she whispered. "You know what you're doing. You gotta give me a few pointers, at least."

"You're doing fine," Melody said, her tone softening. "Just relax. You make a joke out of everything, right? So keep joking. If someone notices us, let them see two women laughing their way through town. Normal. Happy."

"I'd rather be noticed for my fashion sense," Lyla muttered, flinching at the sound of tires grinding against cobblestones behind them.

Melody quickly glanced back. The sedan had turned into the lane, its size ill-suited to the tight stone streets. She brushed Lyla's elbow, steadying her breath. "Keep walking. Don't flinch again."

The street began to climb away from the harbor, uneven stones pushing their pace off balance. Another row of boats bobbed below them while sunlight flared off the water, turning the bay into a sheet of white. Melody used the glare, steering Lyla uphill where the lane narrowed between pale stone houses. Laundry lines sagged above them, the path too tight for anything larger than a scooter.

Still, the sedan followed, its engine straining, a low growl echoing through the climb like a warning.

"Keep moving," Melody whispered, tugging Lyla's arm.

The lane curved sharply, pressed tight against a wall where ivy clung in stubborn threads. Melody glanced again over her shoulder, then pulled Lyla toward a waist-high stone barrier. Without hesitation, she vaulted it, dropping into the shaded yard of a chapel tucked just out of sight from the road.

"Come on," she urged, offering her hand. Lyla scrambled over, heart hammering, her bag catching for a breathless second before she landed hard beside her.

They slipped into the quiet courtyard as pigeons burst upward in a startled flurry, their wings beating against the hush of old stone. Beyond the wall, the sedan slowed, its engine idling low, rumbling through the narrow street like a snake approaching its prey.

Melody exhaled, then pressed a folded scrap of paper into Lyla's hand. "Put this in your pocket and don't take it out until I say."

Lyla looked down at the faint pencil scrawl—dates, numbers, and the name of a Croatian town few people would recognize. "Why? What is this?"

"Another clue from Russell." Melody's voice dropped, fierce and quiet. She held Lyla's gaze as though the words themselves might fracture if spoken too loudly. "It's why I came here. I know it's only been a few weeks, but I'm learning the language, setting up a little house, and making friends in the market. I need the picture to look permanent. Other than the quick trips to Paris and New York to meet Amanda, I haven't strayed far. And I can't for a while."

Lyla blinked. She had imagined Melody holed up in some safe house, curtains drawn, but instead she was wandering cobblestone streets, maybe buying bread from the same woman every morning, and planting herself in a place that was never meant to last. "But…what about the party? Weren't you invited?" Her voice tilted with disbelief. "I thought you'd be spending Christmas in New York with the boys."

A flash of guilt flickered across Melody's face, there and gone before she looked away.

Lyla's hand flew to her mouth. "You lied…to Amanda?"

Melody leaned her back against the chapel wall, stone cold against her shoulders. Her eyes drifted upward to the chapel's tiny bell tower as if it might offer absolution.

"I need them all to think I'm complying. It's too risky for her to know yet. If Amanda thinks that I'm following orders and playing along, she's safer." Melody's mouth tightened. "I've made peace with leaving some mysteries buried. I may never uncover the whole truth of Russell's death. But I know enough, and I think I've figured out what comes next."

Lyla's stomach dropped. "Which is?"

"Disappearing. Now." Melody said it like a sentence she had rehearsed too many times. "My boys know the plan. They're okay with it."

Lyla's eyes widened, her voice rising despite herself. "What? Okay with their mother vanishing? I don't buy that, not for a second."

Melody turned her head, the faintest smile tugging at her lips—not of joy, but of someone resigned.

"It's not forever. Just long enough to get clear. It's safer this way—for them and for me. You shouldn't have been dragged into it either."

"Oh, please." Lyla tried for levity, her throat tightening anyway. "I wasn't dragged. I *sashayed* into this like a dancing queen."

The corner of Melody's mouth lifted, then gave way to an unexpected laugh. She tipped her head back against the stone and let it out, full and hearty, echoing strangely against the quiet chapel walls. For a moment, the weight broke.

"You do bring the comic relief," she said at last.

"Somebody's got to." Lyla hooked an arm around her, grinning through the sting in her eyes. "I hate to break up the band, but if this keeps you safe, you've got my vote."

Melody shifted, pointing to the pocket where Lyla had stashed the note with Russell's handwriting. "Then do one thing for me. Leave that where Julius or Katherine will find it. Let them think I settled in here, see the evidence that I was building a life. When I vanish, they'll spend months scouring the town. My death will be declared soon enough, and my boys will know exactly what to do."

Lyla reached into her pocket and felt for the paper before taking it out and securing it in a zipped compartment of her bag.

"You're talking like it's already said and done." She pulled Melody tighter, her cheek pressing against her friend's temple.

"But it's fine. I'll do it. But you have to promise me something." Her voice cracked. "Promise me you'll find me when it's safe."

"Deal." Melody's head came to rest on her shoulder, the simple word carrying more weight than any oath or signed document.

They hadn't heard anything for minutes, just the whisper of the wind against the stone.

Lyla swallowed hard. "Think we lost them?"

"Maybe," Melody murmured, though her eyes stayed fixed on the stone gate, listening. "The real test isn't now. It's getting you to the airport without being followed. And me onto a train without being noticed. If we're wrong—if those men catch up with us—the plan is over before it starts."

Lyla tried to match her calm but failed, her laugh brittle.

"That would definitely put a wrench in things." She kept her arm wrapped tight around Melody, as though letting go might make her disappear sooner than either of them was ready to accept.

CHAPTER EIGHTEEN

New York City: Christmas Day

TINY PATCHES OF SNOW clung in a thin layer to rooftops outside the loft windows, softening the skyline with its white hush. Now and then, a few stray flakes drifted down, catching the light before vanishing on the glass. Inside, the air was warm with cinnamon from pastries Amanda had reheated, the scent mingling with pine from a small tree they had dragged home two nights before.

Christmas in New York with a partner in her life was exactly as Amanda imagined it would be. The tree lights blinked lazily in the corner, casting a faint glow over the brick wall. Tristan stretched out on the sofa, his head propped up on one side with a throw blanket tossed across his legs. His arm curled lazily around Amanda as she leaned into him, nursing a mug of hot chocolate that had already begun to cool. On the television, the announcer's voice rose over the roar of the crowd.

"Touchdown!" Tristan exclaimed, lifting his fist like he was at the stadium instead of their living room.

Amanda laughed, shaking her head. "You're adorable."

"You love me," he said, pressing a kiss into her hair before dropping his feet to the floor and reaching for another warm pastry from the plate on the coffee table.

She *did* love him—and she loved this ordinary domesticity, the way the noise of the game filled the room, how his body was warm against hers. It felt like she had stepped into the story she was fighting to make true, the kind of life she used to imagine when she was younger. A man she loved. A holiday. A tree, a game, and laughter.

"You know," she said softly, "this is my first Christmas in New York."

Tristan turned, surprised. "Seriously?"

She nodded, brushing a crumb from her lap. "Every other year, I've been with family or... traveling. But never here. Never like this."

He squeezed her shoulder gently. "Then I'm glad your first is with me."

She wanted to hold onto that line, to wrap herself in it, and let it replace the chaos in her chest. Cooper's voice, Katherine's orders, the spy games, and the prototype she'd once carried, now stashed in Tristan's apartment—none of it was suffocatingly close.

The broadcast cut to commercials and then into halftime coverage. Tristan absently flipped through his phone, barely listening, while Amanda curled tighter against him.

"...and now to breaking news in Washington," the anchor's voice said suddenly, cool and measured against the noise of holiday ads.

Amanda's head lifted instinctively. The screen shifted from highlights to a polished image of Governor James Hansen flanked by an American flag.

"Sources close to Governor Hansen confirm he is preparing to announce his candidacy for the presidency in the coming weeks. The announcement, expected early in the new year, comes amid rising debates over technological advances, including the Ocular Grid project, which continues to attract both acclaim and scrutiny. Hansen has been a vocal supporter of greater oversight and strategic use of the Grid, which many believe could become a central issue in the campaign..."

Amanda's chest tightened, the words landing like rocks in her stomach.

Tristan groaned lightly. "Politics. Even on Christmas. Can't they leave us alone for one day?" Disinterested, he clicked the volume down.

But Amanda couldn't tear her eyes from the screen. The photograph of the governor lingered, his gaze steady and commanding, his smile carefully measured. All she saw was Cooper's jawline, the same shadow across his cheek, the same steel in his eyes.

Her hands had gone cold despite the hot cocoa in her grip.

Tristan nudged her side. "Hey. You okay?"

She shook her head, steamrolling her expression smooth. "Yeah. Just—thinking about all of it."

"You don't need to think about anything right now," he said easily, kissing her temple. "It's Christmas. Your only job is to relax. One day a year. Because people like us? That's about all we get," he laughed.

Amanda let her eyes drift back to the tree, but her mind was far from calm. She swallowed hard, lifting her cup to her lips as if the sweet sip could anchor her.

She sat back, curling deeper into Tristan's side, willing the warmth to last. Moments passed as the game surged back from halftime, cheers rattling the speakers, and her phone buzzing against the cushion.

She smiled when she saw Lyla's name flash across the screen. Every Christmas came with a joke—a dancing elf GIF, a Santa meme gone rogue, once even a photoshopped nativity featuring Amanda herself. But this time there was only text: *Merry Christmas, love you.*

And below it, words that felt sharper and out of place: *We need to talk. Soon.* Amanda's stomach dropped. Her thumbs quickly tapped out a reply.

Merry Christmas. Love you too. Everything okay?

The dots bubbled, then paused. She waited while the noise of football droned on, Tristan beside her but engrossed in the game's outcome. Finally, Lyla's message came through.

At the in-laws' for our family Christmas. Loud little humans everywhere. Might've had an eggnog or two. Will explain everything at the party.

A lone dancing lady emoji followed, her bright dress glittering red.

Amanda frowned. Lyla's texts were usually chaotic—memes stacked on memes, gifs that made no sense, long strings of emojis like code only she understood. This felt clipped and performed.

Amanda set the phone facedown on the cushion.

"Everything okay?" Tristan asked, glancing over.

Amanda let out an extended breath and gave him a smile, cuddling back into his side. "Yeah. Just Lyla. She said Merry Christmas."

Tristan turned back to the game, satisfied as Amanda leaned into him. Between Hansen's announcement and Lyla's cryptic messages, this day suddenly felt fragile, like a cracked snow globe that could be shattered with the mere shake of a hand.

She nuzzled herself into his chest, the screen flickering with touchdowns and cheers. But her thoughts snagged on Lyla's message, refusing to let go, until the noise inside her seemed louder than the game itself.

New York City: New Year's Eve

Crowds pressed shoulder to shoulder at Times Square, their collective voices carrying blocks away. Helicopters swept the skyline, humming like restless insects. Horns blared, police whistles cut the air, and the city pulsed with anticipation of midnight.

Inside The Plaza Hotel, the noise softened into velvet. The Grand Ballroom glowed as though carved from light. Crystal chandeliers rained brilliance across mirrored walls and gilded ceilings, every surface catching and multiplying the shimmer of sequined gowns and polished tuxedos. Music swelled from the hotel's Terrace Room just beyond—a jazz band slipping seamlessly between classic standards and holiday flourishes—while silver trays floated past, heavy with champagne flutes etched with a discreet gold "M."

Amanda lingered at the threshold. She closed her eyes briefly, feeling the hush of polished stone, the weight of grand arches overhead, the soft glow of light catching diamond earrings and necklaces, laughter drifting like perfumed air. Vases bloomed here and there with winter flowers, notes of white and green against gilded frames. This was not Tristan's party.

This was his parents', and every inch of it carried their signature of wealth, taste, and control.

Tristan's hand brushed hers, urging her forward. At once, the crowd shifted, conversation dimming as though tuned by an unseen conductor. Faces turned, and smiles curved across a sea of faces as a path opened before them.

"Don't look so tense," he murmured close to her ear, lips grazing just enough to settle her. "They've all been dying to meet you."

She swallowed, forcing a smile. Every eye assessed her. Politicians and financiers, editors and ambassadors, women who wore couture as casually as perfume. This was the city's elite stitched together beneath The Plaza's painted ceilings.

Amanda kept her smile steady as Tristan guided her through the crowd. She had stood beside him at a party like this before in Tokyo, but New York was different. This was their home turf, their legacy, and she could feel the weight of it in every glance turned her way.

The Montgomerys were impossible to miss. Evelyn and Harold stood beneath the gilt arch at the far end of the ballroom, a picture of curated grace, with Olivia beside them in a dress that shimmered like champagne.

"Amanda," Evelyn said as Tristan led her forward, her smile spreading like a beam of light. "How wonderful to see you again. You look...well." Her eyes flicked briefly over Amanda's gown—a crimson décolleté that made its own statement, balanced by understated jewelry—as though she was measuring both choice and fit.

Amanda inclined her head politely. "Thank you. This party is just breathtaking."

Evelyn's fingers brushed Harold's sleeve. "We do what we can. New York expects a certain kind of celebration, doesn't it, dear?"

Harold lifted his glass of scotch in a loose salute, his grin wide and a little unsteady, more bravado than agreement.

"And the Montgomerys never disappoint," he proclaimed, his voice booming just enough to turn nearby heads. "To Tristan's homecoming—and to you, Amanda." He drained half the glass in a swallow, his composure blurring at the edges. "Tonight, we celebrate."

Evelyn's smile tightened. She steadied his arm with practiced ease before turning back to Amanda. "He does like to make a show of things."

Amanda offered a polite smile, unsettled by the change. Harold had always projected control, every gesture deliberate, but now she caught the faint sway of a man softened by more than celebration.

Tristan's voice cut in gently, smoothing the moment. "Thank you, Dad. It's good to be home." He squeezed Amanda's hand lightly. "And I'm glad you're making her feel welcome."

Before Amanda had time to reply, Olivia leaned in as though confiding.

"Amanda, it's lovely to see you. Funny—I was just remembering how Elise always used to help Mother with these events. She had such a flawless eye. The parties practically glowed under her touch," she said, letting the name of Tristan's ex fall between them like a shard of glass.

"Olivia," Tristan said, low but sharp enough to cut the air.

Amanda only smiled, surprising even herself at the steadiness of it. "Perhaps she passed that gift along then. You look radiant tonight, and if you're the one who stepped into her shoes this year, no one would dare make a critique. Everything is perfect."

For an instant, Olivia faltered, her glass pausing midair. Then she lifted it with a tilt of her head, conceding the point with a gleam that was half-smile, half-challenge.

Tristan let out a faint breath of amusement, leaning closer to Amanda, but unwilling to join in any of the banter. He had learned long before that the easiest path with his family was observation rather than involvement.

But before the silence could stretch too far, Evelyn's voice glided in. "It can be a lot, I know—this family, this city, this night. But you're carrying it well, dear."

Amanda met her gaze evenly. "I am grateful to be here."

"Good." Evelyn's hand closed briefly over Amanda's, cool and deliberate. "Because nothing matters more to Tristan than loyalty. He gives so much of himself—sometimes too much. He deserves someone who sees that, especially someone on whose hand he's placed a ring."

Her words dripped like honey, the sweetness almost suffocating, and Amanda absorbed the weight of it—blessing laced with warning—before Evelyn released her hand and let the music swallow the moment. Tristan's arm slipped around her waist again, steadying her against the shimmer of laughter and glass.

"Ignore the theatrics," he said softly, though his smile was still fixed for the room. "It's just family."

"Yes," Amanda grinned, "and just wait 'til you meet mine."

They shared a quiet laugh before his mother touched his arm, directing him to the left. "Darling, Senator Whitman has been waiting to speak with you. Don't keep him," she said, urging her son to remember both his place and his duties.

Tristan kissed Amanda's cheek with a light brush. "I'll be right back," he said before he slipped into the current of admirers, his shoulders disappearing in a tide of Gucci and Versace.

Amanda reached for her champagne, grateful for the pause, but she barely had time to steady herself before Julius appeared at her side. He carried a glass of scotch, his smile broad, and his presence undeniable.

"Miss Hopkins," he said cordially, his voice somehow sardonic yet laced with disarming warmth. "I trust New York is treating you better than Tokyo did. Having to run off like that."

Amanda inclined her head. "Duty called, but it has been lovely to stay in one place for a while."

"Yes," he said, as he swirled the amber liquid, eyes glinting like they saw far more than he let on. "You know, I once knew a courier in Vienna, a young man. The first item he carried was nothing more than a grocery list. A test, you see. Would he deliver it without question, without panic? He did. Whistled all the way, in fact."

Amanda forced her expression to be neutral. "And that was enough?"

"Oh, it was enough to mark him," Julius said lightly, tapping the rim of his glass. "Once you've carried one message, they'll keep giving you more. And soon the groceries turn to secrets, the secrets to burdens, until the poor fellow realizes he can't walk straight under the weight."

Amanda's breath caught. "And what happened to him?"

Julius's grin widened, loose but deliberate. "He stumbled. And men like Malonga—they don't forgive stumbles. Which is why I ask, Miss Hopkins—has anyone slipped you groceries since Tokyo?"

Her chest tightened at the name, but she kept her reply even. "No."

"Excellent." Julius lifted his glass, satisfaction mingling with warning. "Best to keep it that way. Once you carry the first parcel, you'll never be rid of the habit. And Malonga…" His tone softened, the name lingering in the air between them. "He trades in heavier wares than bread and milk."

Amanda swallowed, her mind darting to Katherine. She had been at the facility tour—surely she was here tonight. Julius spoke Malonga's name like a shield, but was it a mask for his own manipulations? The thought gnawed at her as she let her gaze sweep the glittering crowd, searching for Katherine's familiar silver hair.

Instead, she found Lyla—beaming from the entrance, her smile a burst of light against the marble and chandeliers.

"Enjoy the evening," Julius said, his smile returning to something almost grandfatherly. "Dance, drink, toast the year. But remember—watch out for traps." He raised his glass in salute before melting back into the glittering crowd.

Amanda stood frozen, thoughts swirling, when a hand touched her waist. She startled at first, then exhaled as Tristan drew her close again, his smile easy and unaware. "Didn't want to leave you stranded," he said. "Ready to meet a few more people?"

"Oh, I just saw Lyla come in. Let me go say hi first."

"Of course."

Lyla was radiant in her emerald dress, and she waved with the kind of exuberance that cut clean through the dazzling festivities. Amanda slipped from Tristan's side and crossed the room, weaving through a tide of black ties and polished shoes until Lyla's arms wrapped tight around her.

"Look at you!" Lyla exclaimed, pulling back with a grin that was wide enough to look almost insincere. "New York glamour suits you."

Amanda smiled, "Really?" she said, but the note of strain in Lyla's eyes didn't escape her. "And you too—you look incredible."

"Oh, please," Lyla said, tossing her hair with mock bravado. "I'm just here to drink champagne and try not to trip in these heels." She flicked her foot up with a soft kick, then suddenly leaned in close so no one else could hear. "We do need to talk, but not here." And without a beat, she grimaced. "Except now I'm about to say it here, aren't I? Just—don't react too loudly."

Amanda stilled. "Lyla—what is it?"

Her friend's smile stayed perfectly in place, but the words slipped from her mouth like the edge of a knife. "Melody's not coming."

Amanda's breath faltered. "What do you mean?".

"Croatia," Lyla whispered, her glass rising to obscure her lips in perfect time with a laugh nearby. "I went with her. We were followed, just like Katherine said we would be. We dropped the prototype, and then the next day, we were trying to dodge these guys before we made it to the airport, and that's when she told me. She's going to disappear. To let the world bury her before it can destroy her."

"She's going to fake her own death?" The words slipped out harsher than Amanda intended, her pulse hammering in her throat. "And you didn't call me?"

Lyla's eyes glistened, though her smile didn't falter. "She made me swear, and I think she's safer this way. If anyone notices she's not here tonight, they'll only just now start looking."

"Good God," Amanda exclaimed breathlessly. The chandelier light fractured in her glass as she gripped it tighter.

"And the people following... You think they were the ones Katherine meant for us to trick with this decoy plan?"

Lyla's hand brushed her wrist. "I don't know who they were. Men, watching, circling. Could've been Malonga's. Could've been someone else, trying to keep the Hansens from absconding with the Grid—and the White House. I can't tell who's the hunter and who's the prey anymore."

Amanda forced her lips into a smile, though her pulse thundered. She was about to respond when the room itself shifted. A ripple of attention moved through the ballroom, heads turning in unison toward the grand entrance as Governor James Hansen stepped across the threshold. His wife at his arm, their son shadowing a half pace behind. They didn't just arrive—they *claimed* the space. Even the light seemed to bend toward them, applause rising faintly without a cue. It was a family portrait of power itself.

Amanda's breath hitched.

"No date tonight for Cooper Hansen?" Lyla scoffed, noting the woman from the press was conspicuously absent.

Before Amanda could respond, Tristan reappeared at her side, his arm brushing against her waist.

"Come on," he murmured, smiling for the room though his voice was fraught with the stress of obligation. "It's time we said hello."

Amanda lifted her glass, the bubbles rising in a quick, frantic stream. For a moment, she stared at her own reflection, warped in the crystal, her face skewing out of shape. When she looked up again, the Hansens had already swept into the ballroom, the crowd folding around them until they were only steps apart.

CHAPTER NINETEEN

New York City: New Year's Eve

"Tristan Montgomery." Governor Hansen's voice carried across the marble and chandeliers, smooth and commanding, pulling the air toward him. "I reckon New York has been waiting to welcome you back."

Tristan extended his hand with practiced ease. His smile was warm, but Amanda could feel the consummate duty beneath it.

"Governor Hansen, welcome. We're so honored you could be here tonight. And congratulations on the big news."

"Ah, tonight's not about me—an evening like this deserves a Montgomery at the center of it." Hansen clasped Tristan's hand firmly, then released it with a measured flourish. His gaze shifted as smoothly as a lens adjusting, settling on Amanda. "And Miss Hopkins. What's this? Twice, three times in one year—we must stop meeting in such crowded rooms."

Amanda steadied her glass, pulse quickening. "Hello, Governor."

"You can call me James, please." His smile broadened for the crowd, but his eyes never softened. "I was just talking to Cooper earlier—how well you two knew each other back in the day. You were from White Pine, I think?"

Amanda felt the champagne nearly slip in her fingers. The words were phrased harmlessly enough, but beneath them lay a deliberate trap.

Cooper, a step away, inclined his head, expression calm, voice low. "Of course. Hard to forget."

The governor chuckled, the sound of his voice sliding into the hum of music, polished enough to be mistaken for small talk.

"Life has a way of circling back, doesn't it? Old friends reappear, and the bonds that seemed buried prove stronger than anyone expects."

Tristan's arm tightened at Amanda's waist. His smile stayed in place, but a flicker passed behind his eyes—an unspoken question. "I'm sure Amanda has always been remarkable at holding on to the right people."

Amanda forced her lips into a curve, even as heat pressed against her ribs. "And letting go of the rest," she said.

"Wise," Hansen said, studying her with a gleam that veered on approval. "Very wise."

The governor lifted his glass, finishing the exchange with a casual sip, but the words lingered in the space like thick smoke, impossible to wave away.

Before Amanda could draw a breath, Evelyn's voice swept in, warm and melodic. "Hello, Governor, and Margaret, welcome. We're delighted you could join us."

She glided to Amanda's side, her hand brushing Tristan's sleeve, as though tethering him back into her orbit.

Margaret Hansen accepted Evelyn's greeting with poise, her gown sparkling under the lights. "We wouldn't have missed it. Your parties have a reputation all their own."

Harold arrived next, glass in hand, his grin broad and loose at the edges. "To you, Governor, congratulations on the candidacy. Never doubted it for a moment. And to Tristan's successful tour," he boomed, clapping Hansen's shoulder, "and to all of us. A fine year ahead."

His drink sloshed perilously close to the rim, but he raised it high without a care, beaming with pride befitting a lavish host.

Governor Hansen matched the gesture but with smooth restraint. "To the future."

"Always the future," Harold echoed, swallowing half his glass in one pull. Evelyn's smile bristled, her hand at his elbow the only sign of control.

Amanda caught Margaret Hansen's gaze in that moment, cool and assessing, as though she too had registered the slip in

Harold's composure. But the governor's wife said nothing, her silence polished into elegance.

Olivia stepped forward at last, her pale pink gown catching the overhead lights in deliberate sparks. Her mouth curved in a satisfied grin as her gaze landed on Cooper.

"So this is *the* Cooper Hansen," she said, letting the name linger as though tasting it for the first time. "The son we've all been hearing about. They weren't exaggerating."

Cooper inclined his head politely, his expression practiced but steady. "Miss Montgomery."

Olivia tilted her glass, her eyes glinting with mischief. "Please, Olivia. Formalities are for senators and CEOs. With you, I'd much rather be known as simply Olivia."

Amanda felt Tristan's arm tense slightly at her waist, though his smile didn't slip. Olivia's tone was light and playful, but her attention lingered on Cooper.

Evelyn turned with an elegant tilt of her head, fingertips brushing the governor's sleeve as though to draw the attention anywhere but her daughter. "James, Margaret—I trust you found your place cards? We'll all be together at dinner, of course. And the evening's events build so beautifully—the orchestra has promised something extraordinary for the countdown at midnight."

"Of course," Hansen replied smoothly. "We would be delighted." His gaze flicked once more to Amanda before turning toward the wider crowd, already claiming new conversations as if they had been waiting just for him.

Amanda exhaled, her smile still in place. But beneath the opulence and glamour, she felt the weight of his words—the test he had calculated to see how much of her past Tristan knew about—coiled around her like a rope pulled just tight enough to remind her it was there. As the two sets of parents moved deeper into the crowd, the four young people were left sipping their drinks in a moment that stretched longer than the seconds that ticked by.

Olivia's smile lingered, her glass poised at her lips, when Cooper turned slightly away from her and looked to Amanda instead.

"Would you like to dance?" His voice was smooth, and might have been casual if it didn't cut directly through the music and chatter around them.

Amanda's breath caught. She hadn't expected him to ask, not there, not like this. For a heartbeat, she wondered if she'd misheard.

Tristan blinked, his easy composure shifting as if the ground had moved. "Oh, with Amanda?"

Cooper's gaze didn't leave Amanda's. "If you don't mind," he said.

Olivia laughed lightly, but the sound carried a sting of surprise. "Well, I was just about to ask you myself." She tilted her head, feigning sweetness. "As long as you save the last dance for me, Mr. Hansen."

His smile barely moved, courteous but thin. He didn't look at her when he answered. "Of course," he said. "But it would be nice to have a moment." He reached for Amanda's hand. "For old time's sake?"

The orchestra swelled, the first notes of a waltz unfurling across the ballroom. Cooper's hand wrapped fully around Amanda's, and though every instinct told her the floor beneath them was anything but steady, she set her glass aside and let him draw her into the current. His other hand found the small of her back, firm but careful, guiding her into the sweep of the music. Her skirt brushed against his trousers as they turned, the polished floor like mirrored glass beneath their steps. Amanda lifted her chin, forcing her body to follow the rhythm even as her pulse stumbled in his hold.

She rested her hand on his shoulder as shadows splintered across polished shoes and Louis Vuitton gowns, as dancers began moving in concentric circles like clockwork.

Amanda's settled into his light embrace, the warmth of his grip disarming in its familiarity. His thumb brushed slightly against the inside of her wrist, a touch that shouldn't have meant anything but sent heat darting up her arm. Her breath caught on the rise of his chest, and though her smile stayed poised, her pulse gave her away. She could feel eyes on them—Tristan's, Olivia's, others she didn't dare name—but she lifted her chin as though nothing were amiss, as though she wasn't on the edge of forgetting where the music ended and he began.

"I'm not sure I know how to waltz, Cooper. This may be embarrassing for you," she laughed.

"I'm not worried about it. We've always made up our own moves, haven't we?" his eyes sparkled in the evening's glow.

"Cooper." His name in her mouth was little more than a gasp, her throat too tight to shape anything else. The music carried them forward, but her heart thrashed against the measured glide of the waltz.

"So, we only have a few minutes," he said. "Have you thought about what I said?" He leaned in as they turned, speaking low enough to vanish beneath the music—yet Amanda felt the sound as much as she heard it, the vibration slipping through her like a secret meant for her body as well as her ear.

Of course, Amanda had thought about it—his warning, his insistence that the Grid was dangerous, that Tristan wasn't innocent. She'd walked out then with her heart in tatters, and now, here he was, pulling her into another storm.

"I don't know what you expect me to say," she replied softly, keeping her lips close enough to his ear that it would look like nothing more than polite conversation. "I couldn't risk—" She caught herself, shaking her head faintly. "I just couldn't risk it," she said as she clung to the practiced smile that kept the room from seeing her unravel.

Cooper's jaw flexed. He pivoted them gracefully through the turn, his hand steady, though his eyes betrayed a flash of frustration. "So you do know the steps," he widened his smile to mask the words he was about to say. "You blocked my number."

"You think I had a choice?" Her voice was sharp for half a beat, then smoothed as another couple twirled too close. She drew her smile back into place, though her eyes burned. "It's safer for both of us if you go your way and I go mine."

The orchestra rose, the rhythm ebbing and flowing until pulling them into a sweeping arc. They moved closer—closer than was proper for such an audience—his shoulder brushing hers with every turn. Their intimacy was undeniable, as though the music dimmed and the crowd blurred, leaving only the two of them in the sharp spotlight.

"You seem less surprised than I thought you'd be," Cooper said finally, his words threaded with quiet accusation. "About my father. About Tristan. As if you've known all along."

Amanda's throat constricted. She wanted to laugh at the irony—how much more she knew than he could imagine—but instead she let her lashes lower, her face schooled into composure.

"There's so much I can't tell you," she whispered, her voice breaking only slightly. "For your safety, Cooper. For mine and for everyone's, can't you just leave well enough alone?"

He drew her closer as the waltz carried them into another pivot, his mouth near her ear, his breath steady.

"Don't give me that. You've never been the type to stay quiet when the truth mattered. What's happened to you?"

Her heart lurched. If only he knew. If only she could hand him the whole, raw truth—Katherine's dossier, Julius's manipulations, Melody's disappearance, the prototype hidden like a ticking bomb. But the walls around them were too high, the eyes too many.

"How dare you ask me that? You know only a portion of what's happened to me. And that should be plenty to understand that I'm surviving," she let the words fall out, threaded with resolve.

They spun again, the skirts of spinning dancers brushing, every foot sliding in time with the strings. Across the floor, Amanda caught sight of Evelyn's calculating gaze, Harold's loose grin, and Olivia whispering something sharp into Tristan's ear. She felt the scrutiny of them all, the way her closeness to Cooper looked like more than high school acquaintances, much more.

"You're trying to protect him," Cooper said, his eyes narrowing, searching her face. "And I get it. You still believe he's the good man in all this."

Amanda's smile trembled but held. "I believe he's the man I love."

"And love makes you blind," Cooper shot back, though his tone softened at once, as if the words hurt him too. "You already know, don't you? How deep Tristan is in. How close my father keeps him. I can see it in your eyes—you've stopped questioning. You've already made your choice."

Her chest seized, but her face remained light as they turned with the music. "I do ask questions, Cooper. And I care—more than I can say here." Her hand pressed harder into his shoulder, the pressure a silent counterpoint to the graceful sweep of their steps.

His grip tightened at her back, guiding her smoothly into the next turn. To anyone watching, they looked like the most elegant couple on the floor—her gown catching the light, his posture impeccable.

"Then give me something," Cooper whispered, his tone urgent but controlled. "Anything to show me you're not already lost to him. Tell me I'm not imagining that what's between us is still real."

Her eyes lifted to his, the heat of his gaze steady and unyielding. Her lips parted, but no words came. She saw them reflected in each other's pupils—the ghosts of their Tennessee romance, the memory of a child, the burden of years stolen from them.

"I can't," she breathed finally, her voice a frayed whisper. "Please. Not now."

The orchestra surged toward its crescendo as the floor shifted and couples swept wide and closed in again. Amanda could feel her breath receding and the walls pressing in. From the edge of the dance floor, Tristan's gaze cut through the glitz and the music, fixed directly on her. Olivia stood beside him, her lips tilted in a smile too sharp to be friendly.

"You look like you belong in my arms," Cooper said softly, almost mournfully, before he paused. "But, erm, hopefully we're not too obvious because people are looking," he said, a slight laugh breaking the tension he was carrying.

Heat rose to Amanda's face as her breathing hollowed. Her head told her to break away, to push distance between them, but the swell of the dance held her there, spinning until the crowd became a blur around them.

"Then let them see," she whispered, her smile brittle but radiant for the room. "Just hold step and finish the dance without a scene, and we won't give them reason to pounce." Her gaze locked with his, the nearness of him igniting every part of her. Their bodies moved like they had rehearsed, and the ballroom closed in, every turn a reminder of how little space they had left. "But next time, let me come to you, okay?" she murmured.

The music built to its peak, violins soaring, the chandeliers flashing like stars caught in crystal. Cooper guided her through the final sweep, his hand steady even as the air between them vibrated with everything unsaid.

As the orchestra struck its closing note, Amanda found herself standing still in his arms, breathless, their faces too close, their silence too telling. A beat of applause rolled across the ballroom, polite and practiced, but Amanda heard only the roar of her own pulse.

Cooper released her slowly, his hand sliding from her back with reluctance. "I don't want this to be over," he murmured, barely audible beneath the applause.

Amanda lifted her chin, her smile fixed for the watching world, though she felt the ground splitting beneath her.

"It's not," she finally whispered.

The clapping swelled, couples separating, laughter and chatter resuming as if nothing in the world had changed. And as if using a futuristic time travel device, Katherine materialized at Amanda's elbow as the last of the applause concluded, the silver of her gown and hair melding as they flashed before her like a blade.

"Amanda," she purred, taking her in with a single precise sweep. "You look luminous."

Amanda's smile held. "Katherine."

"May I steal you—just for a moment?" Katherine didn't wait for permission. She angled her body to block the path from the floor, positioning Amanda between a column and a spray of white orchids. Tristan and Olivia appeared a beat later, Olivia's gaze drawn straight to Cooper. He met her look with a courteous half-bow, as though the dance had always been meant to end with her.

"Shall we?" he asked.

Olivia's surprise flickered from shock to pleasure. "I thought you'd never ask," she said, slipping her hand into his and sending Amanda a glance that landed like a quiet, satisfied *point to Olivia*. The orchestra lifted again, and Cooper led Olivia into the slow revolve of couples.

Katherine took Tristan's arm. "I must commend you both on the New York tour earlier this week. The site was polished beautifully. Uptake metrics are exceeding Bucharest, and that was already a success." Her tone softened, her approval uncharacteristically lavish. "The whole network is singing," she continued. "Every site is reporting clean, with scarcely a tremor in the drift."

"Good to hear," Tristan said, easing closer to Amanda's side. "I've barely had time to catch my breath since wheels down."

"You'll have more time after midnight," Katherine assured him. "For now, smile, shake hands—donors must feel attended to. Very shrewd of your parents to bring in so many from the Helion group. We'll settle the brief in the morning."

She pivoted to Amanda again, as if to test for hairline fractures. "You were able to do the home base walk-through, yes?"

Amanda kept her voice even. "No, I wasn't."

"Oh. I see," Katherine said, as if Amanda had been called into the office. "Your presence recalibrates the optics. Investors like to believe the future looks like love."

Tristan gave a small laugh. "I'll take any edge we can get."

Katherine's smile sharpened. "The Grid gives you the substance. She gives you the story. Together, that's the edge."

Before Tristan could say more, a polished baritone cut through the noise.

"Are we really talking shop at a party?" Governor Hansen approached with a genial scold. "Evelyn will have your heads."

Katherine nodded with a smile, "Governor."

"James," he corrected, "please." He set a hand on Tristan's shoulder, then let it land lightly at the small of Amanda's back.

"We'll save business for Monday. Tonight, the next Hansen in line owes Miss Hopkins a dance."

Tristan's expression flickered—a flash of surprise swiftly ironed back into composure.

"May I?" the governor asked, already extending his hand.

Amanda placed her fingers in his because there was no way she couldn't. The orchestra unfurled a fox-trot, urbane and bright, and he eased her into the current as if the floor had been saved for this.

"You wear secrecy well," Hansen said lightly, as if simply remarking on her dress. Up close, his smile was exquisitely controlled. "I suspected you would."

"I'm not sure what you mean," Amanda answered, shaping her voice into the casual music of small talk.

"Oh, I think you do." His palm was steady at her back, guiding, not pressing. "I wanted to tell you—bravo. Truly. When Katherine first floated your name because of your history with us, your particular...alignment—I said it was a risk. But some instruments are worth tuning. You've played your part beautifully."

Amanda's steps didn't falter. She felt the floor tilt, but her feet held the count with ruthless precision. "I don't have a part, Governor. I'm just here as Tristan's fiancée."

"And a very good one," he agreed, the compliment landing like a slap. "You steadied the optics at every site he brought you to. And tonight—tonight you reminded us how easily balance can be shifted with nothing more than a smile."

His pleased expression deepened slightly before he continued. "Malonga's men have been edged out of more than one corridor this month. Influence can be such a gentle thing. A word here, a look there. You've done more than you know."

"I haven't done anything." The words slipped out of her mouth before she could varnish them. She caught herself and softened her face into a smile, hoping to take off the edge. "You're giving me too much credit."

"Am I?" Hansen's gaze held hers, unblinking. "At first, I thought you'd protest. But you kept your end of the deal before, so ultimately I agreed you'd deliver. I should have never doubted you."

He guided her through a turn that made her stomach spin. "I admit I thought the tapestry of our woven pasts might snag. But look at you. Not a fray in sight."

Amanda's chest held breath she couldn't spare. She pictured Katherine's cool hands arranging lives like place cards, pictured a dossier fanned open to a page that should have been locked forever.

"You're mistaken," she said softly.

"Rarely." The governor spoke with a tone that never changed.

Tristan stood at the edge of the floor, his jaw locked, Katherine's eyes cool and unreadable. On the far side of the ballroom, Olivia's laughter spilled into the air, her head tipped back in a charmed gesture, while Cooper leaned close enough to keep her attention fixed.

Hansen's voice softened, meant for Amanda alone.

"Consider this my thanks for your discretion. It's such an unglamorous virtue," he grinned.

A ripple of applause cut through Amanda's thoughts as the orchestra quieted and Hansen bid her farewell with a veiled sneer. Evelyn's clear voice rose above the din, calling guests toward the dining room, where gilded doors had been drawn open to reveal a cascade of candlelight and silver. Couples moved as one, trains dragging, velvet swallowing the shine of marble, as the crowd was carried along by ritual and the flow of champagne.

Lyla appeared at Amanda's side, slipping her arm through hers as though they'd planned it. "There you are," she said brightly, her voice pitched for nearby ears before lowering it for Amanda alone. "You look like you've seen a ghost."

Amanda forced a laugh, but the sound cracked in her throat. "Maybe I have."

Lyla's eyes searched Amanda's with a glimmer of warning. "We'll talk," she whispered, so soft it was nearly swallowed by the music starting back up.

Amanda nodded, then the night swept them forward—seating charts, endless toasts, the rustle of velvet and silk. She ate nothing. The wine turned metallic on her tongue. She caught Tristan's smile, Olivia's sharp glance, Katherine's poised stillness, and Cooper's gaze flicking her way with questions she couldn't answer. Lyla kept close, laughing at the right moments, but Amanda could feel the tension in her friend's body, the unspoken torment they both carried.

And then midnight pressed close—ten, nine, eight—the ballroom alive with voices, crystal raised, the orchestra thundering as if the whole of Manhattan hung on the count.

Seven, six, five—Tristan's lips brushed her temple, his arm a steady prominence at her waist. Four, three—Olivia laughed loudly at something Cooper said.

Two—Lyla lifted her glass with a dramatic sweep.

One.

Confetti suddenly burst in silver arcs, champagne foaming as fresh bottles popped, and the ballroom erupted in cheers as the year turned over in a roar. Tristan caught Amanda's face in both hands and kissed her—deep, unguarded, triumphant. Guests around them clapped and whistled, the orchestra striking a jubilant chord as if it were written just for them.

Amanda let herself melt into the kiss, her arms circling his shoulders, her smile dazzling when he drew back to lift their joined hands high in the air. Flashes sparked from cameras at the edges of the room, catching them in perfect light—her lips parted in laughter, his arm raised like a victor's. To everyone watching, she was radiant, swept away in love, the picture of a woman beginning her new year exactly where she wanted to be.

Chapter Twenty

New York City: New Year's Day

To Amanda, there is always a tenderness to the first morning of a new year—the way light stretches slowly across the skyline, the way voices fall softer, careful not to disturb the fragile memory of the night before. But by the time she and Tristan had stepped into the Montgomery penthouse for their traditional New Year's brunch, that tenderness had already been forced into formality.

"Tristan, darling," Evelyn said, gliding forward from the far end of the room, her silk blouse catching the pale daylight. "You're early. How very like you." Her eyes slid to Amanda, cool but courteous. "And Amanda—you look fresh. That color suits you."

"Thank you," Amanda replied, offering her a polite smile. She kept her coat draped neatly over her arm, uncertain whether to set it down or wait.

Harold appeared at Evelyn's shoulder, a mug of coffee in his hand, his smile suggesting he was drinking away last evening's scotch. "Early risers on New Year's Day? That's discipline." He clasped Tristan's arm, his voice booming with cheer. "Good man."

Tristan chuckled. "Just trying to beat the traffic, Dad."

"You've beaten everyone," Evelyn said with a satisfied little nod. She took Amanda's coat and passed it off to a waiting attendant.

"Olivia's still upstairs—she insists on a dramatic entrance. But no doubt she'll be down before the other guests arrive." Evelyn's smile curved faintly. "In this family, appearances matter."

Amanda smoothed her palms together, careful to keep her expression even. "Well, she'll certainly make one."

"Indeed," Evelyn replied, already leading them toward the dining room.

The centerpiece spilled forward in drifts of flowers and winter berries, a tangle of abundance that drew the eye down the table's length.

"Do you enjoy traditions?" Evelyn asked, her smile precise.

Amanda glanced at Tristan, then back at his mother. "I do. They make the world feel steadier somehow."

"Good answer," Harold said, sinking into a chair with a satisfied sigh. "Evelyn insists on brunch every year. Says it sets the tone."

"And it does," Evelyn replied crisply, smoothing the linen beside his plate.

Amanda smiled again, but her chest felt tight. Every word in this family seemed to carry two meanings—one spoken, one implied. She reached for Tristan's hand briefly beneath the table, grounding herself. They had barely taken their seats when the elevator chimed.

Evelyn's head lifted after smoothing the linen at her fingertips. "Ah," she said softly, satisfaction curling through the sound. "Our other guests have arrived."

Tristan's brow creased, almost imperceptibly. Amanda felt the flick of his glance, the silent acknowledgement that *this wasn't tradition*. The Montgomery New Year's brunch was a family rite, sealed off from the outside world.

The elevator doors parted, and Governor James Hansen stepped into the room, immaculate in a freshly pressed suit, Margaret beside him in gray silk. Cooper followed a pace behind, his expression polite, unreadable—though Amanda felt his eyes linger on her for a beat before sliding away.

"James," Harold said, rising enough to clasp hands. "Welcome."

Evelyn's voice cut in smoothly. "We'll wait for Olivia before serving. She'll want to greet you, too."

"Of course," the governor said, all poise and grace as his gaze moved to Tristan. "Good to see you too, son. You're looking well even after the big bash last night."

Tristan inclined his head, his hand steady in the governor's. "Thank you, sir. Happy New Year."

"And Miss Hopkins." Hansen's voice deepened ever so slightly as he turned to Amanda, taking her hand with more formality than warmth. "Always a pleasure."

Amanda kept her composure, though her pulse had already stumbled. "Governor. Happy New Year."

"You look right at home," he said, holding her hand a moment too long.

Evelyn interceded, her tone light. "We were just admiring the table. Please, sit. We'll have coffee brought."

As Margaret settled gracefully into a chair, Cooper caught Amanda's gaze. For the briefest second, his expression softened, an unguarded flickering of hope barely visible, before Olivia Montgomery's voice cut across the room.

"Cooper," Olivia said brightly, gliding toward him with a champagne flute from the mimosa bar already in her hand. "So, you did come. I was worried the governor would keep you chained to a desk all morning."

"Not today," Cooper replied, his smile polite but markedly distant as he took a seat.

"Good." Olivia tipped her glass toward him. "Because brunch is always better with fresh company." She tipped her glass toward him and claimed the vacant seat beside him, the pairing a matter of polite symmetry, every couple aligned neatly, leaving the two of them drawn together by process of elimination.

Amanda forced her eyes away, focusing on Evelyn guiding the governor's wife with a hostess's precision, the setting itself shimmering with a practiced, almost theatrical harmony. She could feel Tristan beside her, calm and cordial, unaware—or unwilling to admit—how quickly the room had tilted.

The governor's voice filled the silence. "I trust you'll indulge me later, Tristan. I'd like a word about the Grid if we can steal a moment."

Evelyn's hand landed lightly on the governor's arm. "After brunch," she said smoothly. "Not at the table."

The governor's laugh rang out, genial but sharp at the edges. "Of course. After brunch."

With coffee poured and the first plates of smoked salmon and delicate pastries set down, the conversation began to circle like a current looking for its drop point.

No one would have expected the plunge, but with Olivia at the party, she was sure to find it.

"Well," she began, her flute poised in her fingers, eyes bright with mischief. "I suppose it would be rude not to comment on the dance last night."

Amanda's head tilted, her smile careful. "The dance?"

"Yes." Olivia leaned forward, her voice carrying lightly down the table.

"You and Cooper. Quite...comfortable. More so than I would have guessed." She let her gaze flick between them, then tipped her glass in mock innocence. "Must be a Tennessee thing."

Tristan set down his fork with quiet precision. "Olivia." His tone was still mild, but carried a brotherly warning on its fringes.

"Oh, come now," Olivia pressed, her grin sharpening. "I'm only teasing. What was it, Cooper? Tell me—were you the jock and Amanda the nerd you remember picking on? Or maybe she was the girl in the corner with her books, and you never noticed her until much later."

Amanda's cheeks burned. She opened her mouth, but the governor spoke first.

"My son was never a bully," James Hansen said smoothly, though his gaze slid toward Amanda with something heavier than paternal pride. "And Amanda was never invisible."

The weight of his words made Amanda's breath hitch. *Careful,* she told herself. *Smile. Always smile.*

Tristan's hand tightened over hers beneath the table, a small, grounding pressure.

"I'm sure it was nothing," he said lightly, though his voice carried an edge. "Old acquaintances catching up on the dance floor. Olivia, you know how people talk when they don't have the whole picture."

"Do I?" Olivia's smile sparkled. "Because from where I sat, the picture looked fairly clear."

Evelyn's voice cut in, soft but commanding.

"Olivia," she sang, smoothing the moment for the room: "Families are complicated, especially when they carry history. We all know that."

The governor's eyes traveled the length of the table before coming to rest on Amanda, the pause weighted enough for everyone to notice. "Indeed," he agreed, lifting his cup in a genial salute. "Loyalty is the backbone of family, wouldn't you agree?"

He paused again as if his question warranted a reply before he let out a quick breath through his nose and a light chuckle. He tipped his cup toward Amanda as she felt heat rushing to her cheeks.

"Loyalty steadies us when the rest of the world is in chaos," he finally concluded.

"Loyalty." Harold let out a stifled laugh from the other end, his mug still steaming. "That's what I taught Tristan—loyalty to your name, to your work, and to the hours you put in. None of this...sentimentality."

Tristan's jaw flexed. He lifted his eyes from his plate, voice calm but precise.

"Yes, of course. Loyalty meant boarding school at eleven. Loyalty meant proving yourself every day, so no one questioned whether you belonged. Loyalty meant work, not warmth."

A hush fell, subtle but sharp. The strain beneath Tristan's composure was unmistakable. Between the distance he and Amanda still hadn't resolved, the sting of her dance with Cooper, and the raw discomfort of having the Hansens at the table, he was wound tighter than anyone could have expected, even for someone under the stress he was facing. This wasn't a trait they often saw.

Evelyn, always a pro at keeping up appearances, straightened her spine with a subtle cough. "Tristan," she said, her tone clipped. "That is hardly the spirit of the new year."

"No," Tristan agreed, his smile tightening. "But it *is* the truth. I think Amanda has a different view of loyalty." He turned to her, his expression gentling. "Don't you?"

Amanda couldn't decide if this was a challenge, a threat, or a test. She felt every eye tip toward her again. Her pulse quickened, but she steadied her voice, regretting not making more of an effort to connect more deeply with him after seeing his face when she was on the dance floor.

"I suppose loyalty, for me, is less about proving and more about...staying. Standing with someone, even when it isn't easy."

"That's... romantic," Olivia all but scoffed.

"And dangerous," the governor added, his smile cool. "Because standing with the wrong person can cost you everything."

"Or it can be the only thing that matters," Cooper said suddenly, his voice quiet but sure. His gaze lingered on Amanda before he reached for his coffee. He blurted it casually, then carried on as though nothing had slipped. But everyone who was staring at them the night before was staring at them now.

Amanda swallowed down a sip of coffee, suddenly wishing she had opted for the mimosas instead.

But Evelyn stepped in, redirected swiftly. "Family is where loyalty is tested first, of course. The rest of the world is negotiable, but not blood."

"Except when it is," Tristan countered, his words noticeably quieter, yet steadier. "Blood doesn't always mean loyalty. Sometimes it means expectation. Obligation. Sometimes it means you spend half your life trying to live up to someone else's definition of your worth."

Harold bristled. "What's gotten into you? That's an ungrateful way to speak."

"Is it?" Tristan asked, his tone not exactly polite, though his eyes gleamed. "Or is it honest?" The edge in his voice wasn't only defiance—it was suspicion, frustration, desire, and old wounds colliding in the space between them.

Amanda felt it gathering like a storm, and she wondered how long he could keep his control from breaking. The silence tightened, then immediately loosened under James Hansen's practiced laugh.

"Every family wrestles with its definitions. Mine as much as yours. Loyalty, expectation, obligation—none of us escapes it. The question is, who survives it intact?"

Margaret's hand brushed his sleeve, her smile still fixed. "James," she said softly, a gentle plea for civility. "I'm not sure about the subtext of this conversation, but perhaps we're all still workin' off that buzz from last night. Should've turned in a little sooner, I suppose," she laughed as she ironically pulled a flute full of orange juice and champagne to her lips.

Amanda sat a little straighter, her hands folded carefully in her lap as her heart thundered. Evelyn lifted her cup, her smile cool but impeccable.

"Well. Perhaps we should toast to loyalty in whatever form it takes. To family. To the new year," Evelyn suggested.

All glasses lifted, crystal and ceramic chiming together like a dissonant chord before side conversations about the food choices and the weather began to emerge. Coffee was refreshed, plates cleared and replaced, and the conversation reassembled itself with the determined cheerfulness of a tradition refusing to misstep.

Amanda could feel the fault line running through the table in the way Tristan's thumb traced the rim of his cup, his gaze flicking—covert, then blatant—toward the end whenever Cooper spoke.

James Hansen blended into the chatter until choosing his moment with a statesman's patience.

"Tristan," he said, as though recalling something trivial, "you mentioned in Tokyo that the New York site would be decisive. I've been thinking about that word—decisive." He tipped forward, elbows propped in a mimic of casual ease, though the sweep of his hands carried the cadence of a speech. His smile was the same one he wore at political rallies. "Decisive how?"

Tristan set his cup down with care. "Uptake. Throughput. The U.S. drives a quarter of the world's gross domestic product—the sum of everything a nation produces. If we're responsible for a fourth of that globally, it matters whether you're selling data or physical goods. New York alone would rank among the top economies on the planet. So how Manhattan behaves becomes the model for everywhere else."

"For everywhere else," Hansen repeated, tasting the phrase. "What a tidy way to say *influence.*"

Harold chuckled, pleased. "Influence is the whole game."

"Influence is the polite word," Hansen said lightly. "Power is the honest one."

A faint glimmer passed across Evelyn's eyes, gone before it fully formed. "James," she murmured, hostess-smooth, "we said after brunch."

"We did," he agreed amiably, and then carried on anyway. "Tristan understands. The Grid isn't a parlor trick. You stand at the edge of a position men have chased for centuries. It will either be leaned on by the reckless or stewarded by those who think beyond the quarter."

"The Grid is not a weapon," Tristan said, and then caught himself, sanding down the heat in his tone. "It's an instrument. It amplifies what already exists."

"And who tunes it?" Hansen asked, pleased by the opening. "Instruments do not tune themselves. They also go out of tune faster than their creators like to admit."

Tristan's mouth tightened. "That's why Helion's already been chosen as the operating partner. The framework is in place to keep it balanced."

"And frameworks bend," Hansen countered. He didn't raise his voice; if anything, he softened it. "Sooner or later, someone decides where the weight falls. Don't pretend you don't know that. Agreements change. Partnerships shift."

The servers appeared with grapefruit and marmalade, but Amanda barely noticed. Her eyes stayed fixed on Tristan, who was no longer only defending the Grid but himself, his decisions, his motives, and seemingly, his place at the table.

"Better to place the center where it belongs," Hansen continued. "With people who can shoulder the responsibility. Who can steer the weight without breaking."

"And you think that's you," Tristan said flatly.

"I know it's me," Hansen said, genial as ever. "And I think you know it too. Which is why I'm curious what you imagine your part is."

Tristan let out a breath that was half a laugh. "I imagine my part is making the Ocular Grid work as it was intended. Not turning it into a politician's baton."

"Not a baton," Hansen corrected, as though humoring him. "A stage. A presidency is only as powerful as the tools it carries. Imagine standing where no one else can stand—on the fault line between information and decision. You, Tristan, have built the fault line itself."

The table hummed with delicate clinks. A server set down a platter of sliced citrus, the scent bright and clean. Amanda watched Tristan's jaw tighten and release, tighten again. He wasn't just weighing Hansen's words; he was trying to keep three separate plates spinning: the governor's argument, the question of optics, and the line of sight between Amanda and Cooper that Olivia had painted for the room.

Cooper asked Margaret for the marmalade, and Olivia laughed softly at something he didn't quite say. The sound made Tristan glance. His smile didn't change, but his hand shifted a hair closer to Amanda's on the linen, as if to remind them both of where they were anchored.

Hansen watched the movement. He hid his satisfaction with the skill of a man who'd won too often to celebrate aloud.

"Here's what I'm offering," he said, as if discussing real estate. "Stability. The kind that can't be bought with a tranche or a press release. You build the instrument. I run the stage. The audience wants symphonies, not sound checks."

Harold beamed. "Now that's the sort of poetry I can drink to."

Amanda's pulse stumbled. Tristan's fork scraped softly against china, but his eyes flicked across the table again. Olivia caught his glance and she smiled slyly into her glass.

"You good, brother? I'm usually the scandal, but today you've stolen my thunder. Fine by me—I'll just tell them it was the champagne talking."

Tristan lifted his glass in mock salute. "Happy New Year's."

"Cheers," Olivia replied. "What a party. And quite the midnight display," she added. Her tone sparkled, but her eyes narrowed. "The photographers adored it. Mother says the pictures are everywhere."

Amanda's cheeks warmed, and Tristan pulled her hand to his lips with a kiss.

"I call it a victory," Harold boomed, oblivious. "Every man should kiss his fiancée like he means it. That's loyalty."

"Loyalty," Hansen echoed again, nodding slowly, happily bringing the conversation full circle.

The words landed like stones in the middle of the table, everyone averting their gaze from each other. Evelyn's hand tightened around her coffee cup, her smile unshaken. Harold cleared his throat, as if another toast might dissolve the tension.

But Tristan leaned back, his shoulders squared. "So this is the new year," he said dryly. "Breakfast with family, a lecture on power, and a reminder that loyalty is never free."

"Free?" Hansen said, tilting his head. "Nothing worth having is free, son. Power, least of all. Don't tell me you're not one to handle pressure, " he laughed, his tone always emitting the same jubilant sound. "The only question is whether you admit the price when you pay it."

The rest of brunch moved forward because it had to—a conversation that forked off into safer channels before circling back to the inevitable. By the time plates were cleared, Amanda's smile had grown sore at the corners, and Tristan's silence had stretched more tightly than his tone.

When at last Evelyn rose to lead the migration toward the sitting room, Tristan touched Amanda's arm. "We should go."

Olivia's voice floated after them. "So soon? Shame. We were just getting to the good part."

"Early morning," Tristan said with a smile that wasn't at all believable. He shook hands he didn't want to shake, kissed his mother's cheek, accepted his father's clap on the shoulder, and nodded politely to the Hansens. Cooper stepped back, without a word, letting them pass, but his silence felt louder than Olivia's laugh.

The elevator swallowed them and sealed, the penthouse's hum muted into a mechanical hush as the numbers flashed downward. For three floors, Tristan said nothing.

Then, still facing the seam of the doors, he asked softly, "So, just how long have you known the Hansens?"

Amanda blinked. "I told you. Our high school did stuff on their school's campus. We had interactions. But everyone knew the Hansens. You couldn't be anywhere near Knoxville without knowing that name."

Tristan's jaw shifted. "You seemed...comfortable with Cooper."

"We were just dancing," she said.

Tristan turned to look at her. "Well, Olivia suggested it meant more when I mentioned it. I mean, I get it. I'm human, I don't enjoy seeing the woman I love in another man's arms, so I can't act like it didn't bother me, but if my sister saw it too?" he stopped before saying more.

Amanda cleared her throat. "Olivia sees blood in the water and calls it sport. That's all."

Tristan nodded once, then twice, as though filing it beside other doubts. His voice stayed quiet. "And Lyla? And Kyle? How well do you know them—really?"

Amanda's mind began to race, her breath shortening. She pressed her fingertips against the cool brass rail, grounding herself in the motion of the car. "Kyle is your friend. My best friend just happened to marry him. I haven't been lying about that. Why would you even ask?"

"Friends of friends," Tristan said, the words flat. "Blind-date setups. Coincidence. I've started to distrust coincidence. Was our first date one of those coincidences, Amanda? Or something planned?"

Her stomach dropped, the kind of plunge that left her breath caught high in her chest. "Planned? Of course, it was planned. You sent me flowers. Your friends and mine were in cahoots to bring us together in Rome. Remember? You called *me,*" she said before taking another breath. "But does it matter *how* we got together?"

"It does today." His voice was soft, frayed. "My father talks about loyalty as obedience. Hansen talks about loyalty as leverage. To me, it's honesty. And I look at you across the table, across the room, across the dance floor—and I don't know if I'm seeing the truth or fiction."

Amanda's pulse roared in her ears. She wanted to tell him everything, but the words stuck like glass in her throat. "I... love you. That's what I know."

Tristan's jaw loosened, not with relief, but with something akin to exhaustion. "I know. I *think* I know."

As the doors opened, he stepped back just enough to let the sensor activate, pause, give up, and close again. "I need it all, Amanda. I need trust and honesty, and I need to know what I'm standing on before I keep building."

"It's stable ground," she said. "I've got you." She could feel her whole body react to the way she slipped a lie and a vow into the same breath.

He nodded, then offered his hand the way a diplomat offers a truce, and she took it. They stepped out together into the lobby's cold light, into a new year that had already chosen a direction.

Chapter Twenty-One

New York City: The Next Day

Amanda was still curled on the sofa in Tristan's loft when her phone rang, a late morning glare spilling across the apartment floors. Tristan had gone quiet after the debacle at their family brunch, barely speaking to her in the twenty-four hours that had passed. He was intent on losing himself in emails at his desk with a furrow between his brows.

Evelyn's name glowed on the screen, and Amanda answered, breaking the silence. "Hey, Evelyn."

"Good morning, darling," Evelyn's voice bloomed like an opening flower, "I trust you're recovering from yesterday's excitement?"

Amanda straightened herself on the cushions. "Good morning, Evelyn. Yes."

"Perfect. Because we cannot sit idly by while the men bury themselves in all this tedious work. They refuse to take more than a day off," she laughed. "We didn't even get a chance to discuss wedding options yesterday, and I feel like I've failed as a mother-in-law already."

"Oh, it's not a big deal, honestly. We haven't even talked about wedding plans yet," Amanda wanted to protest any discussion of the sort. She didn't think she had it in her to pretend things were okay for another moment.

"I won't take no for an answer," Evelyn insisted. "I've arranged all the appointments—a proper New York bridal tour. We'll start with gowns, then a venue, and we'll grab a bite after. Olivia will join us later, of course."

Amanda swallowed. "Actually, I found a dress in Paris—"

"Oh, splendid," Evelyn interrupted without missing a beat. "Paris always produces divine fashions. I'm sure it will make a charming gown for one part of the day, but you'll need at least three, dear. One for the ceremony, one for the reception, and one for the farewell. A bride's trousseau isn't complete otherwise."

Amanda pressed her lips together, glancing at Tristan, hunched over his laptop. "Three?" she gulped.

"At minimum. Now, I'll send a car. Be ready within the hour. We'll make the rounds while the men are busy building empires. Our task is far more pleasant," she chimed.

Her voice glowed with satisfaction, the brunch gone wrong already seemingly eradicated from her memory.

A sleek black car waited for Amanda when she exited the building, Tristan's doorman following as she stepped near. The driver whisked her through the winter-bright city, frozen droplets shivering against pavement, until she was deposited in front of a glass-fronted atelier on Madison Avenue. Inside, gowns shimmered under strategically suspended lights—silk, lace, and beading twinkling like frost. Evelyn was waiting for her, drink in hand, immaculate in her winter cream coat. She kissed Amanda's cheek like a seal of approval.

"You're radiant. Exactly what a fiancée should look like."

Amanda smiled and nodded, unsure of what to make of this overly friendly side of her future mother-in-law. The first time they had spent time alone together, she had felt Evelyn's searing, calculating gaze, and in public, she was utterly proper. But now, with no one around to judge them, Amanda expected less than flattery.

Stylists glided forward with practiced grace, wheeling in racks where textiles swayed gently as if the fabrics themselves breathed.

Evelyn was in her element, in love with her craft of finding and making textiles for the perfect occasion; she became more of a commanding presence than ever. She moved ahead, hand glancing over a hanger here, a sleeve there, her voice clipped yet velvet-lined.

"This cut is too sharp. That one—lovely fabric, but hopelessly common. Not that silhouette, it belongs at a garden party, not an altar."

Amanda trailed after her, caught between amusement and unease. When the stylist finally pressed an approved gown into her arms, she disappeared into the fitting room and let the cool silk fall over her shoulders. It whispered down her skin, settling with the weight of expectation.

"Out you come, dear," Evelyn called, her tone lilting.

Amanda stepped onto the low pedestal beneath a chandelier. Mirrors flanked her on three sides, multiplying her image until she seemed surrounded by versions of herself she didn't quite recognize. The gown clung at the waist, the skirt spilling wide in a frock of satin.

Evelyn's eyes swept once, then narrowed. "Better. The neckline frames you beautifully. But the waist? Dreadfully uninspired." She flicked her hand at the stylist. "We'll see the next."

Back in the dressing room, Amanda sighed as another gown was lifted over her head—this one lighter, a river of lace with a back cut daringly low. She caught her own profile in the mirror as the stylist fastened the last button, the contrast between softness and steel almost startling.

Stepping out again, Amanda proffered an opinion. "I like this one. It feels...modern."

"Mm." Evelyn tilted her head. "It is striking, I'll grant you. But modern ages quickly in photographs. We're not designing for a single night, Amanda. We're designing for memory."

Amanda bit her tongue, then smiled faintly.

The stylist murmured, "Shall I fetch the Parisian silk, madam?"

"Yes," Evelyn said smoothly, though her eyes stayed on Amanda's reflection. "Let's see how that reads under light."

Amanda held her own gaze in the mirror, steadying her breath. The gowns changed one after another, fabrics whispering, zippers closing, mirrors multiplying her, while Evelyn's quiet commentary threaded through each reveal.

By mid-afternoon, they swept from Madison Avenue to a venue overlooking Central Park with vaulted ceilings and candelabras like inverted constellations. The manager spoke of spring weddings, blossoms spilling across the terrace, and the humidity of summer avoided with perfect timing. Evelyn nodded at each detail as if she had written the script herself.

"A spring wedding, yes," she said as they stepped through the ballroom's golden doors. "It's the only sensible choice. Summers here are dreadful. You'll thank me when you look back."

Amanda traced a hand over the carved banister, her mind drifting. "Spring is lovely. But I'd like Tristan's voice in this, too. We're not making any plans today, right?"

Evelyn linked her arm through Amanda's with the ease of possession. "Trust me, he'll be happiest when he sees you radiant and celebrated. That is the Montgomery way. He carries the legacy; you carry the light."

Amanda's stomach twisted. She smiled anyway, letting herself be led toward another showroom before the day finally paused for a meal. They came to a restaurant hovering above the city like a glass jewel box, sunlight spilling across linen-dressed tables and vanishing into tall windows that framed Central Park in its winter hush. Silver glinted through a crown of crystal hanging above them, and every detail whispered of quiet wealth made visible.

Amanda trailed her hand along the curve of her water glass, the faint chill grounding her after the whirl of gowns and mirrors. Seated across from her, Evelyn spoke easily with the maître d', smoothing every detail as if she could prevent this meal from taking a steep turn.

Olivia swept in as if on a gust of cold air as she kissed her mother's cheek.

"Well," she said, tugging her napkin open with a flick, "I see Mother's already begun shaping the wedding of her dreams. How lovely for you, Amanda, since her own daughter will likely never be a bride."

"Olivia," Evelyn said, the name precise on her lips. "If you insist on making trouble, I'll count you the only common denominator," she said, her eyes holding a warning her words didn't.

Amanda kept her expression steady, smiling. "Your mother has been generous," she said. "I'm so grateful."

Olivia's smile sharpened. "Yes. She does love a good project."

Menus appeared, the servers hovering, but Olivia barely glanced before continuing, her tone drifting into false nonchalance.

"Speaking of projects—Cooper was excellent company after you and Tristan left the brunch. Did you know he broke off his engagement?" Her eyes flickered. "Tragic, really. But perhaps it leaves room for something better. I might even manage to make Mother proud after all."

Evelyn's fork hesitated just long enough to betray her distaste. Amanda pressed her napkin tighter into her lap, keeping her face smooth.

"Well, that would keep everything in the family, wouldn't it?" Amanda said evenly.

Olivia's gaze held hers, sly and unblinking. "Business and pleasure?" Olivia winked. "He's rather fascinating once you draw him out. Don't you think?"

Amanda's pulse thudded, but she refused the bait. She lifted her glass, her tone calm. "I wouldn't really know. I only knew the boy, not the man. Tokyo was the first time I had seen him in years."

Olivia leaned back, satisfied, while Evelyn steered the conversation into calmer waters about menus, venues, and the agreeable safety of spring dates. The daughter's sharp edges dulled beneath her mother's practiced hand, and the meal carried on with the rhythm of civility.

By the time their late afternoon cappuccinos were served and plates cleared, Amanda realized she could weather almost anything the Montgomerys set in her path. She had smiled through their testing, sidestepped Olivia's barbs, and learned just how far Evelyn would go to bend a moment back into elegance.

At the curb, Amanda declined the waiting car with a polite smile. The subway would be quicker at this hour, and she craved the solitude of its rush with time enough to let the noise of the day settle before she returned to Tristan's apartment. They parted with air-kisses; Olivia softened just enough to leave Amanda with the sense that parts of their rendezvous had even bordered on enjoyable.

By the time she reached the door of the loft, she was met with the kind of quiet that pressed against her ribs before she even stepped inside. Her eyes landed first on the bags—*her bags*—lined neatly by the door. For a moment, she almost imagined she was meant to be traveling, until the precision of their placement told her otherwise. This wasn't preparation for a journey; it was the quiet choreography of exile.

On the table, the prototype gleamed faintly in the winter light, an object that seemed at once inert and alive. Its presence there was deliberate, an accusation requiring no words. Tristan stood barely apart from it, his frame caught in shadow, his gaze anchored to the prototype on the table as though it might detonate with a glance.

He didn't move or speak as she entered. His silence was more scorching than any outburst could have been.

Amanda closed the door softly behind her. "Tristan."

He lifted his eyes, the look on his face not exactly anger but a sorrow so raw it hollowed her chest. "Where did you get this?" he asked, voice low, as if the prototype itself could be listening.

Amanda's throat constricted. "I—" Her throat constricted, the start of a word dying in her mouth. She reached for him on instinct, but he drew back, his rejection of her cutting sharper than expected.

Tristan's hand rose and hovered over the metal case, then dropped to his side. "I need you to leave," he said. I have to clear my head, and I can't do that with you here."

Amanda's chest ached under his stare. "Tristan, listen to me. I didn't ask for this. I was forced into it."

He laughed once, bitter and short. "Forced?" He gestured at the prototype with a sharp flick of his hand. "You're standing in my loft with the most controversial piece of technology in existence, and you expect me to believe you just stumbled into it?"

Her throat tightened. "I didn't stumble. I was chosen."

His eyes narrowed. "Chosen," he echoed. "So you admit it. Someone planted you here. With me. To watch me. To... what? Seduce me until I could be thoroughly manipulated?"

"No!" Amanda's voice fractured as she reached for him again. "Not...not exactly. To watch you...yes. But I hardly knew what I was supposed to do; I was given orders, not explanations. I promise, everything between *us*—it has been real. You know it is."

She reached his arm, taking his hand into hers, but Tristan recoiled as though her touch burned his skin. The sorrow she saw in his eyes flickered into a fury that blazed with suspicion.

"How can I know anything anymore? Who are you working for, Amanda?" he boomed, arms spread wide.

Amanda's vision blurred with hot tears. "I didn't want this. I wanted you. Us." She pressed a trembling hand to her chest. "But when Katherine put this in my hands, she made it clear—if I didn't take it, someone else would. And I couldn't trust anyone else. They aren't who you think they are, babe."

She had to let a piece of the truth slip through. Even though, at this point, Amanda still felt a slight affinity for Katherine, the strange woman who approached her in Rome with a cryptic message that plunged her into madness.

Tristan's jaw clenched, the lines of his face carved deep by grief. *"Babe?"* he spat the word back at her. "I don't know who the hell you are, and you're calling me *babe?*"

She faltered, her lips parting on words that refused to form.

"I didn't mean for any of this to happen. If you just let me explain—"

"Explain? Yeah, you do have some explaining to do, but I can't wrap my mind around this right now. I just need you to leave," he repeated, tilting his body away from her to underscore the directive.

"Okay, I'll go," Amanda agreed. "Can we talk in the morning?" she asked as she mindlessly put her hands on the carry-on bag that used to hold the prototype.

Tristan's voice dropped into a gravelly hum. "You *used* me, Amanda."

The silence that followed swallowed everything—her protests, the echo of his words, even the faint buzz of the city outside.

Amanda's breath hitched, but her feet stayed rooted to the floor.

"Go," he said again, louder, turning his back to her as though the sight of her was unbearable.

Amanda's body refused to move even as his words reverberated through her chest. When he turned fully, moving past the table as though the prototype demanded his allegiance more than she did, she knew there was nothing left to salvage in that moment.

Hands shaking, her fingers slipped as she reached for the handle of her first bag, then gathered them one by one. The soft scrape of luggage against the floor was the only sound filling the cavernous quiet. With each movement, she felt the finality pressing in.

She lingered at the threshold, lips parted on a plea that would never cross the space between them. Silence pressed in, thick and merciless, until she could do nothing but yield to it, letting the corridor swallow her whole. As the door closed behind her with a softness that reverberated like thunder, the scene echoed in her chest as the elevator carried her downward in its slow descent. Each floor dropped away beneath her feet, each passing number a tolling chime she couldn't help but notice, until she left the building, the brittle air of the city rushing up to meet her. And through the noise of rushing blood in her ears, through the fracture of thought and breath, one name rose steady, insistent, and impossible to silence: Cooper.

By the time she reached the tower, her pulse had steadied into a numb rhythm. Cooper had casually mentioned his room number at the hotel, being his old address at the New Year's brunch, and Amanda had filed the detail away without knowing why. Now it felt inevitable.

At the elevator, she pressed the button, her reflection splintered across the brass doors—a face strange and unfamiliar, almost not her own. When the doors opened, she stepped inside, and moments later, the hallway unfolded before her, hushed and expectant.

She followed it to three-fifteen, the numbers on each door blurring until she stopped at his. Her breath caught. She could still turn back, vanish into the night with only her bags and her grief, let this moment dissolve into silence. She stood there long enough to feel the weight of the choice before her, knuckles hovering in the air. At last, she knocked, soft but urgent, and the door opened almost immediately.

Cooper Hansen stood framed in the light, his jacket unbuttoned, tie loosened, and expression shifting from surprise to concern in a breath.

"Amanda." His voice was low, steady, and nothing like Tristan's. No accusation. No edge. Only a quiet gravity that reached her before he did.

She leaned forward, the hush folding around her like a fragile shelter. Her grip gave way, and the bags slid to the floor with a muted thud, the sound too small for the weight it carried. Her eyes stung, her breath caught, and still she stood there, facing him, unable to move closer yet unable to step away.

"I didn't know where else to go," she whispered, her voice fraying.

For a heartbeat, he only watched her, his brow drawn as though he carried her pain in his own chest. Then he closed the door, the soft click sealing them into silence. He reached for her with measured steps, not rushing, not pressing, but the weight of his gaze consumed every corner of the room, leaving her nowhere to look but at him.

He closed his hands around hers, his eyes fixed on hers with a gravity that left no space between them.

"Then you came to the right place."

About The Author

Shelly Snow Pordea is a storyteller at heart, known for her exciting novels that connect, heal, and spark meaningful conversations. She first captured readers' imaginations with *Tracing Time*, a time-travel romance series that remains a fan favorite in its category. In 2021, Shelly and her brother placed in a top screenwriting contest for a co-written family drama based on their experience growing up in a cult—an exciting step into the world of film storytelling.

Her 2024 novel, *The Cheating Wife*, was inspired by a real incident of public shaming—a woman's property vandalized with the words "cheating wife" scrawled in graffiti. "After witnessing graffiti on a woman's property, blatantly accusing her of being a 'cheating wife,' I knew I was going to write a story about how far we've come—or haven't—from the days of public shaming and scarlet-letter-wearing," Shelly says. "The patriarchy is alive and well, and this book is my attempt to remind us all to take a look at our part in it."

Shelly is also the author of the *Flight Risk Spy Series*, which follows a high-flying heroine who stumbles into the world of espionage. She has based the travels of her protagonist, Amanda, on locations she's been lucky enough to visit. She and her family maintain a residence both in Brașov, Romania and St. Louis, Missouri.

Beyond her professional pursuits, Shelly is a dedicated mother to three incredible adults, loving wife to her favorite guy, George, for nearly three decades, and Buni (boo-nee) to one enchanting, magical granddaughter. She invites you to join her journey on social media, where she shares her insights and creative endeavors. Follow her @shellysnowpordea for a glimpse into the world of a multifaceted storyteller and advocate.

Also by

Shelly Snow Pordea

"A fun, engaging travel adventure with a female James Bond vibe that keeps you turning the page."

Books in *The Flight Risk Spy* Series:

The Night We Met – One encounter changes Amanda's life forever. March 2025

The Last Flight from Tokyo – Amanda's hunt turns deadly as she races against a ticking clock in Japan. June 2025

The Flowers of May – Back on American soil, Amanda discovers betrayal blooms closer to home than she thought. September 2025

Unfollowed – When everything goes offline, Amanda's past is sure to catch up with her. December 2025

From chance encounters to near-deadly escapes, this high-stakes series takes Amanda across continents, through smoky backrooms, and in a race against time. Each book peels back a layer of deception as Amanda learns that flying under the radar might just be the hardest thing of all.

Fasten your seatbelt! This spy series is a trip you won't want to miss.

"So original, imaginative, and captivating."

The *Tracing Time Trilogy*, **Book 1:** When Anna Wright's husband disappears abroad, her search for the truth draws her into a time-bending experiment that will test her love, her courage, and the very fabric of history.

Book 2: Fourteen years later, Anna and David's daughter Maggie uncovers her family's hidden ties to a secret time travel program, and finds herself pulled into a past that refuses to stay buried.

Book 3: A new generation steps into the fight as Maisy discovers her destiny as part of a family of time travelers—and leads the charge to free them from The Company's grip once and for all.

★ ★ ★ ★ ★

"A story that stays with you long after you've finished."

Morgan Conner had it all—until the words *cheating wife* appeared spray-painted across her property, turning her world upside down. Suddenly, her picture-perfect life is in pieces, and the whispers of her community grow louder by the second.

Caught in a storm of judgment and betrayal, Morgan must dig deep to fight for her truth and her survival. In a society where appearances often mean more than facts, can she rise above the scandal and find her own voice?

Dive into this powerful story of resilience, redemption, and breaking free from the expectations of others.